CW01209010

# Psychomachia
## Kirsty Allison

*"You're either on the bus, or off the bus..."*
Ken Kesey

*"...the compensation of a very early success is a conviction that life is a romantic matter. In the best sense one stays young"*
F. Scott Fitzgerald

*"Die young, stay pretty"*
Blondie

**Psychomachia**
Kirsty Allison

All rights reserved. No part of this book may be reproduced, stored in a retrieval system or transmitted in any form or by any means electronic, mechanical, photocopying, recording or otherwise, without the prior permission of the publisher.

ISBN 978-1903110751

First published in this edition 2021 by Wrecking Ball Press

Copyright © Kirsty Allison

All rights reserved.

Dedicated to Gil, and all the vagrant lovers.

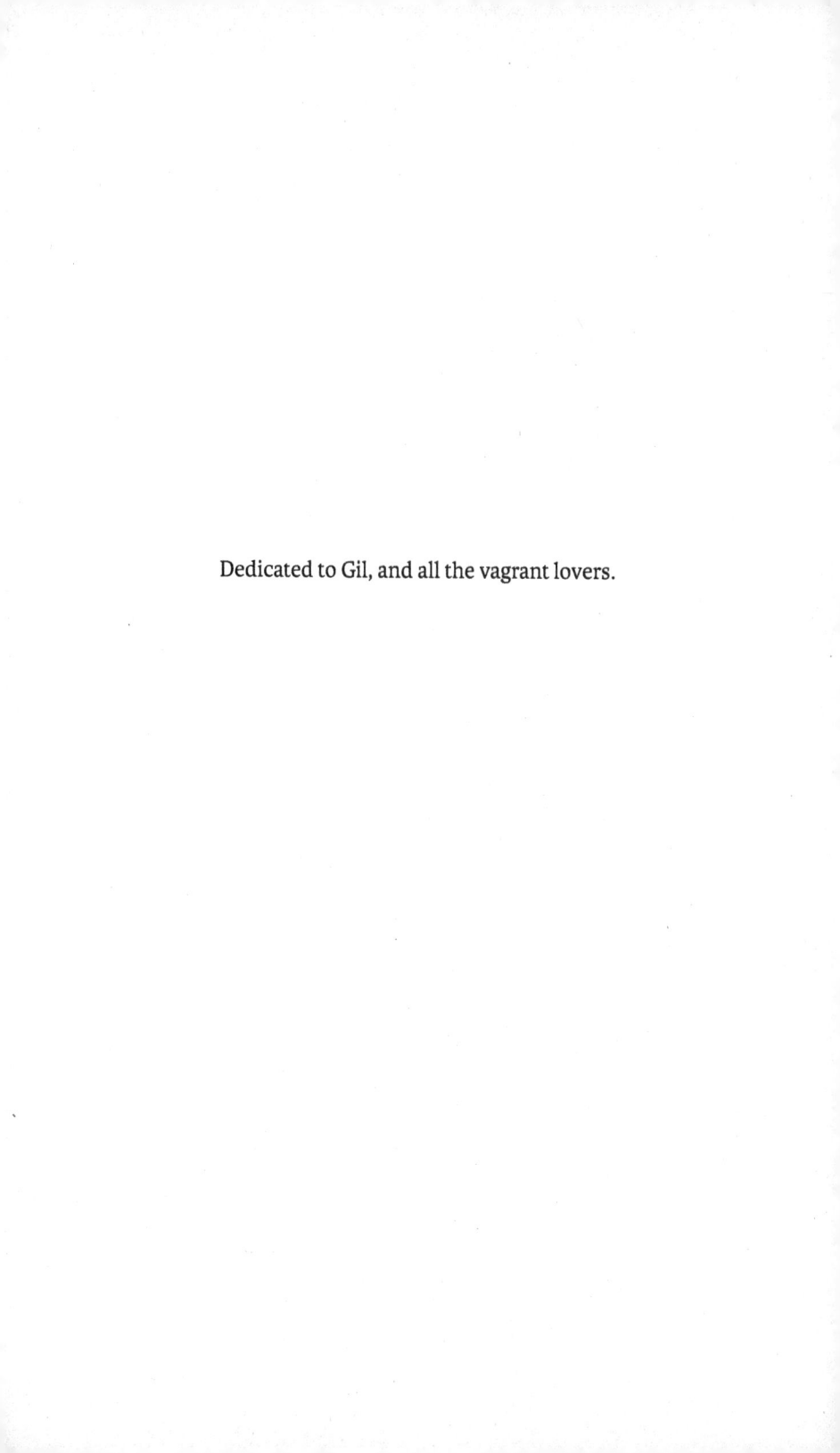

# PROLOGUE

### HMP Holloway, February 1998

I suck on the shit-stained bristles of the toothbrush I found rammed behind the cold iron radiator. It looks as fucked up as I got in Shoreditch: from snow white plastic to the broken virginity of Nightclub-Floor-In-The-Morning Black. The handle's snapped away, lost forever, and I chew the remains. Tonight, again, the water's off - it's like a bad rave.. The screws think we'd flood the place. They're right.

In London, everything looks good, sounds good. *The piss-yellow glow of gold.* It's all fiction, right? Like my admission to murdering Malachi Wright, of Wright States International Touring.

I had every reason to kill him, dear, dear reader, I am sure you will agree.

I look at my old diaries brought in by Harry the lawyer, a posh wide-boy with more anarchy than the Sex Pistols.[1] Telling me to go through them, and get a grip on what was really going on.

I find a note from when I first met Ruby Moon. She was sheathed in a silver catsuit and leant over her mirror ball shop counter in Portobello. Her advice: *"London is a game. It's full of people in disguises. It's all a look. Use these streets like they're supposed to*

---

[1]. John was a lonesome punk growing up in Ibiza, but found friends in a gang of Johns in London. Born John Simon Ritchie (10 May 1957) he became John Beverley when his mother remarried in 1965.

The Johns prowled the King's Road and most of them shared a Finsbury Park flat. The leader was John Lydon* who became Johnny Rotten, joined by John Wardle AKA Jah Wobble, John Gray, and John 'Rambo' Stevens (Lydon's left-hand). There was also John 'Boogie' Tiberi, who later became tour manager. All being called John was confusing, so adopting nicknames was essential for the sense of self they championed. John Beverley became Sid Vicious when, apparently, Lydon's hamster, Sid, bit him: 'Oi, Sid's vicious!'.

Before joining the Sex Pistols as bassist, John Beverley was frontman in Flowers of Romance with Viv Albertine (who was later in The Slits). Sid learned to play from a Ramones record, although Lemmy, for one, debated how much that taught him. Either way, he oozed style and attitude, and was undoubtedly smart, playing drums for Siouxsie and the Banshees at their first 100 Club gig.

*be walked on, don't let them use you."* I didn't get what she was saying. It never made sense, but the words chip at me like I'm white bathroom enamel. I was so distracted, thinking her mouth was bigger than her face, I squirm in my grey prison tracksuit.

The memory blends with WPC Pizza Face, on my way here:
*'Who do you think you are, taking someone's life?'*

Her chip-fat hair splattering around the vaults of the police station in Covent Garden after the party to end all parties.

Even she knew I should have been more neutral. More Calvin Klein. I threw my head back ninety degrees, as if my neck snapped, rocking back on the metal legs of the black PVC seat at the cop shop - sliding down deeper, my eyes on the glass bricks flashing in the ceiling, to the pavement above, each little window going light and dark with people walking on top, reminiscent of a recording studio desk - bumping up and down with levels. I wanted to know what shoes they were wearing. I should know, I thought, working in fashion. But like my admission to murder, fashion is all a great game of pretence, manufacturing illusions of perfection. That's why I was so bored, and made the detour into porn. I was only pretending to be crazy, ma'am. I giggled, sheltering in the colour of the night, the glorious noise of fried-neon pain, dripping in sequin smithereens

---

*The Sex Pistols split on 14th January 1978. Sid stayed in the States (despite he and the Pistols' criminal records). He was with Nancy Spungeon, a former sex worker who was more than kicked by the boot of punk's patriarchy. After the Pistols split, Sid performed in a one-off band with Johnny Thunders, and another with Mick Jones of The Clash. Nancy once appeared as a backing singer but apparently was so strung out that both her and Sid's amps were turned off.*

*Vicious died in New York after his mother ordered him some heroin following a compulsory detox and a fifty-five day prison sentence having glassed Patti Smith's brother, Todd, in a New York disco. Sid fell cold on 2nd February 1979. Undoubtedly stressed, awaiting trial for murdering Nancy. She was found dead in a room at the Chelsea Hotel with a stab wound in her stomach on 12th October 1978 (the blade was Sid's. He'd bought one like his hero's, Dee Dee Ramone, which in turn had been given to Dee Dee by Stiv Bators of The Dead Boys). Various Chelsea residents suggested a drug dealer had been present when Nancy died, and it's likely that Sid expected drugs on tick, as he had received them in London, but New York rules are different.*

*Sid was 21 when he died.*

*\*John Lydon escaped death by missing the 1988 Lockerbie Pan Am flight with his wife, Nora Forster (whose grandfather owned Der Spiegel newspaper, her former lovers including Chris Spedding and Hendrix, also mother to The Slits' frontwoman, Ari Up). The Four Tops were also due on the plane.*

across a blood-splattered canvas. Darling reader, the patina of our experience was SHRIEKING.

After I compared myself to a hyena, finding this hilarious. The only mangy flea-bitten bitch on the hill.

'You're high, alright, Scarlet.'

This is a mess. I'm a mess. These flashback loops are enough to strangle a girl. Every time, I laugh less. Plus, Malachi's ghost's been fucking me all night. The dark lord enters as I hover above the metal toilet to pee, I know it's him. I spasm three levels inside: pussy; spunk tunnel; womb. My heart stops, I burst atomically, wild sexual energy ratchets me into the dark corners of this cell, his vibes sling lightning through the iron bars. I wouldn't water the vinous-faced cunt's grave by squatting on it; and still, he takes the piss, my piss, my power, from this perch in Hell. Mainlining me to the black, male cord of rock n roll which roots across the astral planes.

# CHAPTER ZERO
# WHAT HAPPENED AT READING STAYS AT READING...

*The vandals take the handles* - Bob Dylan

### Reading Festival, 1988

Shifting through the festival crowd for The Toothless Bulimics, I vaguely recognised the sailor top, talismans, and silver and leather belt around old-man black jeans of Malachi Wright, or perhaps it was the power of his Access All Areas passes. Using any erotic capital at thirteen years old may seem on the spectrum of precocious, but a girl is always in training, by expectation. Girls are just holes to be filled in. I knew Malachi was the guy I had to talk to, to get anywhere. It was an instinct. It was my fault. I was attracted to his long hair and air of being 'on permanent tour' with his measured yet wild smile. All the boys I like have that. And girls. I love dreamers. People who live in the clouds. Reading the shapes of cumulous claws as tea leaves of the sky, the clouds as reasonable a guide as any god, angel or demon. Their metamorphosing consciousness is as reliable as any i-Ching, chant, hymn, or tarot. Clouds, at least, are actual parameters of existence, skies are real boundaries, like a book cover - when there are endless words ahead. I feel freedom in that known restriction the story can go anywhere but it will end.

But sometimes the script's written for you and the game is over before we realise we enrolled.

I grab Malachi's arm noticing a tattoo of a severed horse head, its neck drips with blood. I ask what he does. I told him I was taking photographs for an 'arrrr' school magazine, lying but not lying, art school, older than I was. Desperately trying to age myself. Hanging with a generation or several wiser than mine: an assortment of punks from Smacklesfield. Teasing me about wearing flower fairy flares, with hopes of a utopia of peace and love.

'My parents know you.'

He didn't ask for details, and going on about my Dad when he's in a prison-phase is never easy, but Dad and Mum used to speak of Malachi like a legend, his father was the biggest hitman in the Republican army, who made him shoot his own horse when he left Ireland for the bullion promised on London streets.

I let my mates know that this guy, who was about to escort (only) me backstage, was a pal of my Dad's. They hate the elitism of the eighties and backstage hero-worship bullshit. I would have my own backstage pass if Dad was out, here, working.

I'd told Mum I was staying at a friend's. She would want to join me, if I told her, but I wanted freedom, which, although life's too short for regrets, was where this all began. Freedom without justice is useless but none of either are even worse... so I said I was staying at my friend Melanie's house. Just doing each other's hair all weekend.

'It's the next band I'm really into.'

'Come with me, love, if you wanna meet Fore Skin properly...'

'It's the Four Flaws, Malachi.'

After the gig, watching from stage right, Malachi made me wait in the backstage bar.

Loitering uncomfortably, knowing no-one, everyone in gangs, laughing beneath the plastic tented roof. I could feel people judging us when this power ranger returned with the Four Flaws in tow. Father? Daughter? Lover? Child?

'Awright?' asks Cass Vet, singer. Their *Last Man Down* album had been number one for weeks, obviously I'd been into them since way before that.

Shaking hands with the people I had cut-outs of on my walls, cheesy moody shots of boys with triangle bobs, I mumbled around in my dungarees, eyes on their Adidas, staring down like I wasn't there. Wanted to be cool. I don't feel like people get me. It's not like

I've killed someone. Ha ha. I seriously don't remember doing it. I know that's no defence, but *faaaaark* - really? I don't think I've got that in me.

Soon the Four Flaws were surrounded by others, Cass Vet's eyes diverted: girls in groupie outfits, grabbing the attention of the boys too fast-witted to hack a nine to five. The life drains from me when I realise I've lost the band. They were from Manchester too, near me. Maybe Cass knew my Dad. I should have asked. Everyone in the music industry has a story about my father, known and loved by all as Flash Barry - onetime frontman of The Wanton Habits. Dad's wild. Makes us all feel square: the time he tried to cash Elvis[2] cheques; the time he built a missile using fart cushions, PVC guttering, speaker wire and too much gun-powder; the time he drank five litres of mescaline.

Been visiting prisons regularly since I was six, so I know I can hack it. Christmases were a blast, of bullshit, splattering down the scraggy tinsel of visiting-room walls; but if he was out, it was always fun, making up for lost time.

Dad's coming to see me. I am looking forward to it. Finally he may get what I'm going through.

The only person I knew backstage was Malachi Wright. Passing me a pint of snakebite and black, 'You are gorgeous!'

His Wright States International T-shirt bears a logo I grew up with, Dad working for him, seeing the S for States snake slaggily below the W that held up a stage - promoting bands on flyers, posters, tickets, everywhere. No-one had ever called me gorgeous before. His belief made my insecurities flush away. I wanted the rush of his attention to last forever.

---

2. *Elvis, the King of Rock n Roll, was the twentieth century's best-selling solo popular music artist. Big in the late fifties but taking big to a whole new scale in the seventies, he suffered from an enlarged colon, glaucoma, high blood pressure and liver damage, likely brought on through drug excess. Codeine, Valium, morphine, and Demerol were some of the drugs found in his 46-year old dead body. It is said he was constipated, and died on the throne of his Graceland bathroom.*

'Kiss me, baby girl!'

And I did.

Sharing his mouth was an extension of the love I craved. Lips cushioning together, inside his jaw, hot tongues, new worlds. It made me giggle but I liked the silliness of our mouths becoming a cave twirling with serpent eels. Would he touch my 'secondary sex organs'? I hoped not. Blackboard sex sounded disgusting. School was bad enough without clingfilm wombs and intercourse education videos. Clunky fuckers: managed to take the love out of sex. Between that and Just 17 and Jackie magazines, we didn't stand a chance.

*Stretching out on the prison bed, I put my hand down my tracksuit and hold on to myself. I am not sure I would kill Malachi Wright.*

The kiss, my first. A step closer to adulthood. He's a difficult farker not to be slightly in awe of, laminates swinging, and he was using every trick in the book, offered to walk me back to my tent, trying to kiss my neck, soon begging me for sex. It meant he really wanted me. On and on, louder and louder, he pleaded. My periods had started four months previously. I hadn't imagined it to happen like this. He persisted and persisted.

'Where would we do it?' I eventually ask.

'Here,' he says.

No. I continue to refuse. No, No, No, No, fucking *No*. It is dark, we can't tell what we are walking on, I'm still half-tripping from the night before. I'd always envisioned a four poster bed. At least. Champagne. A bubble bath. Tonight there was not even a moon in the sky. No stars. Zero points. The voices of campers, drinkers, men.

'I want to have sex with you,' he kept on saying.

'LET HIM HAVE IT, LOVE,' shout the guys who couldn't see my age (and wouldn't care) lurking inside their tents, drinking cans. Men always side together. Hunting in packs. We walk, falling into each other, the ground mangling with guy ropes, around the curve of the festival field, thud of The Twisted Melons in the distance. The guys in the tents, 'GET IN THERE, LET HIM HAVE IT.' I was going to have to do it for an audience. Couldn't make a fuss, keep the show rolling. I am overvaluing the moment. Everyone I know: the ex-psychedelic warriors who I'm a bit embarrassed to be seen with, even here, at Reading where it's full of people like them: none are virgins. It is something to lose, not hang on to - some girls in school reckon we're still in Jane Austen times, they're so prim, holding on to their dignity like it mattered. And everyone's been raped at some point, right? It's not such a big deal. It happens every day in war, photoshoots, and places of conflict. Women are the n****s of the world - John[3] and Yoko were right.

Malachi pulled me into his armpit, steering my neck, his blue piggy eyes scan my big brown irises which plead him to send my lack of desire FOR THIS, his sweat-riddled hair entwining itself with my never-dyed mane. His tongue spiked like aloe vera through my lips. He told me it was only sex.

'C'mon, let's do it,' he whispered.

I still didn't want to. I'm not sure. Taking my hand, he escorts us over the little country wooden bridge to my life as a woman. I would be fully grown up, finally. The smell of damp mud and nettles, the high notes of a death ditch[4] swelling with stinking black disease, laced by the sound of larvae eggs hatching, mutating. Less holding my hand, more gripping, he pulls us twenty metres into the field, in silence, my ankles negotiating ugly ravines from the cows trampling before it stopped raining this summer. I unreel the grasp, and stop. He slips away, into the darkness, only to return as an overbearing body.

---

3. *John Lennon, former Beatle and husband to Yoko Ono was born in Liverpool on October 9th, 1940. He was shot dead outside his apartment on December 8th 1980 by Mark Chapman who had asked for his autograph two hours earlier. Speculation that Chapman was a 'robot' assassin for the CIA resurfaces regularly.*

*Lennon was not the first Beatle to die. Stuart Sutcliffe, the fifth Beatle, passed April 10th 1962 in an ambulance. He had left the band to paint, but there has been speculation that head injuries were sustained through a fight with John Lennon which occurred four months previously. Cause of death is more likely to have been a congenital aneurysm or arteriovenous malfunction. He was 21.*

4. *Shep Sheppard (The Heartbeats, Shep & the Limelights) was found in a ditch with a bullet in his head, said to be murdered by Morris 'Moishe' Levy, whose activities of swindling artists were said to be a front for the Genovese crime family syndicate.*

'Lie down.'

I submit to what I've got myself into, and sit down, knees to my chest. Having dragged me here, he kneels into me, frustrated at my metal dungaree buttons. I rescind the possibility of a temper tantrum by helping him take my overalls' front flap down.

'Let's get these off, shall we?'

He grabs the bottom of my trousers and I slide out. Stakes of grass pierce my arse. Holes are being made into my skin by the sun-scorched spikes of cut hay. I don't want to be uncool, to wail. Oak trees gaze, crab apple bushes shake their prickles. My once-favourite long-sleeve T rides up so there's nothing private. This guy who I photographed because he looked like a real life pirate with bad black sneakers pulls my legs open, wider and wider than ever before. His hips crush mine. The pressure of his chest asphyxiates mine. I CAN'T BREATHE. I DON'T WANT TO DO IT LIKE THIS.

'Too late,' he said.

Undoing his buckle, black jeans fall to his knees, allowing a raw, creeping sausage to stand above me, all Olympic torch in a moonlight silhouette. I think of the blushing Napoleon hat of his cock, embarrassed to be a part of him. Flying towards me, his skin hangs off his face like an air-cooked bat-sauscison, swinging off the ceiling of a catacomb. I can smell the filthy heat of his insides, black-blood cooking in his toxic bain-marie. His warm spit slavers - dog who can't reel it back in. Man-drool waterboards my face. Ripped-nail stubby fingers force my palm around the top of the grotesque reason we're here. He makes me hold on to his penis, wraps his hand around mine to wank him off as he keeps me pressed down beneath his knee and arm. He then dribbles on his fingers, pokes my vagina and rams part of his hand into the small slit of my never-fuckedness. It all feels wrong. My pubic hair is still new - and I'm not sure what is going on. He mounts his hips to mine, grinds in, his weight crushing me into a depression I'll never shift. He holds his dick as he wedges it inside me, pushing pushing pushing - my legs are opened wider and wider and wider - medieval torture - he's splitting me - skin squeaking as he pushes inside. It's like a cramp that won't shift. I take ownership of being there, of kissing him, of letting him be my first. I don't scream. I don't yell, I don't resist, I have to take take take. Him, finding his way inside me. I open up and my bruising is my own. I feel small as he tears and pumps and hammers, overtaking me.

'TURN OVER.'

He demands; I don't know what he means - and can't move. Before he explains, he cums. I don't know if I've kind of wet myself. I feel hot mucus inside me as he pulls out. It drips. I stare into the nebulae above, imagining they are my Dad's lasers above us in the sky, the ones my punk lightweight associates believe, taking bad acid, are the sign of a third world war.

'ARE YOU ON THE PILL?'

'Of course not. I'm thirteen.'

'STOP SAYING THAT.'

I'm feeling numb now. I want to lie here, in the outside. Let the ground hold me. He makes me stand up and pull my knickers up, get dressed. There's no thanks; he's sorted.

'AH, THAT'S BETTER, LOVE.'

He should have just called me FUCK - love and fucking are very different things.

I reassemble myself and reach for his hand. I want to pretend that this was okay. We walk in silence towards backstage. One of his hips drags slower than the other. Halting in the St. John's Ambulance tent to get a morning-after-pill. It's an acid M*A*S*H - a carnage of casualties, people who'd caught fuck-knows-what from being capsized in Portaloos. He tells me to make up a name.

'Like what?' I asked.

Alison Von Deland. A name I used later with my best friend Orlando, when we go for AIDS tests in the Chelsea and Westminster Hospital. He went as Freddy Mark Curiosity.[5] We were lucky.

---

5. *Freddie Mercury, singer of Queen, 1946-1991. Zanzabari-born to parents of Farsi and Gujarati descent, he was educated in Mumbai and moved to London at seventeen, studying art at Ealing College. He died from bronchial pneumonia, resulting from AIDS, something he never publicised, not wishing to become one of the tragic statistics that defined an era and latter attitudes.*

Celebrated with champagne in Kettners, cash from the T-shirts we'd been selling down Portobello Road - the ones that got me thrown out of school. We just wrote in permanent marker on Ts I bought in Acton, three for a quid. Everyone loves them. Big sellers:

LES BEAN, MOI?
GENIUS, JUNKIE, WHATEVER
and:
I SUCKED A LOT OF COCK TO GET HERE.
It was the latter that my Catholic nuns deemed inappropriate.

Malachi sat down next to me in the St. John's tent, pulled new socks from his pockets, ripping the labels off with his yellow teeth. He said his concession to touring was to put new socks on everyday.

'You wanna come here, and kiss me, baby girl? Pretend we're all in love?'

I sit on his knee briefly. In the ambulance tent, swallowing pills that takeover my body with seasickness.

And that was the last time I hoped I'd ever see him, leaving me with a weird, Sicilian wave - cracking his elbow out away from his body to ninety degrees, flipping his hand backwards, opening and closing all the fingers at once, like he's Burt Lancaster in Il Gattapardo, thinking the wave gives him personality, but he's just a cunt.

It has taken me my lifetime of twenty-four years surviving to write this book. I lived raw, for every moment. That's how my Dad made me. My Mother - the victim of being born a woman, in Cambodia - there was no escaping the sex trade. It's no wonder she married a guy in the music industry. I thank them. Writing is nothing without experience, and although, perhaps, this may have benefited from a re-write, life is too short for that, my life is too short... This story, if it can entertain you, will mean something. We can glide through London, New York, Ibiza, when all the sanitised people are doing sanitised things, and we will inspire, disguising our naked bodies in costumes of invention. We are artists. We are covered in drag as soon as we are vomited from the womb, we wear the grain of our experience. I know I will never feel young again. The skin like parchment, it cannot stay pristine in a dirty world of death drugs and bruises of others; reverberating, pustulating, infecting our conscious spirits.

There are no blinds on the windows. Each room on this floor is a single. Maybe they think I'd actually kill a cellmate.

## DIARY ENTRY: 1988

School was shit. Teacher = thick. I walked out. Said I could teach myself better. Got pissed, played cards with the old punks in the crappy park. I'm crying. I hate Mum. Dad's left her to rot. I can't tell her anything - she's in her fug of television, smoking, sleeping on the sofa.

I wanna leave this place.

I only told my Mum about it several years later. I had to tell someone because keeping secrets hurts. That perfect PR smile; never complain, never explain. Aching, festering, twisting like a tapeworm. I explained my mystery fuck was older than me, and made me do it. She's always so stoned, and went through far worse, getting out of Phnom Penh as a girl. Mum had full sympathy but never acted like it was major news. I never grassed. It was supposed to be a summer of love - when ecstasy washed up like a revolution. Dear reader, the long days of feeling alone were dealt with by nights that went on forever. I started bunking school, and the train down to London. I hate Macclesfield, it isn't even a city, flung on a slag-heap to be forgotten forever. Schmacklesfield aka Shitsville, cesspool of the universe, wedged like a lucid dream between the swamplands of the Peak District where moss is all that will grow against the aspirations of Cheshire.

I hate the people, the lack of prospects. Hate.

'You'll be needing this!' shouted out a Rasta guy I later knew as Tony the Toerag. He passed me a Rolling Stones album as I walked down under the Westway to Portobello Market, smoking a joint, seeing the London people I'd read about in Jackie's Tab and Jet Trash magazines, surrounded by antiques, dead men's glory, treasures of life.

The next visit to Toerag's stall, I'm wearing my black velvet flares (you can't see the zip on the side) and a little black leather jacket under my Mum's original Afghan coat, which is cream, stinking of rotten, wet sheep, and the soaking I gave it of Nina Ricci's L'Air Du Temps. Toerag officially qualifies as a giant. I pass him a load of my Dad's old tour T-shirts: Hawkwind 1971, Yardbirds, Free Mandela, Motorhead's first tour, Elton in USSR.

'They're mint, child.'

I wince. Hate being young. It's so lame. No fags without ID, can't get booze, just have to nick Mum's dope and get my mates to exchange it. I told him I'd been playing *Exile on Main Street* on my Dansette 'til the grooves stopped working; he just nodded.

'He won't remember giving it to you, love!' said a blond-swishing, Converse-wearing, double-denimed Orlando Moon,[6] sashaying over from a stall selling shirts with pointy collars and poppers instead of buttons. Style was dripping out of him like a hot lard sandwich.

'I'll take them all,' he said. Which turned into an exchange for clothes on his stall, and began a habit of swapping, and later, creating our own clothes. It was the first time I'd worn designer

---

6. *Keith Moon "The Loon" - drummer of 1970s British band, The Who, died in Flat 12, 9 Curzon Place, Shepherd Market, Mayfair, 1978. His death was ruled accidental after he matched his age with the the number of Clomethiazole tablets he consumed, taking thirty-two of the pills used for alcohol withdrawl.*

clobber, and it came with the cosmic revelation that they felt so much better than the mass-produced masses. I knew I'd learn stuff off this new crew.

'You'll learn nothing good from me,' Tony warned. But I later became skilled in skimming from him, I minded his stall when he went up to Finch's, the pub. I'd just tell punters things cost more than he would have done, and kept the difference. It wasn't bad.

They introduced me to Terry Vision, who was DJing that night. They want me to go. Orlando's fabulous. He's vegetarian, I'm vegetarian. He had a sofa, I needed a sofa. He was abused as a child, I had my sex-thing when I was barely in my teens.

Orlando thinks I should move to London, if I want to write. Since I could read, I've wanted to write. He knows loads of people and promised to introduce me to people on magazines down here that I can work for.

He skins up a six-skin spliff, and we become a genie's spirit, floating above bad T-shirts and bad leather jackets. Dreamcatchers twirl in the same incense Mum uses, Nag Champa. Totally prefer it here to Kensington Market, where I've been with Mum, to see her mate Marj who has a shop there, selling clothes from distant lands, skirts with mirrors. They loved dressing me as a little hippy. I mixed it with vintage denim from LSD, or the T-shirts in Sign of the Times. I nicked one from in there anyway.

Smoking a joint, my Mum and Marj sat in the shop complaining about the throb of techno downstairs, the lack of windows, but I made my excuses to get lost in the bends and curves and stalls. Leaving the dark caves of stickers and graffiti and patchouli oil, crossing the road to Hyper Hyper, diametrically opposite in all ways - white, and sleek and rave and on. A new world.

Orlando and I would move our stalls close together. I got enough money to go out at night, just missing a few days of school to begin with. We'd laugh like we were the only people in the world, tight as a rubber catsuit, ready to lob fruit from our turrets at the badly dressed, Hell-dwelling plebs below.

*Scratching a leopard-skin pattern into the enamel-tiled walls of this cell. Everyday arriving in the same place, never leaving. I think of Orlando, darling Orlando. I miss us. Before he even got scouted for modelling, or doing it for friends, he was so perfectly Shallow, Shallow, Shallow to those who couldn't reach his head-in-the-clouds attitude where only supermodel necks reach. That's the thing about spring onion models, giraffes, they stand out amid a crowd of normals. They always seem moody to people they don't know, with accusations of being superficial or pretentious, simply because they are jealous, ugly, intellectual, or short.*

# CHAPTER ONE
# FRESH BLOOD

*Thirsty walk along the water, to a room without a view* - Judy Nylon

It was a million parties after Reading Festival that I saw Malachi again. 1995, I am twenty-one. My past far behind yet all the splinters have bound into an entire being.

'It's going to be sooo Toulouse Lautrec, Scaz. You have to come!'

My flatmate that I rarely see, Ruby Moon, insists we hang out. Blood, the new red vodka are taking over the Tramshed in Hoxton. The party to end all parties. Everyone's going to be there. Of course. As ever.

Heroshima are playing. They're ahead of me in the queue, and Ruby whistles "The Boys Are Back In Town"[7] as the band sidle towards her clipboard.

'You like my look?' she asks, not to me, more seeking approval from singer Iggy Papershoes. A long black cape reveals sequinned skin over her stripper pose. Her capacity for frontmen is slag legend. Ruby fucked Iggy on first sight. In a phone box, outside the pub in Clerkenwell. Her Wonder Woman fuck. I've told her she should do her own Rock n Roll Rubysutra. He took her back to his 'space' in Old Street and she became obsessed about leaving our traditional housing of Ladbroke Grove, and taking over this Jack the Ripper territory between the lands of Clerkenwell, Murder Mile and Brick Lane. We could become pioneers of disused warehouses, gutted factories, and vacated lofts. We would be the next generation of Shakespearean superstars, finding our own Factory scene in this crepuscular ghost town, with no cash-card machines, nowhere

---

7. *Phil Lynott - frontman of Thin Lizzy, the brains behind 'The Boys Are Back In Town', had lost his way by Christmas Day 1985, when he collapsed at his home in Kew under the influence of heroin and alcohol. He was diagnosed with septicaemia and died in intensive care of pneumonia and multiple organ failure on 4th January 1986, aged 36. He is buried in his hometown of Dublin.*

to buy anything. That's okay, we don't eat, and we make our own clothes.

*It was dark, and we ran like fireflies. Our playground of dreams, with stolen electricity, rare heating, live/work secret bathrooms. Sheltering in the corners of expansive factory floors, renting studios out for raves; we are blind to the council estates. Only have eyes for others who dress and talk as rarely as ourselves. We were few. A recessive species. Oh so special, surpassing our pasts, in these factories of dilapidation. Hosting the rich, skint, and infamous in our warehouses of dreams: shooting videos, showing clothes, being the party. Acres to play in, be seen in, and get lost in.*

I pretend not to have seen the band, or Iggy.

Behind us, queues of people line up in wait. Desperate, displaced victims of a greater agenda. They look towards Ruby as if she's the golden supplies truck from the United Fashion Nations.

'We've just been in the Blowers, after soundcheck,' Iggy tells her.

Orlando's been playing bass on the two-month tour they're just back from. He is no musician, talent dwarfed by ambition (like his sister's). We've drifted since he's come out properly; he doesn't really like spending time with me. But living with the pair of them, in Whitecross Market off Old Street - we have an old shoe warehouse and my bed is between hospital dividers, on wheels - it's hard to keep affairs quiet. I hang fabrics over the vile mint-green plastic curtains, to prevent seeing Orlando at it through the slits. Now, he twists his angel neck back, spots me, puts his hands in the air for everyone to make room as he walks over and gives me a massive hug: 'Where have you been, Junior?' Like he ever tells me where his night meanderings lead him, unless he's boasting...

'Oh, just working, really hard, y'know...' Uncomfortable pause, which I fill: 'Eyes on the grindstone...'

'Well, keep it up, treacle-cheeks!'

Maybe he doesn't mind me as much as I thought.

Ruby asks Iggy again, 'You like this look?'

'Aye, beltin', doll,' says Iggy, not meaning it. Wanting to laugh like the crowd, who also know better.

'Yeah, Hallowe'en's come early...' says Orlando.

'It's Hallowe'en every night in my world, darling.' She's a witch queen, alright, tapping her guest list like a blackmailer, tossing cherry-pop hair, 'So, Iggy. How was the Euro-tour? Behave yourself?'

Iggy winks, 'Yeah, pretty wild. Can't wait to get back out there again...'

He looks back at me, our eyes catch, I'm playing it casual, in my chiffon nips-out top, black jeans, death spikes. I've always had a crush on Iggy. His face. The way his clothes hang from the haunches of his body. Tonight, a black silk Japanese bomber jacket drapes his angular shoulders, all glorious urn of Victoriana death. I like his darkness. He spits sex like a fuckstick. When I brush against his lean arm, he feels strangely grounded. Iggy's jacket is embroidered with a dragon. He holds up a smashed-up black wax coat in one hand, his guitar in the other. I've never really spoken to him much. He steps to the side as the familiar ravine opens between Ruby and I; moving in to kiss her on both cheeks. She casts her eyes up and down me. We're supposed to be best friends, living together: 'So glad you could grace us, Scaz. Saint Foreign have just gone in, you're gonna love them. They're so off-bias. You must write about them. Druggy vibe...'

'Yeah, sounds up my street, thanks.'

Fifteen years older than me, I will always be Ruby's plaything, her rock-slut protégé. She makes these vile announcements in front of people, to show me up. And yet, she saw herself in me - and vice versa - when we first met in Portobello Road Market. Walking amid old furs, Indian scarves, pocket watches, books of any description, crap records, bad emeralds, and the full gamut of vintage clothing, aside piled stalls of old brass, fake silver, moth-eaten, woodworm-tunnelled, flea-munched, time-worn, much-loved, never-loved, damp, sun-warped, out-of-time possessions of the dead, moved-on, nearly dead: smelling of l'Eau de Granny Tabac and Auld Sex. My instinct was not to like Ruby, face strapped around her like a mask, her noise abnormally loud and dominating. But she is entrancing, fascinating - she is a character study. They all are. I was so impressed. Ruby's shop beneath the Westway was the bomb. She'd lost her Manc accent, which I immediately did my best to follow. I was about fourteen. Took her picture for a magazine I wasn't working for, she twirled, reeled me in. Force-fed me with ecstasy so I'd work in Tuesdays, for free. I don't tell Ruby what I'd like to say, ever: she's too scary, basically; but I thought we were going to hang out tonight. She didn't tell me she'd be doing the door, got me down here, said we'd catch up.

I say hi to Iggy, shyly, and remember my hand squeezing Orlando's arse, like I'm some kind of dog cocking its leg.

I check my shoes - welder's sparks fly as they hit the ground. Designed by a fetish guy for the recent Kalvin Stein catwalk debut, a present from Joe Delaney, the editor of Jet Trash, for my birthday. Rich potent exclusivity drags us past medieval garlands of green, white, and black, adorning cavernous doors as we walk into the party. I catch the eyes of someone I used to speak to when I knew no-one, and leave them back in the trenches as I march into the cathedral of the night. We are greeted by can-can sluts serving cherry red cocktails. This is the kind of Have To Do event that Everyone makes an appearance at. It's about being seen and knowing where the cameras are. Shock and awe, darlings - we pout because our lives depend upon it. Pump up the pout, pump it up, while the place pulsates with self-promoting strut-tastic, future fashion overlords, nodding and smiling, whilst more engaged in what their jawline looks like under the light they're standing in.

'How do I look?'

'Not as great as me...'

'I'm Fanny Fricking Fabul Arse, who are you?'

'Is that thing you're wearing from the shoot I heard you did, with Lars von Schplinker?'

'Ya, I worked with him, years ago, y'know, before he was getting paid.'

'I knew him before he was getting laid.'

'Funny. Remind me, what can you do for me?'

We act like we care.

Tell me about yourself: What do you do? i.e. Can you aid any personal progression? Introduce me to your Gods. I love what you're wearing. Did you make it/did your friend make it/were you given it on a shoot? i.e. You work in fashion? Or something else? Are you useful? And by this point, IF we're still talking, the final assessment: is your taste in line with mine? Because we are the tastemakers and the taste, we are partying like it's 1999, as if we'll never reach the sci-fi years ahead, because it's so far away. The future, 2000AD.

Are your heroes dead yet? If not, do I know them? Surely not? The newest new reformation of the newest new band? Soda Streamers? They're *whaaay* too obscure, like they only gestated a minute ago and we were surely the only ones to know about them because the frontman used to model for Flannel. I was there when that band formed at lunchtime, for fark's sake. The singer wore one of my old T-shirts. They've not even worked out their bass lines yet.

We're so pre-trend the lights are still off when we walk into rooms.

*Old Street is a game; roll a six, hold on tight, read the right lines in Jackie's Tab or Jet Trash magazines, and you'll get sent straight to the Windblower's Arms, where you may see Chernobyl, the band, drinking pints served by Cherry Gonorrhoea.*
*Every night there are auditions for debuts in our classless society in front of the royalty of promoters, editors, advertisers, PRs, A&Rs, and drug-dealers. We spot you coming like snacks on a sushi belt. Come, Fresh Blood!*

There's not been a party in this space before. The competition to be the first either to host or find a new location propels our world from day to day.

'Come with me!' demands Ruby. She's swanned in, got Kyrie Eleison-Adetayo covering the door. Of course I have to follow her or I'd lose any currency in fashion. My life would be Over. Always having to prove they're having a good time. The best time. Ruby's medieval bludgeon of a tongue whips emotions outwardly before anyone can approach her. Never the sort of person to have a quiet affair, she had nothing to hide. Sex was the only true guide through the tangled web of confusion of life. She'd fuck and fuck and fuck towards the light. Cold. Calculatingly devious in her quest towards domination. Or notoriety, or fame, or whatever it was that drove her. People are always scared of women like Ruby but allow them into their worlds. Overgrown she'd never let her world become. Straight forward as the Titanic. Born unhappy but her shrewdness made her appear successful and complete. Her swooshes of fabulousness made everyone feel she was having the best time. And I think we were. It was all extreme but Ruby liked hanging out with me, knowing I'd stay up all night, by her side.

'Do you want another E, you crazy little weirdo?' she asks as we hustle into the dressing room for The Tin Foil Satellites, who are onstage. The walls are projected with leopard skin and gold. Ruby hasn't slept with a girl, that I know about, since me. And I've been into guys since. It was just a reaction against men being such arseholes, for both of us, I think - and caning pure grade ecstasy.

'Maybe just a nibble of yours.'

I hate the taste of pills, it's easier to swallow them whole, but I've had two halves already. I can hardly talk.

'Really, what I'm trying to do is Art.'

'Fucking on film is always porn, Scarlet. Just admit you want to be a porn star.'

I wish the ecstasy worked on Ruby. All I want is to shoot something with more authenticity and truth than all the naked fash shoots I'm getting involved with. Everyone is always so naked, so why pretend it's fashion? Why not be honest and say it's about sex, and beauty, and create something radical, a new genre? I wanted to make porn, but make it look good... reinvent sex films as *fashion*. I want women to do the fucking. Realism not representation. The tameness of fashion. The conservativeness of Everything being so Spring/Summer or Autumn/Winter, and a wedding dress.

'Love it, Scar! Debbie Does Dalston! Horny in Hoxton.'

'The Clitorises of Clerkenwell. Slags of Shoreditch.'

'Bow Belle Ends! If you can do it...'

She's prepping foil, pulling the folded squares from her pocket, maniacally straightening it out between two fingers, putting her nail through the centre to create a ravine for the burned smack to slip. She rolls up a tube to inhale it with. She always has to be in control - even though I paid for half the drugs. She takes the first chase before passing it to me. I wipe her lipstick off the tube, onto my leather jacket.

'Making porn look good, it would be fab, I think you're right.' Rare encouragement from the woman who is her own biggest muse. Narcissism doesn't even cover it.

Before clicking the lighter and inhaling. I puke. Alive enough to read the sign on the back of the door:

### No drugs. The Management.

'Aren't they artists, the people that own this place?' I ask.
'Photographers.'

'They can't be very good if they're that straight.' I spark up the lighter and inhale more smoke. I swallow it. Such a shandy-lightweight. Ruby puts make-up over make-up. Her paper-white knuckles come smashing towards my face. She's wearing jaw-denting armour, brocaded with silver orbs of hard-bitch decoration. I duck in slow motion. But her don't-get-on-the-wrong-side-of-me skull rings merely brush an eyelash gently from my cheek. The chink galvanises us. She sprinkles glitter across my eyes. I think of the old days, of us selling pills at Dionysus. Nigel the Neuron calling me Les Bean. As if! Lesbians are so fucked up. Farrrrrrk's sake.

'Do you want me to be in one? Is that why you're doing it?' Ruby asks, swilling Blood.

'I dunno - do you want to?'

'Not really,' she says. 'Maybe... depends who it's with. Would you do it?'

Sometimes I feel I finished with her, rather than it fizzling out. But that doesn't matter now.

'Same.'

We march back through the party, grabbing another five free drinks as we go. People act like this night is no big deal but they're all here, working the scene. It's as full of aspiration as any hustle joint the world over. Vaudeville girls swing from the ceiling, red velvet enshrines every wall. There are photos and flashes; it's a decadent inferno. My company of a drink, pretty with its black lace trim, my real best friend. I do my hardest to look content but the warehouse does not give me my answers. I smoke a joint. Takes the edge off existence. Makes me see another, funnier, parallel universe where this is all a charade. I look at the models snogging models, the musicians and filmmakers trying to work out their identities. Everyone wanting to be the most beautiful person in the room. In their iron bubbles. I feel like a ballerina in a jewellery case, all eyes upon me, the star of a musical rising above the chorus. I drink fast and swivel for another. A glass is placed in my hand. More purple this time. *Purrr*fect! I announce it to no-one in particular and find Iggy Papershoes in front of me. We're forced to speak because it makes us look popular. We talk about our current projects.

'If I do your porn film, will I get the cover of Jet Trash?' he asks. I'm staring at him but too nervous to look into his eyes.

'Maybe. You know the editor better than I do.'

'That's debatable, Scarlet.'

Sex between Joe Delaney and me has been getting weirder. Videos, gaffer tape. Him tying me up. He likes me kissing models that he invites to his flat for castings. Girls and boys. Sometimes both together. He still won't call me fashion editor. I'm starting to hate him.

'You're still seeing each other, right?' checks Iggy, scratching his hair out from his eyes.

'Not really. I'm kinda over him. It was just one of those things, y'know?'

I hold Iggy's gaze for a micro-second, his eyes flash green. So many secrets. I can't read him. It's too intense; I turn away.

'We've got a song called 'Fame or Glory'. I want to do something that's performance, but not performance.' I couldn't tell where his persona and truth collided. Maybe he was just one hundred percent cool. I wanted him to be.

He stands close, spider-leg jeans, long-sleeved sailor-striped T-shirt: goth-gardener chic. His arm presses into mine. There's something very warm and comfortable about being this close to him. We'd fit so well together.

'You should be in it...' he suggests.

'Nah, not me...' His lips are stained with Blood and my cheeks blush to match. I shake my head, shy. 'You need hot S&M girls preening over you. The Belgian triplets, they're fit...'

'Not half as beautiful as you are.'

I don't know how to acknowledge this. Whether he's flirting with me, to get in a video, to get in my pants. But there's an attractiveness that there's no doubt in his mind that he's going all the way, baby. He's not here to claim his rock n roll crown; he's stolen it already. The real deal, and there's a dawning that I fancy the hollowed-out cheeks off him. Oh, no. I am really into *Him*.

The Malfunctions come on. It's not a stage, it's a floor with amps and monitors and wires all over it. The singer, Jake the Rake, groans so hard he looks like he's taking a shit (he wants it so bad) but people keep on walking behind him, getting caught between the keyboardist and the drum machine, then turning around getting caught in the wires.

'I'll kill anyone if they try to walk through my set,' says Iggy, his body slightly pressed into my back.

'You've got more presence in your little finger than any of The Malfunctions, don't worry.'

'Pretence maybe, love.' He didn't know I cared, and takes my arm and grabs Ruby, escorting us into a new room behind the stage. This is Heroshima's dressing room, his black wax jacket strewn over the table. Iggy chops out a line of coke at the back of a desk, Ruby's standing by the door to prevent anyone coming in. His lines are over six inches, and fat; the measure of my men - he goes up in my estimation. At last, something in common. We sigh in relief as it hits the back of our throats. Ruby doesn't seem bothered that he's talking to me.

'Do you want to make this happen, Scarlet?'

'What?'

'The film? Let's do it soon. We could start tonight.'

His pushiness makes me a little anxious, but I need to do something beyond writing stupid sentences about stupid T-shirts that aren't called T-shirts.

Back out on the dancefloor, DJ Woodworm plays the remix of Heroshima's 'Fame or Glory'. I'm feeling pretty hip with Iggy Papershoes by my side, asking what we'll call the new genre we're creating. Pawns, now? Prawns, no? Fashorns? Pure brawn.

'They all sound a bit...'

Cold draught, right up my side. My past: The two-week on tour trousers of Malachi, I can smell the scabs of the crinkly-arsed fucker. Ordering an associate to plug something in, spit globule-ing out of lines around his mouth like old lady lipstick. His balloon-shaped head covered by a black baseball cap with some kind of crap graffiti logo. That stupid dressing gown that he thinks is a trademark 'don't give a shit' statement with his initials sewn on like he's the owner of the Ritz.

He's clocked me and is coming over. It's like the whole gig stops for the chink of his silver jewellery rattling forwards. Fear is weird.

I lumber in to Iggy's ear, 'Come back to mine later. I have to split.'

I leg it. Ruby doesn't notice me leave because she's speaking to Mark Spye. Orlando's off on one, talking to the newest new actress who's everywhere. Sliding through people, annoying them with my urgency, I slope towards the door, nearly running, without looking like I'm being chased. This dark shadow who rolled me so I lay with my face in the grass, arse in the air, my dungarees twisting around my ankles, making me feel all messy and unprepared, like I couldn't get up and walk; he hoiked my bum up to his kneeling crotch, grabbing my hips, so strongly, his fingers bruising my pelvis, I felt tears down my face. My vagina, he made it a distant part of me. I didn't wank until I got here. To prison.

He groaned a vile groan. A monstrous, deep roar. Pulled his cock from me like a pine-tree of razors. COME ON THEN. He instructed. I was crying. I couldn't help it. All my straps tying up my ankles. The bottom of my long-sleeved stripy T-shirt was wet with mud and spunk.

I run back down Old Street towards home. Alone. My stupid see-through shirt, naked into the night. Looking over my shoulder to see whether I was followed. The streets are empty except for a few trucks and cabs at the petrol station. Those guys freak me out too. Driving in the night - staring at the road - hunting prey.

I run and I run and I run. Until I reach Joe Delaney. He has a nice flat in one of the nice squares in Islington, all classy, soft, grown-up. His kitchen is matching Alessi. Joe was the kind of guy who preferred me stoned. He was only into me if I'd drunk, initially. We'd swizz through town, jump into the decadent Gatsby basement of the day, swill cocktails and flounce gesticulations of self-importance through the thick cigar-and-Marlboro Lights-filled air - I'd contemplate adjusting my gold-plate Mayan eyes in the dark glow of the bathroom mirrors before levitating back to Joe's arms; but there is no need because I am super-fly. I do an Uma (Thurman, *Pulp Fiction*) in the mirror, sniffing the power of my reflection - I'm riding through this town on my jewel encrusted horse and I'm not stopping. Neigh! Looking kinda corpse-y. Draws the cheeks in, focusses the eyes. I never found protection beyond getting trashed - and few of my friends had either.

Joe, however, found armoury in blinging out on the old status symbols of yuppie excess. He wore a platinum watch which only works if it's placed against his electro-magnetic pulse, that's how he knows he's breathing. His sports car is silver. No-one else has a car in the city. When everyone else wears designer friends' samples, his pleasure is an understated logo that he flashes at every opportunity. His jumpers all bear Westwood insignia. His work surfaces are the best for taking coke on but we mainly do harder stuff now. Needles[8] are so 80s, no-one wants AIDS, and chasing it isn't addictive. I know people who have been chasing heroin for years and aren't really junkies. H is actually really good for you - stops you ageing if you get it pure enough, and what no-one seems to get is it's just SO MELLOW. My mission in life translates into a will to get more loaded than any era ever. That's the problem with being spawn of Thatcher: the competitive edge. I will beat our heroes and heroines at something. The nineties will be remembered for being hedonism verité. J'adore the Belsen-look, it's so anti-commercial and... I'm about to gag, at the door. I'm a hyperventilating mess. It's as though I've run through the fields of Reading Festival. The extra wend-y path, past hawthorn trees and ditches.

'Let me in, you fucking bastard!' I shout through the buzzer.

---

8. *Robert Quine, virtuoso guitarist - played in Richard Hell & the Voidoids, and Lou Reed's band, and recorded with Tom Waits and Marianne Faithfull. At 61, in 2004, he died from a self-inflicted (or, reportedly, assisted but never proven) heroin overdose - surprising, as although he'd lost his wife a year previously, he'd never been a fan of needles.*

# CHAPTER TWO
# BOMBS N SHACKLES

*I'm so happy, 'cause today I found my friends* - Nirvana

'She wants to write,' said Orlando, pushing up the sleeves of his stripy cheesecloth shirt, to dive into faux-sausages, beans, toast, and hash browns at the veggie caff on Portobello Road. I'd ordered a poached egg on toast, because it's cheap. 'She's been out with us last night.'

I was so desperately impressed with the international names falling from Joe Delaney's perfect mouth, two tables away. His endlessly long pointy legs, encased in grey fine-cords with hand-stitched Jermyn Street boots on the end, were a refined echo to the slow-motion bounce of his floppy hair. His cologne stank of a botanical garden, a Raj-esque greenhouse, a sanctum of lush, fresh, insect-free growth.

I'm barely allowed to speak, they don't care what I have to say, but I gush: 'Oh my God, I love your magazine!' I thought it was a bit expensive but don't tell him that.

'Sausages are so good here,' nudges Orlando.

'Don't really feel like them...' Couldn't look at any sausages after seeing Malachi's dick.

Joe's elegant cashmere-clad chest chose to join us: grabbing a seat from another table, he twists it around Christine Keeler. Resting his chin on the pyramid of his interlinked fingers, elbows on the table, Tiffany ID bracelet and matching necklace make him look money. He rubs his strong white teeth with the pad of his finger, like he's polishing them. I hate the squeak but later learn it's one of his less weird habits.

'Do you need any, like, can I write for you, do work experience or something? I'm from up North, I was born down here,' I explain, nervous at the power he could wield over my future. I will say whatever I need to impress him. 'My Dad's away a lot, works in the music industry.'

'Oh yeah? What does he do?'

'Flash Barry lighting.'

'Touring?'

'Yeah, but sometimes he does long stretches in all kinds of remote places.'

'Interesting. Have you written for magazines before?'

'Not really.'

'Apart from X, the one in Manchester, right?' says Orlando, lambasting me with the schneide-sausage on his fork, pointing it at me. Sure, X, the magazine I made up when I first wanted to impress them and get them to like me, said that was why I needed to take their photos and introduce myself better.

Orlando's slack jaw forgets to keep his mouth shut as he digests. I love that about him: he eats like a cow. My poached eggs were getting cold; I didn't care. Meeting Joe was amazing. Every page in a magazine offers a new start. Like fashion. Every season. New.

"Take your time, get in touch again when you move down here.'

I was clearly grateful, squirming like I'd wet myself.

It took several years to ball up enough courage to go see him at Jet Trash. I was too impressed by Joe and his people. I'd see them gliding about at various 'things'. At a house party, I was reading Rimbaud in the kitchen, by myself; he came up, threw Rimbaud out of the window, and told me to dance - it was a party. I learned. Their eyes would scan up and down, like I may have a bomb in me. It wasn't until we moved east, where their new offices were, that I felt it natural enough to drop around in a look that was so rolled-out-of-bed-next-year.

I'd stayed up all night getting the words in the best order. I went to Tuesdays East, Ruby's new shop where I worked sometimes, and put a floppy disk to use with the printer before going to the headquarters in Charlotte Road. Words ready, I borrowed the best clothes from the shop - a denim catsuit, boned, and a long leather mac. Spike heels, big bleached hair (Ruby and I have done ours together, we're like little and large: my hair is long, hers was shorn close, she cut it all off after the old double-dicked imbecile she wanted to move away from in Ladbroke Grove - Rudi Speinhardt who ran a record company - fucked his secretary, and his wife).

I'd seen the ceilings of the Jet Trash offices at one of their parties: high, fluorescent stripes of light twist with snaking pipes. Windows are masked with coloured gels and tracing paper. The place doubles as a photographic studio. Walls swagger with pictures of new models, test shoots, photos - some framed. Phone numbers to the rich and infamous, scrawled haphazardly on painted bricks of the ground floor. There are five desks around the edges of the cavernous warehouse. One for design, one for accounting, and the others are empty. This is where the writers I have grown up with write. There's a legacy and a class. I will join the tapestry of underground culture by having my name printed beneath this threshold. I walk over the concrete floor towards Joe. He's a bit Citizen Kane, sitting as the yolk in his eggy Eames chair, bang in the centre of the warehouse. He's wearing one of mine and Orlando's 'Sex and Blood and Rock n Roll' T-shirts with Westwood boots and dirty white denim. Stretching out, his T-shirt rises to flaunt the hairs above his belly. I roll my tongue back in. Men's stomachs, they get me...

He directs me to pull up the large silver bean bag to sit upon. Bit slidey and slippery. I lower myself down, 'So, you're embedded, finally, Scarlet?' My jumpsuit slips down and I don't think he catches sight of my nipples as I pull myself back in and try to get comfortable on the cushion. Shop size stuff is always too big. Even when I borrow it from Tuesdays.

'Can I cover fashion week for you?'

'Hold your horses! Let me see how you write.'

I knew this was going to be difficult and pass him the print-out of my work about Bobby Bandit. I feel mega-nervous.

'It's all I ever wanted to do.'

His eyes pass over me as he puts on blue-lensed NHS-style glasses which burn into the paper.

I get up after five minutes - I've not written much; but he gets out a black-inked silver fountain pen from his shirt pocket and makes marks all over the paper like a child scribbling wildly.

'I read slowly. I take it all in,' he explains.

I get up and pace, looking at all the swag that's been sent to the office - without appearing overtly nosy. There are piles of books, records, invitations, press releases, T-shirts with shop names, jackets with brand names, scarves with fashion names, balloons with band names. I return to the stupid cushion, this time holding on to my bodice. He's still writing on my print-out. I flick through back issues of Jet Trash. Joe sighs and scribbles. Tuts come from his mouth and after fifteen long, arduous minutes, he hates me:

'This is so under-developed. It's like you're baking bread with no yeast. You have enthusiasm but no boundaries. No facts. I do not know whether to encourage you or banish you, to be quite honest, Scarlet... writing is a lonely sport, not for those without hearts of steel. You have your life ahead. Are you quite sure you want to go ahead and use all your energies - and it will take all of them - to succeed here?'

I want to crack bolts into my skull and send an electric current across my face. What the fark does he think I'm doing here? The humiliation of having my writing criticised kills the excitement I had of waiting two years to come and see him. My soul is dragged to the centre of the earth in a gasp of silk through a molten ring. I am a bleeding blue steak. My buoyancy deflates.

And I cried.

Could not stop. So hideously ashamed. The taps won't turn off. Oh my God. The shame makes it worse. My nose blubbers.

After an eternity, Joe returns bearing rough, white, scrunched-up loo roll. Thrusting it towards me, embarrassed.

'Would you like me to help you, with your writing?'

Oh, hello, casting couch. I want to run, rather than be subbed down to a fraction of original beauty. I pretend I'm cool with him helping me, but I'm not. Sensitivity swishes like I'm being born. What is this universe? Why am I here?

I take a leap of faith.

'I want you to help me. I'd love you to,' I lied. He gives me a really?

look and I nod. 'Yes, please,' and here our subservient, dominating relationship is established.

He instructs me to start small: write one-hundred-word pieces about single garments. Then one hundred words on three garments as trend pieces - 'One's alone, two's company, but three's always a trend...'

'Thanks,' I say, and feel like I should walk backwards away from him, crouched in the deepest bows of exaltation until I am not even the slightest bit of lint upon his horizon. He addresses me with a statesman's glide, walking to the door with the reverence of someone experiencing a Messiah complex. I leave with mascara running.

### DIARY ENTRY 1994: no date

I've written ten pieces and Joe hates them all.

He told me what PRs do. One girl is nice, Kyrie Eleison-Adetayo. I go see her at the Soho showroom, down Meard Street, in what looks like a house. I'm sure her sofa is pull-out. She's manic, bonkers corkscrew hair, doing publicity for designers and shops. It's weird that we're both mixed-race. It's not something I ever talk about. Britain has the upper hand on both our identities, and heritage is not something that second-generationers are always ready to embrace. I was used to getting called a Paki at school. She's been to Jamaica, hated it; I've been to India - and will likely go back. Cambodia, I'm not bothered about. I used to pretend I was Native American at school. A northern Native American.

'Remember, you're in control of this, not the PRs. They can write press releases, but it would be a conflict of interest if we didn't hold a critical role and published gush about everyone all of the time - we edit what is good in the world. PRs need you to write about their clients. Get tough.'

They're only words. I don't know why it matters to him so much.

It's not until the twenty-first story that Joe published me. Seeing my name in print makes me think that I exist. I call Mother. When am I going to see her? I can't leave London. I might miss something. I hang about in the Jet Trash office every day and have stopped doing the T-shirts with Orlando and focus only on writing. And going to all the parties. I go to every launch, every show that I'm invited to, every press event, every single opening of a letter. I gain opinions I think I am entitled to. I worship at the church of New. I call designers who are good 'artists'. I wear clothes for 'artists'. Clothes are freedom, they are an expression, escapism, belonging; they are *art*. I muse. I am a muse.

I am anti-stale - I believe fashion is progress. It signifies hope and prosperity. We are Art. Haute sculpture. I have my picture taken. Our old 'Satan Rokk' T-shirts sell out:

'Oh darling, they're soooo amazing. Erudite and minimal, so NOW... actually, can I have one for the photo-shoot I'm doing next week?'

No.

'You'll model, won't you?'

No.

'You want a line, Scaz?'

Yes. Easy. Go on, take the T-shirt. Sure. If I only have to chop the sleeves off for people to give me free drugs... I'd be dangerous if I put any effort into my life. I prefer working under the influence. I exchange my sense of humour for the ability to pronounce impossibly difficult names as though they're the new apostles. I gossip when I need to and keep my mouth shut when I don't. Kyrie, the PR, and I become friends. We rear an enjoyable cocaine habit. Her coke will have been on expenses to a client. We pay for nothing. Floating on airs, graces, and free samples; we expect everything to be laid on because we are doing the world a favour by making everything look so fabulous. We are applauded for this, everyone wants to know us. To see what we're wearing. To be inspired by us. The drawback of such an existence is only that we are actually supposed to live on air. Free drinks are great, but no-one sponsors my rent, so the council pay it. I get a cab to wait outside a dole office on my way to appointments. Orlando is doing well, he signs on too, because although his profile is increasing there's no profit - not after five grams of coke each week. The landlord is unaware that the state surreptitiously supports our freedom. Our influence. Our cultural capital. We are not yet in an era of corporate compromise, where our begging bowl has to say, YES, I'LL DO ANYTHING to reach your audience; nor are we in an impossible loop where it is only the independently wealthy or those with manic energy, or a well-known surname who can survive. Grants don't yet suffocate the arts. But we cannot continue alone. Independence is a bit seventies. We want to be bigger than those who have been before, sleeker, more branded.

I'd been writing for twenty issues by the Blood party. I had been faithful to Joe Delaney. I never even really liked him. I carry on ringing the buzzer. The lights are on, I can see movement. He's got someone else there, I can tell. I've always been his slave. I rarely get emotional. It's stupid and doesn't help, but tears fall down and my shirt sticks to my naked breast. After Reading Festival, I fucked other people, and fucked and fucked, so they can't hurt me. The problem with being fucked by someone is you want to fuck other people over, or don't bother to connect at all. And I didn't connect with anyone. Not even Ruby. I slept with guys with shorts hanging in colour chronology, guys from Manchester, guys with surfboards from Newcastle, guys with skateboards from down South, guys with guitars, guys with Technics, or in the car park raves after FaceDance when the pigs suddenly get all righteous about not overcrowding the fields. We'd all popped. All two hundred of us. Police and security tried to stop us from from turning up the bass bins on our cars, where we stuck our heads in the boots, to really connect with the vibrance of repetitive beats. We scaled warehouse roofs. I fucked two guys on some platform at Afrodizzy, in 'nam. Cheltenham. Separately. Mental. Actually, one of them I didn't sleep with, his cock was so big I didn't see how it was possible - it was gigantic, like, to his knees, or my knees. It was wrong. I ran away, put my head back in the car boot.

I crumble, foetal, on the steps of Joe's front door. I look down at my knees. They are grazed, full of grit, from where I flew onto the pavement outside the party, running, out of my mind - sozzled. I don't even remember getting here, my head is against the entrance door to the building. It's cold. The floor so damp it feels I may have pissed myself hours ago. How long have I been here? Passing in and out of a lucid, jagged sleep. I couldn't face waiting upstairs at home alone, recounting Reading all over again. My summer of hate. All the years after, spent dreaming of slicing Malachi's cock off, razoring off shavings of his penis, thin as scrapings of parmesan, lock him up, bacon-fry layers of his vile stump, shove each piece up his scaled arse, leave it there for weeks, starving him, so all he can do is pick his cock-flesh from his itchy arsehole, into his child-raping mouth. Chained up in a dark and lonely cage where there was no hiding from his past. I didn't want to kill him. I wanted him to suffer. Every day.

Heavy thoughts to carry around. So I vowed to destroy him if I ever saw him again.

I ring the buzzer repeatedly, I don't care if it's annoying. He doesn't deserve caution or care. The lights change - the front balcony French windows open.

'Fuck off, Scarlet. Go home. I'm not interested.'

He's smoking. I can hear someone behind him, laughing. Neither will show their face.

'But what about writing for you?'

'You can't bloody write for toffee, love. Fuck off.'

# CHAPTER THREE
# BLACK ROSE PETAL SHOES

*And you used to be so sweet, I heard you say* - Culture Club

'I just went out for some milk,' I explain to Orlando as I come up the stairs. He sports a pirate's hat at a five AM slant and a huge bit of art is casually flung around his shoulders - an oil canvas of burning money:

'We're just in.'

I never know who's upstairs or what scene awaits. One of us is usually entertaining someone. But it's just Orlando, his usual mad, non-stop party-in-his-pants self... but he's here with Iggy, wrapped in our cheetah fur. I am so happy to see him. I hope he doesn't see that...

'Heya, hi - you're here?'

He smiles: 'You missed my gig.'

Orlando twirls around pouring champagne in a tea cup.

'I would have come sooner if I'd known you'd got these records.' He stares. Into me. My pussy blooms.

'They're mainly my Dad's. Sorry I had to run off.'

He's put some of the music on; broken metal music reverberates across the floor. It's Can. There are three bottles of champagne, mainly empty, and a mirror with cocaine debris across it. We never normally have enough cash for champagne. Welcome to my harbour, Iggy boy. I shall bash these flagons to our bows and sail us to the cape of no return.

'Cheers! Welcome!' I say, drinking the bit left inside straight from the bottle.

The early morning sunshine breaks through our frigorific metal windows into our zenhemian emporium. We're on the corner of Banner Street and Whitecross Market. We have foil all over the walls, for insulation (never admitting to one another that it's because we're gutted to have been born too late to have joined Warhol's Factory). With rolls of toile canvas, we built bedrooms around the mattresses we hauled back from Oxford Street in shopping trolleys, pulled them up on the winch. And the hospital-style dividers; all our furniture has a story. Trophy scavenges, high society heirlooms. Orlando has vertigo: the old winch gate gives him the horrors, he's petrified someone will fall out like a bag of sand, splatting on the street, at a party.

'Can I open it?' I ask him.

'Yeah, if it's just us...be careful.'

In love with the day, I lean into the sky, stripes of grey and blue, and the trash of the market rolls down the street as confetti.

'What happened to you last night?' asks Iggy.

'I felt a bit sick.'

'Why do you get so wasted?'

I want him to like me: 'It's like tugging thirty fags in your mouth at once, smoking them to try and put yourself off. It's just what I do sometimes...'

'You sure you're not just gorging yourself in misery, love? You seem, a bit off-colour,' he stands next to me, looking out at the market traders setting up. He wipes the hair from my face. I feel so embarrassed, I'm probably covered in dried tears. I bet make-up and salt track down my face.

*'Slight shade of lost...'* he starts singing.
*You got your black rose petal shoes on*
*Your motorbike burning*
*You got your rebel haircut*
*And you're still not learning*

It's so soothing and reassuring.

'I've been up for three days,' I try to explain.

*I take a Polaroid to remind you*
*Of this grunge tropicana*
*Glitter suicide baby*
*I wanna take you higher*
*Hiiiiighhighhigh-highayyyer*

'You ever been on tour?' he asks.

'Kinda. My dad...'

'Yeah. Wanton Habits. Kings of the road. But that must have been tough, after...'

'It is what it is,' I bite my lip.

'Don't do that, darling. It makes you look nervous.'

I am nervous, mate. You're in my house.

We're above a betting shop, and a pie n mash caff that I've never looked in. This is it: home sweet desolation. Our secret network of Steppenwolf doorways where, once behind the plain unassuming factory gates and anonymous entrances, your world opens to a series of huge warehouse kingdoms. Where I no longer have any status, because Joe's stripped me of honours.

'You want a cup of tea? It's breakfast time,' asks Iggy.

I swig on champagne. 'I doubt there's milk...'

Our kitchen: a toaster and a kettle - the toaster is for lighting cigarettes. Food is off-menu. I don't remember eating for years.

'Why don't we go on the roof?' I ask. Orlando hates going up on the roof, thinks we'll fall through the glass sheets and past the wooden beams of our ceiling, but we all troupe up, swaying like sailors.

'Woah, we're halfway there...' sings Orlando.

'You like a bit of Jon Bon Jovi?' I ask my new friend.

'Living on a prayeeer...' finishes Iggy. 'Hate them. What do they write about?'

He holds my hand and tries to make me join in singing one of his songs. I don't, too self-conscious, but still feel good; secret sunrise crew - my people.

Traipsing to the top of our building, there's a big space covered in gritty old black-and-white-squared linoleum; the morning air greets us, the sun smacking our faces. Lo and behold, hark the farkin' angels sing - I hear Ruby. She's wearing a black leather catsuit, tall boots, her hair is half-beehive with an Alice band. Sitting on the red PVC sofa we hauled from Brick Lane however long ago, she's got a roof tile with coke on it, and Malachi Wright is sitting next to her.

My heart stops. My vision goes tunnel.

'Hi, Scarlet - how are you?' he asks. His face has got even uglier. I pause. I'm gonna have to front this out.

'Great. How are you?' My voice is pipsqueak quiet.

'You wanna line, love?' It explains the champagne. He'll have brought it. I cast my eyes over the new docks of the city, the glistening towers where money lands from every half-bit blagger of fiscal fisting fuckery on the planet. Why didn't Orlando tell me Malachi was here? Why would he? He doesn't know it was him. None of this lot does.

'Sure. Why not?'

'Scarlet's planning to make porn films,' introduces Ruby.

Malachi leans over, passing me a line on a roof tile - like why would we need roof tiles?

'So that's what happened to you? Always thought you were a goer. Tell me more...'

I take a rolled bank note from Ruby.

'Beautifully lit, sexy film for people like us - well, y'know, like us...' I say, pointing at Orlando and Iggy and me and Ruby, 'who need intelligence to get off.'

'We didn't need intelligence earlier, did we, darling?' replies Malachi.

Oh, no.

'Are you calling me stupid?' asks Ruby, fake-slapping him.

Does this mean he's going to be here all the time? Iggy takes the roof tile from me, and the note.

'Never go back, eh, Scarlet?'

What? He knows about Malachi?

And then I realise. He means Ruby. He thinks I'd be jealous of Malachi fucking her. I was fifteen or sixteen when we were doing whatever it was we were doing...

'I only go forwards.'

'Oh - y'know, I'm not the only man who'd love to see you two back together.'

Why is every guy a victim to girl-sex? Oh, this is so faaarked up. Ruby pretends to be in a huff. Lips pouting.

'Never again...' I slur.

'Sorry to bring that up - it was in my mind, for some reason.'

'Can't imagine how, son!' says Malachi, gallow-laughing, raspberrying his lips together.

'Did you enjoy the party last night, Scarlet? Who did you cop off with? Did Joe turn up?' asks Ruby. I wish our friendship was longer than a line of cocaine.

Iggy physically moves away from me.

'Nah, I left. Felt a bit, um, sick...'

'Alright now, though?' Ruby perseveres.

'Sort of.'

'You weren't in bed downstairs, were you, we didn't wake you up?'

'No, nothing like that. I went for a long walk...'

'To Jet Trash Joe's?'

'No, actually...' I am out of my comfort zone. I wonder if I should take Malachi to the edge of the building, and push him... and Ruby, too.

Orlando snorts up and says we should leave them to it.

'Oh, no, stay!' begs Ruby. 'I'm hoping Malachi can find you a distributor who's not your BMX, for your records. Maybe put you on tour, eh, Mally?' She's furiously chopping out more coke. 'We'd better get Fish Shop Frankie to drop by some more. Need a morning delivery, don't we?'

'You'll have no nose left,' Malachi tells her.

'The party never stops up my nose.'

I look at Iggy, *can we leave?*

'Malachi, brilliant meeting you. Look forward to next time. Be great to work with you. Maybe go for that cuppa, eh, Scarlet?'

No way. We're going to the pub.

We flee without pause. No further goodbyes. Hanging with Iggy immediately becomes my preferred state. He made me feel special. And a star. He talked about me in the third person: What would Scarlet Flagg do? The sexiest, coolest girl in London. The world.

# CHAPTER FOUR
# ALWAYS BLACK

*Wait 'til their Judgement Day comes, yeah!* - Black Sabbath

Iggy and I cut through the brutalist spiked tower blocks of the Barbican. They stake around us, sweet protection from the morning. Fountains splash loudly into lily pools in concrete. I could almost share my secret within the safety of these harsh dictums, layers of mish-mash granite greys, and the maze of liveries and Ripper alleys blocking out the sky, polished skeleton marble guarding the vessel of the city, honey-comb limestone, thick walls to keep the money in. Corpse city blues as we slide down towards the river, edging the meat market. We duck from suits, their focus on buying suits, and more suits, until their lives are over and all that sits on their suits is dribble. These outlying alleys have a charm all their own. 'Saturdays and Sundays, eh?' asks Iggy, when I tell him those are my favourite days for city walks, when it's dead, in the Bladerunner-ness of banker-free cityscapes, when they've all gone home to the country or launched off to plan their cyber-home space retirements.

'It's Wednesday today, right?'

'Thursday...'

'They're just labels.'

'Every day's Saturday night in your world, eh? So what was it with you and Ruby?'

'What, that friction, on the roof?'

'Are you a lesbian?'

I laugh. I like how direct he is. 'No. I just liked her, what she stood for - she was an escape from where I was at. Y'know, I was living in Macclesfield, right? Dad was locked up. She let me stay at her house, in Portobello.'

'In her bed...'

'Yeah. She's not gay either, it was just a weird thing, y'know... it was sisterly.'

'Sapphic, I think the word is.'

'I don't know. Queer times. We were on a lot of E when we snogged the first time. I'd had a weird thing happen with a guy, and it seemed like she cared more. She came up to my Mum's place, we'd go out to raves.'

'She's a control freak. That's what I remember about her.'

'Ha. We've more in common than we thought. But she told you about us?'

'Proudly, yes.'

I change the subject to his old bands: Chernobyl, and whether he regrets leaving them, because they've done so well; The Peking Poppies; The Fanatics. He tells me of the in-band squabbles that led him to push towards being the frontman - he used to play guitar. The old drummer, Dan, died. He was a junky, offbeat. Maybe three months ago now. Each show since, they've placed a white garland on stage, hung around the 808 machine, in his memory. Each road-stop marked with the memory of his 'pick n nicks'. Emptying white chocolate mice into his pickpockets from the sweets at service stations. Orlando never calls him dead, says he's out mouse-hunting. Dan the Drummer kept a pair of drumsticks in his dirty leather belt and exchanged T-shirts with support bands at gigs, gave up washing.

'Heroshima's a good name for a band,' I tell him.

Ig changes the subject to my Dad. 'I just wish he'd had half the success of the people he's worked with, the ones we wear as badges. He's helped them all out...'

The heroes. The heroines. The under-listed. Dying peak-time at the altar of excess. The dead at 27 club always felt so far away.

We pass through city alleys of livery secrets.

'He always said he was happy to move back up North, but they'd ended up there by default because they fucked up their house in Chelsea, where I lived 'til I was six: the Chelsea pad was always full with beardy pals and people en route between Indochina and New York. We kept chickens in the basement.'

'Chickens?'

'Yeah. Y'know, having me, he kinda had to give up the band, and lug sound gear around the world, or he always said it was sound gear. Even in court. And that's how I got packed up to Gwanny's when he went inside the first time. And why, when he got out, he partnered up with Jack Bentaloiz - you know him?'

Iggy shakes his head. Hair falls in front of his eyes. I want to reach out and touch his face.

I explain that the Jack Bentaloiz deal enabled Dad to buy the largest house opposite his old school to prove he'd succeeded where they said he'd fail, to demonstrate that he was the colonel of everything.

'Colonel of Everything. Good song title.'

I feel a soft smile on my face, and want to tell him more of my history. 'I went to the same school, they said I'd fuck up too.'

(It's too poetic that I was cast a Class A fuck up in the era where anyone could become anything they wanted to be.)

'You know I was born in Scotland, deftly dull after, did some time in Cyprus, being an army brat... 'til Mum left Dad, it was violent, so I grew up mainly in Streatham...'

'Moving around, uh?' It explains his soft vocal twang, not going in too loudly anywhere, slight wistfulness.

'No one wants to move around Streatham. I'd pretend I was part Mexican.'

'I heard that.'

'What, that I'm part Mexican?'

'That you lied about it... s'alright, I did it too.'

'Y'know what I've been meaning to ask: that guy, Scaz, that Ruby was getting it on with - your dad must know him?'

'Malachi. Yes.'

'Y'know he's the biggest booking agent in the industry. Be great if Ruby stays with him for a while...'

'What, to get you a deal?'

'You think that's likely?' His dreams are circling, I'm the last person to want to bat down any of his desires. 'I think he knows who Heroshima are. He was watching our gig.'

I change the subject. 'I'm sorry I couldn't stay... I suddenly remembered... a deadline.'

'It's alright, you've seen us loads of times, right?'
'Yeah, just a few...'

I love their music. I'm such a groupie, I know all the words. We cross over Blackfriars Bridge, stopping in the middle with the Thames beneath us. We look west, and into the waves of the water. It's carrying the dark matter of parliament, all the city ambition and greed, out to the sea to be diluted.

Iggy comes close, he touches my face, gently, gentlemanly.
'Can I kiss you?' he asks.

What? Most people just go for it. 'Sure.'

Cold lips, skin smooth inside, the breeze of the city drawing from the ocean, the water dispelling the frantic, electric ambition of the city. His mouth engulfs me, tongues dance and twine. His dark bristle is soft on my face. He smells like leather. I fizz with his tonic, our eyes open, embarrassed, but I wait for him to close his eyelids with long, dark eyelashes. I want to kiss him again. Together. We hold hands along the riverbank. It's my favourite place in the city. And his. It feels like it's meant to be.

In the bar of the National Film Theatre he tells me about Freya, his ex, a designer over in Paris. She works for Steve Stalin - they have such a strong aesthetic. It's kinda Japanese samurai but more utilitarian. Always black. Always male, but women wear it. He met Freya in an ashram in India where "clothing was optional". He regrets that he forgot his dreams while being with her. She distracted him from city elixirs. Interception of the finest deceit. He won't let that happen again. It scares me, his focus. World domination from a four-track recorder. I don't know if he would put me before him. Covering his eyes with shades, he licks his lips. Fark. 'You're Scarlet Flagg,' he says. 'You can do anything.'

I have never been out of control in love but there's some voodoo class magic riding my way. I watch him at the bar, ordering us pints of Belgian beer. I think about the stupid article I'm supposed to be writing for Latex magazine, a feature on 'the nu-goth wave'. Fuck it. Fuck the PRs. I'll call them later.

By channelling wild, it's what we all became. My mind drifts to the night when Ruby and I became blood-sisters, binding our wrists and spirits, vowing by candlelight that we'd get whatever we wanted on our own terms. Wrist to wrist. Blood to blood. Sister to sister. In the deep cover of four-in-the-morning silence, the end of the Sonic Youth record circled its spindle, d-dum, d-dum, for hours. The birds were about to let loose and go ballistic for the day. She brushed my cocaine moustache to her gums with Matador-red talons and growled her Steps of Rock n Roll towards me.

'Here's what we have to do, Scar,' she rasped. 'One: we admit we are powerless against rock, and get ourselves a rockstar boyfriend;

'Two: Give yourself up to him;

'Three: Turn yourself into the press - get in the papers with him;

'Four: Get hitched;

'Five: Get babies;

'Six: Remove him. Get divorced;

'Seven: Be totally famous, without apology;

'Eight: Be totally rich and let everyone know it;

'Nine: The world is ours...we can do anything;

'Ten: Create a business: a new clothing line/interiors line/candle company;

'Eleven: through prayer and meditation, reveal the inside of the former love-nest in a newspaper before selling it for major profit;

'Twelve: REPEAT.'

Ruby's the high priestess of having her life planned like a chess game. She thinks she's got it all mapped out, like she's some kind of groupie cartographer. She rates herself as such an oracle, swashbuckling through the achievements of feminism, power-shag by power-shag.

'I dunno, Rubix; isn't being a wife kinda old school?'

# CHAPTER W14
# DADDY'S BACK

*They get what they want, and they never want it again* - Hole

*I visualise blood cut on fingers, touching other bloodied fingers, wiped over skin, lust. The stickiness as it dries and gets repainted. I think of the sex with Iggy. Him taking me out on my period, to the best place to that feeling. Then I think of the first time he met my father.*

'When I...'

I interrupt Dad, he's already been on a sesh with the Tramp Set, stashing vodka bottles around the country, dog hiding his bones. His skin stinks. Pickled like an onion. His alcofrolics taking him well over the edge of his dreamer's blag and cent of talent. And he only got out a week ago. He's telling us about the time his old mate, Ken Market, supplied the horse that rode into Studio 54, with a nosebag full of chang...

'Horse-power!' Iggy guffawed, lacking his usual control.

In his alco-state, Dad pretends our reunion is higher than it will ever be. He came towards me, awkwardly self-conscious - knowing I was judging him in his current office, the back seat of a pub in West Kensington.

We're back from a tour of the UK. The van broke down near Loch Ness. Or it ran out of petrol. Orlando was driving, looking for Nessy. Met Iggy's Mum. She's amazing-looking. His genes would be fab. A prime baby-maker: witty, tall, handsome, stylish. Slightly dominating. After I've become a famous wife of rock, I'm looking at repopulating the planet with a baby me, baby he, and maybe baby three and four, enough to make a band. He introduced me as his girlfriend. It feels as right as the way our bodies do, folding together. Him holding me, lifting me, my leather boots entwining his neck. The gentleness of him turning to a thrust inside me, his pretty cock.

'How are you, my rebel with a clause?'

'It's so great to meet you,' Iggy bows like he's adulating the ruler of the state he's in.

'Mum sends her love...'

I know I'll have rolled my eyes.

Haven't seen him for four years. I adjust the gaffa-tape on my tit, re-sticking it beneath my gauze black dress. I wish I'd borrowed a T-shirt from Iggy, I feel I've been in these clothes forever.

'I fancy you,' whispers Iggy into my ear.

Dad looks over to Iggy: 'So what have you been doing with yourself?'

'We've just been on tour...'

'Were you writing about it, Scarlet?'

'I write about fashion, not music...' *Jesus.*

But he seems to like my boyfriend. 'Bit of a poet, are you?' he asks him.

I squiggle about on the pub bench as they impress each other with their musical knowledge. They spin in neon atoms of their rock n roll brilliance, yay, double yay, fugtastic, brillobollocks. Makes me want to spray all the white warehouse walls with a black spray-can and firebomb the whole of East London.

'So you know Malachi Wright?' There's a stalky side to Iggy's focus. Can't he just go off-the-job for a second?

'We did USSR together, with Elton. Hawkwind. The Clash - so many tours. So yeah, we know each other.'

'Scarlet's flatmate, Ruby, is going out with him.'

Dad doesn't look surprised. 'We should all go out on a double date, or whatever you kids call it...'

'Oh, yeah, ask Mum down. She can bring her bong.'

My rockstar-to-be pokes me in the ribs. He twists the silver-chain bracelet I bought for him. Dad doesn't pick up on Iggy's desperation, or ignores it.

'Is old Mal still married to Suki Varenza?' asks Dad.

'Not for long if he is, Ruby's kinda determined.'

Dad goes on to explain, Suki Varenza is the reason Malachi killed his own brother. Because Suki was fucking him. Liam Wright got 'electrocuted' onstage while trying out a guitar for Tommy

Helsinger. Les Harvey[9] could only happen once. Like Malachi Wright's domination of the touring industry, the Varenza fashion mob are not a family you fuck with, they racketeer the levies on all the right sort of drinks at clubs in London and across Europe. Started in Italy. They do the same with fashion. The Varenzas and Wright States International Touring are a force you can't fuck with. Rinsing money through nightclubs. A power couple that it is so much better to be friends with. Shootings get covered up as gang-related incidents, but there's only ever one gang in their clubs.

'And by the way, the reason your Mum's not here is because she's got cancer, again.'

That's why he wanted to see me.

It's in her lungs. I kind of knew. My premonitions and fears becoming the same thing. Dad makes his excuses, says he's got to meet a dog about a man.

## DIARY ENTRY: unknown date

Ruby's pregnant and wants to keep it. She thinks Malachi'll give her enough cash to buy a Mercedes and live in the manner she'd like to become accustomed to. She's such a power fucker, thinking she can raise a kid on her own. It'll end up like me; or worse, like her.

'I was on E when he got me pregnant,' she revealed in a proud whisper. 'It's going to be a proper happy baby.'

It's going to be one-hell-of-a-comedown baby.

---

9. *Les Harvey of Stone The Crows was electrocuted by a microphone on stage in 1972, and died. Age 27. On a similar note, also 27, Gary Thain of Uriah Heep plugged himself into an amp in 1975 and electrocuted himself. It didn't kill him, but it is said he never recovered and was fired shortly after. Three months later he ODed on smack.*

*Peter "James" Bond - drummer of Spinal Tap and latterly Buddhahead, mysteriously exploded on stage in 1977 at the Isle of Lucy Jazz Festival.*

Of course, Malachi wanted nothing to do with her now she was carrying his child.

'I just can't be fucked with him anymore. I don't want to walk down a jet-plane aisle with him, let alone doing it in a white dress. You know he's married right?' Drama twanging off her like a badly-tuned guitar solo, she told me it was over. I was super-relieved.

'I didn't know if they were still together...' I lied softly.

'You know Suki Varenza and I go way back? She nicked Jake from No Logo from me; I loved him, so I thought her husband was fair game.'

Which explained everything, I thought Ruby only slept with singers, sperm of frontman. But after lecturing me on the merits of getting babies in the bag, so you could control these men and be in their star-fucked lives forever, Ruby Moon got her fifth lovechild aborted. It had been conceived in a bouquet of hotels.

We went to the Marie Stopes Clinic in West London, hiding, in case anyone saw us, had to walk past a picket-line of Christian bitches telling us we were going to Hell.

'We're going anyway,' she responded.

I wanted to think she hurt inside.

# CHAPTER FIVE
# BORING IF YOU'RE BORED

*I got my cock in your pocket and I'm shoving it through your pants, I just want to fuck you and I don't want no romance* - Iggy Pop & The Stooges

'I can't help it, Iggy. It's hardly my fault, is it?'

He's angry that I didn't make the double-date happen with my Dad, Mal, Ruby, and the pair of us.

'It's too late now,' he strops. 'Why couldn't she stay with him long enough to sort us out?'

This is our first moment of conflict. I defend Ruby, like I'm on a march for the mistresses and wives of rock, explaining that Malachi got her pregnant and wasn't willing to support it, at all, threatened to blow up her shops if she spilled to his wife, Suki Varenza.

'He's not fucking about when he says stuff like that.'

'I just really thought Heroshima were about to get taken on by him.'

He stews.

Later, in The Blowers, where he's DJing, he's all pouty and distant. I get drunk[10] on red wine, the kinda drunk that gets you in trouble, the kinda drunk that helps you forget you have a body you should be inhabiting. We have a further dispute, about me not having any money, and I throw the wine all over the decks when he asks if my father could help with Malachi.

'Maybe pass me on his number?'

Arrrrrghhh - awkward, pushy, annoying.

'Is that the only reason you're with me?'

---

10. *Dave Alexander (aka Zander) was at school with the Asheton brothers who formed The Stooges in 1967 with Iggy Pop. Zander played bass, but was fired in 1970 at the Goose Lake International Festival for being too drunk to play. He died five years later of a pulmonary oedema, related to his drinking.*

If I don't make this happen, he's going to blame me, we'll split up. It's the only way Heroshima will get to the next level, by signing with him.

Nursing my glass, I explain to Cherry Gonorrhoea, who's behind the bar, that I'm skint and stressed. Without the money from Jet Trash, however little that was, I'm signing on, doing a few bits of writing here and there, helping Ruby occasionally too, but I hate working in the shop. It's soooo boring, the hours are so slow, like I have nails hammered to my wrists. I really don't want to go back to Tony the Toerag and have to beg to work on his stalls either. I still want to do my fashorn films. And write a book, maybe about the new wave of designers around here, and us lot, the creatives. It's why I live, for experience, to turn it into art.

After two days by myself, not taking drugs, going swimming at Ironmonger Row, because I know Iggy prefers me straight, I ask if he'll cut me in, on tour money if I do the intro.

'I should speak to Orlando, really... but fuck it, I'll give you cash out of my half, if needs be...' he decides.

'Are you sure?'

He kisses me on the cheek. 'Course - anything for you, moon, stars, sea, m'love.' He's so kind. I forgive his dense moods, knowing it only comes from frustration from not having made it.

We're at the Barbican, there's an exhibition opening for Helmut Newton. Everyone's here. We're both wearing black floor-length cloaks. We love dressing the same. I leave him smoking outside, with the Tin Foil Satellites, and go to the public phone in the dark-lit foyer. There are always weird guys in long macs and strange, design-obsessed nuts wearing abstract glasses. I ignore them and put a call in to Mum. I think of her stupid face, she looks like a cat, her hair reels out, black string to her knees. She weighs about four and a half stone, including hair. She eats three peanuts and thinks that's a meal. It's a disco[11] throwback. When Dad came back from wherever he'd been (touring or jail), Mum'd cook beef like she did it everyday and would recite amazing meals we'd had that were figments of her imagination. I got all the bad chromosomes from both of them: the jealousy, the square-pegged-ness, the junkie-ism, the rock, the roll, the wretchedness. The bitter resentment. She picked up, coughing: 'Hi Scarlet. You up to no good?'

'As you would expect. Hello full moon mother.' Her name is Channary Rae: *full moon*.

'When are you coming see me?'

'When you give up the forty a day and an ounce of grass.'

'Not on phone, Scarlet!' she scolds. Why would I aspire to be anything like her, if she's the best definition of grown-up? Silly cow thought she was doing me a favour by marrying a half-British guy, that I wouldn't carry her skinnier-than-Karen Carpenter[12] deficiencies. That I'd lactate milk and honey.

'And don't pretend you are better than me.'

I shrug so she can hear it.

'Mum, I'm sorry I've not been up to see you.'

'Your daddy tell me you have boyfriend...'

I explain that's why I'm calling. That I'm happy. That he's in a band and needs some help. One of the guys in the macs is staring at me. He is so listening.

'Mum, you remember Malachi Wright? Mum?'

---

11. *Sylvester, popular for singing, You Make Me Feel (Mighty Real) and later, Do You Wanna Funk, was an American disco and soul singer, and performer with a very high voice. He kept hits flowing through the eighties but will always be known best for sharing the Queen of Disco crown with Gloria Gaynor and Donna Summer. He died at 44 from complications with AIDS in 1988.*
*Other AIDS deaths are too extensive to tribute, from Robert Mapplethorpe to Reinaldo Arenas, to Liberace, the pianist who took camp on more trips than the Scouts, his wardrobe was obese in its opulence. He died age 67, in 1987. Ricky Wilson, 32, of the B-52s, in 1986. Ray Gillen of Black Sabbath, age 31, in 1993. Easy-E, of NWA, age 31, in 1995. Wayne Cooper, the original funkster-falsetto singer in Cameo, is reported to have died in 1984, age 28. It is likely he was informed he had AIDS because in 1981 other rumours of his death begin to circulate, and continue until 1985, including him going down in a plane crash in 1983. The band are best known for Single Life and Word Up! released in 1985 and 1986, respectively. Tracks such as Shake Your Pants and Find My Way were huge on seventies' dance-floors. His family were fairly traditional and devout. The wipeout of a generation is impossibly devastating. The effect of AIDS on culture-at-large can be discussed via Fran Lebowitz: "'The first people who died of AIDS were artists. They were the most interesting people."*

12. *Karen Carpenter, best known for singing We've Only Just Begun and Close To You with her brother in The Carpenters, was also their drummer. She died in 1983, age 32, from a heart attack, the result of abusing her body with anorexia nervosa. Very little was recognised about the illness at the time. The fashion industry in the 90s was criticised for glamorising anorexia and the look of 'heroin chic'.*

'Wright States International Touring, Malachi?' She hesitates.

'The one and only. I need his number?'

'What you need Mr Dick Damage for? He play fuckity fuck with everyone, you know.'

Uh, yeah.

'I know, he got my friend pregnant.'

'Eagle doesn't change his feathers.'

'Spots, Mum. Leopards. I can get the number from someone else, if it's a problem...'

Mum knows I rarely connect with guys. She blames herself. Thinks Dad being in the nick on and off has left me with trust issues. *Maybe I could discuss these things more if she could be bothered to come see me here in prison.*

'They're good. Heroshima. Mum, are you okay? Sorry I've not been back home for a while...' She sounds pretty sick again. I don't know how bad. I don't want to. 'Mum, we both know Mal's a wanker, but he does what he does really well, right?'

'I give you number, I meet your boyfriend?'

'Sure, but he's on tour a lot. Iggy Papershoes. He's got no record deal, no publishing. I might do a film with them.'

'I thought you were writing?' Cough, splutter, cough.

'Yes. It just gets a bit boring.'

'You boring if you bored. Maybe film is good, if writing not working...'

'Thanks, Mum...' She doesn't get that all I want to do is write. Her nails tap restlessly on the receiver. Then she goes into her bureau and reaches for her address book.

'This is home number. Ibiza. If you go there, and he will want you to go with new boy, okay, Scarlet? And you come see me, this weekend?'

It's like she knows I'm going to dance with the devil. And you only dance with the devil in his playground.

After the Barbican opening, we go to meet friends in Primrose Hill, and end up scouring the loo shelves of pubs NOT lined with Vaseline. They say gak's not addictive, but the effects are, and pubs are scared it's putting people off their lager. Surely they can see it makes us drink for days. The injured becomes the injurer. You become the stereotype of the stories that impress you. We crawl around the basement of an actor's house, veering towards narcotics as the hours pass.

'Still can't hold it down, girl? I don't ever want to tell you what to do, but I really think you should get off the horse before it kicks you, darling,' says Iggy, as I hold bile down, swinging in the nest inhabited by artists who have produced Heroin's Greatest Hits.

"Find what you like, and let it kill you..." was one of Dan the Drummer's sayings. Habits police the ego, pacing with vanity extremus, to bullying comedowns, but what often begins as an irregular occupation surreptitiously becomes more frequent, galloping into the era of false promises, Tony Blair waiting in the wings, for us to vote him in. The good times fading. Rising ladette culture murdering the feminine, and everything propagated by ecstasy. The only way to behave was as a metal-hearted warrior, geezer-hardcore, iron-suit. So I persist. All the pre-globalised eras go in cycles of psychedelia, moving through to cocaine, uppers, to heroin, to finding oneself in eastern esoterica, and back to the wishy-washy weed fug. I've done all the gateways. One day we will meet a Buddhist ohm, or the apocalypse, whichever comes first. I see no future. *I am the impatient inpatient, the prisoner, lying on a prison bed below, crying, for the first time in years. I miss Iggy, with daggers through my body. I sleep all the time, hoping to dream of him, and me, in fur. I used to see arrows in the sky, connecting us. That shield is dying. The fantasy of who I was, or could be, the writer, the sidekick to his dreams, it's fading with my vision to the future... you find what you like and let it kill you. Clothes, sex, drugs, music.*

# CHAPTER SIX
# NU BEAT

*Elvis was a hero to most, but he never meant shit to me* - Public Enemy

It's days until we wake up again. Daze. Bang. Bang. Dead head. Thud. Bang. Shake hair over face. Bang. 'Scarlet, are you awake?' Grumble. Grumble. Misery is me. Hair's stuck to the gak around my mouth. HeadACHE. Bang. Bang. Hello, is that the shadow of the Grim Reaper at the bottom of the bed? Alas, no. It's Iggy Papershoes, tweaking his ear-stud, looking all garage-mechanic rockabilly. Fark. He's so together. I consider pretending to be asleep, but he knows I've clocked him.

'Farking hell, what is it?' Gah. He's not seen this side of me before. I want to be perfect, and kind to him. I pull the manky duvet around me like a mole's bonnet. Kinda hoping it's cute.

'I've been up already and pawned my guitar.' He's only got one guitar. Isn't he supposed to need it? 'I want to take you to Ibiza. I need you to be with me, my spirit angel. You're my good luck charm.'

He sees something in me that I've lost.

My nostrils are joined together. I can't breathe. I've soldered the channels to my lungs shut, bad drugs. My eyes roll to my left and there's a kebab lying next to me. The light is dark outside, the birds are crying, it's either dawn or dusk. Where am I? Why am I? I feel my face. It's still there. Paranoia pops like burnt toast. Have I got clothes on?

'Ibiza? Isn't that the naffest place on the planet?' I am cold, shivering, having an affair with a sliced meat and chilli sauce. I seem to have been in a wet (red wine) T-shirt competition. I pull my fingers through my No Bypass hair. I remember meeting Beanpole, the Polish drug dealer, under Marble Arch. You give him a coded phone ring and he gets there within half an hour, fully loaded, full European embrace. We went to Mayfair after, stumbled back around Elephant and Castle, skirting another dawn.

'Do you know how gorgeous you are, with all your exotic blood, and sexy skin - you are gonna look amazing with a bit of sun... we're gonna get out of London, sort our shit out. We're gonna go to Ibiza, you and me, do the deal with Malachi. Straighten out in the sunshine, baby. And I'm gonna take you shopping when we get back with all that money. Mother-fucking Gucci, baby.'

I sit up. He holds me. My glamour, now an obvious panache. This is raw, fucked up me on a dead day. There's no light from the glitter I was scattering all over us last night, bought down Bethnal Green Road, from a sari shop, where they thought I was one of them, but via another planet. I want to tell Ig about Malachi. When we're away - by the ocean, on a beach of sand and moonlight. First we must get out of London. It's a hard town, a dirty town, full of dirty tricks and whores. London is a mean town, a cold town, a filthy smelling grey town. It's the Hollywood of Europe, a place to smile, not be weighed down. It's a small town network that I no longer want to surround. A web of old establishment stealing nu town ideas. A Hitchcockian fear shudders this sheet-less mattress - I'm having a sobriety quake. I'm splattered. Trampalicious. Bon Scott.[13]

'Am I still a virgin?' I ask him.

'Ha. Unlikely.'

You're going to find this weird, but we've still not slept together. Shared several beds, been intimate, but he's not yet been inside me. It's not that we're so wasted we can barely fuck (let alone leave the country), it's that I've wanted to hold out.

'Scarlet, there's another reason for us to get away.'

'I know, I want to make it special too.'

Our wires cross like the confusion in his brow.

'Oh, baby. Yes. But no - they're watching us. We've got to split.'

'Who's watching us?'

---

13. *AC/DC's singer Bon Scott passed out forevermore, after a night out at the Music Machine in Camden with his friend, Alistair Kinnear, on February 19, 1980. Kinnear drove home to Dulwich in his Renault 5 and left the singer inside the car to sleep it off rather than drag the 33 year old inside, as a guest. Bon Scott never woke. A known asthmatic, hypothermia or inhalation of vomit have been suggested, as have the usual conspiracies. The Coroner's report reads: acute alcohol poisoning & death by misadventure.*

'Oh, man, like the CIA, FBI, MI5, MI6, y'know the drill, doll face - Deuteronomy 32: "For their rock is not as our rock."'

'Where are They?'

'Outside, in an unmarked car.'

He's worse than I am. I look up and around, there are pigeon feathers everywhere.

'Seriously, they're out there, Scaz. Can't trust anyone. People are trying to poison me.'

He appears to have given up his place on the last tour and moved in here. His wardrobe has exploded with mine. I pull out black, drainpipe jeans and a spidery top from a clothes mountain. I need to get my passport, asking him if he has his.

I have no intention of physically seeing Malachi, I'll just send Iggy, and Orlando, if he can come too.

Creeping down the stairwell, the only way to see what's on the other side is to open the door and step right through.

'You first,' he says.

I pull the hood up of my floor-length black goatskin cape. Iggy's wearing Orlando's old Portobello stock - combat gear, from dead Italian soldiers.

The real world.

'Farrrrk, it's bright.'

We retreat back inside for shades.

Lensed, we try again.

'That's it...' Iggy points at a long Volvo estate down the side-street, down towards the graveyard on Moorgate, where William Blake was piled in a grave with his wife.

Whomever's in the passenger seat slips down, trying to go lower than the window.

I know exactly who it is.

*Knock knock*, I tap on the glass. JD Frank. Ruby's coke dealer. His bad leather blouson squeaks against matching seats.

'Mate, what are you doing here?'

'I'm on special ops, aren't I?! What do you think? I'm waiting for Ruby, she owes me five hundred nicker. Where you off to?'

'Travel agent.'

Iggy pokes me in the ribs. Naughty. Never let the enemy know your plans.

'Going somewhere nice?'

'You'd have to arrest us to find that out, mate,' sniggers Iggy. 'Laters!'

We scuttle like beetles to a travel agent near Liverpool Street station.

'I don't trust him,' conspires Iggy. He scratches his leg like it's bitten with paranoia. His hair is longer than it's been for a while. I cut it a month ago, but he's so full of man, hirsuteness pours out of him. Rivers of spunk will soon stick us together.

Budget posters for coach trips to Calais, Bruges and Dublin are taped to the windows of the travel agent in Liverpool Street. Black-block type is printed on sun-faded fluoro-pinks and acid-yellows. They clash with the rainbow of YSL shirts coming into Liverpool Street from Essex.

The travel agent's badly-bleached, below shoulder-length hair stands wizened like a cliff-top gorse tree, behind her is a mirror, from which I spy a tired face staring back. Little has survived the past week, I'm left with worn-out smiles. I look sixty. Finally, I'm ageing.

We'll leave later that afternoon. Iggy's guitar pays - he sold a watch too. 'It was my Dad's, it wasn't important.'

A gypsy harangues our space on the other side of Liverpool Street Station. 'Would you like some lucky heather?'

'I can pick it myself, I reckon.'

'Round here? Curses will fall on you, young lady.'

'Your lucky heather's done you a lot of good, hasn't it?' I hurl.

'I've got a three-bed semi in Chelmsford,' she snarls.

Iggy pulls me back, he senses the city people surrounding, staring in conservative horror as I lose the plot, the rise of me swearing.

'Your journey is doomed,' she cries. 'The devil's going to get you.

And you, young frizzihead, won't know his face, mark my words...'

'Oh give me a break - sage of Shoreditch - like you're going to sell all your shamrock and make enough to buy the council house you've been put in because fifty of your children are in care after you sold them for a caravan.'

The last person I need in my life right now is a shyster soothsayer blackmailing me with plants she's stolen from a garden centre.

My protector moves in, telling her to leave me alone. I am so hungover, I can hardly see. I need to eat a fried-egg sandwich, it's the only thing that'll sort me out. We turn homewards, rattled. Cutting through backroads.

'If she was for real, she'd be able to sense she should have given me a wider berth.'

Iggy leaves me as he goes off to score at the end of Brick Lane.

'Don't do a Glenn Miller[14] on me, all right?'

'Scarlet, I'm walking! I'll see you down at the Blowers. Five minutes behind you. Okay? I don't want you coming where I'm going, but I'm behind you, alright?'

Alone, I'm approached by a city suit. 'How much, love?'

'You couldn't afford me. Fuck off.'

Kyrie, Peachy, and Bobby Bandit are in the pub. Peachy, who models and had a hit with a house record, is boasting that she's nearly off, made a few quid on her kiss and tells about The Luzers, sold the pictures of him pimping methadone outside the housing office on Pitfield Street - one way ticket to Thailand at the weekend.

'I'll look up your relatives,' she says.

I hate groupies. Can't they do something that makes girls look good? Distracted by something familiar in her handbag.

'I've read that,' I say, peering in.

'What? This?' Confused, she brings the book out for all to see.

---

14. *Glenn Miller, a popular American bandleader disappeared, age 40, in a Norseman aircraft over the English Channel in 1944.*

'On your way in, Scazzer?' asks Bobby Bandit. 'It's the freeeakin' A-Z of London!'

'I was joking,' I lie. 'Passed the Shoreditch entrance exam by reading the whole thing, got as far as Zeitgeist Street, didn't I?'

After I've levelled out, five vodka and sodas later (because it's low-calorie), Iggy calls the pub to keep me on track, and I go home to pack.

Ibiza is a massive Shazzy disco. All my mates from up North used to get taken there on holiday.[15] Piña coladas all 'round. It's going to be super-cheesey-feast. I'll be okay if I'm with Iggy. We're gonna have fun. I don't have to see Malachi.

I put my prize-travelling essentials into a velvet, leather and patchwork duffel bag:

- ☑ Chanel No. 5;
- ☑ Bach's Rescue Remedy;
- ☑ a toothbrush;
- ☑ grey pashmina;
- ☑ fun make-up;
- ☑ fun knickers;
- ☑ fun bikini;
- ☑ and fun death-spike mules.

I take three dresses: a baby pink, hippy, psychedelic mini in fat jersey with delicious Bloomsbury flock velour on both the front and reverse; I roll up a black, slutty, fishnet, cowl-necked, short prototype leopard-skin thing with zips all over it; and a classic,

---

15. Billie Holiday was 44 when cirrhosis of the liver and drug abuse overshadowed her beauty and unique jazz voice which belted out over one-hundred recordings. Recognised for melancholic tracks like Gloomy Sundays and revolution touting Strange Fruit (the story of a lynching recorded on Commodore, not Columbia her regular label, it became one of her most famous songs). Billie started recording in 1935 after moving to New York from Baltimore to be with her mother, although it took years of playing clubs to get there, she was determined after getting arrested, not long after arrival, for prostitution in 1929. By the mid-forties she was on screen with Louis Armstrong in New Orleans, but her drug use led to a deteriorating stasis and she died in 1959.

black halter-neck that flares from under the empire line. And a slinky black short number with a zip down the front, it ruffles like an 80s curtain pelmet. Okay, four dresses. Two days. I add one leopardskin print sarong, another with sun salutations printed all over it from a yoga village in Goa (picked up after scattering my grandmother in Varanasi, just after Reading Festival. It was the funeral my Dad wants, not his mother. Staying in zillion rupee palaces every night in her memory, for several months. She would have hated it. And it skinted him, showed him up on the bank's radar, forced that last haul he got caught out on).

I pull a hoody, with Survivor printed on it in silver, frat house lettering, around my waist. I'm wearing black jeans, Stones[16] T-shirt and grey-spider cashmere jumper and leopard-print coat. Together with Mum's silver Ganesh trinket, we're ready to fly.

Ibiza, we're coming for you.

---

16. *Brian Jones died, age 27, July 2nd or early morning of the 3rd July, 1969. A known liability, particularly on drugs, he was found at the bottom of his outdoor swimming pool at Cotchford Farm in East Sussex. Reported as death by misadventure, murder is common gossip, and speculation as to whom varies from odd-job man, Frank Thorogood to his former band, The Rolling Stones who released hundreds of white butterflies in his memory at a gig in Hyde Park two days later. To prevent looting, Brian Jones is said to be buried twelve-feet deep, in Cheltenham, England, his hometown.*

# CHAPTER SEVEN
# BLURBERRY, VUITTEND AND SLAMSONITE

*Tropical the island breeze, all of nature so wild and free* - Madonna

Our friend Valium guides us through the crowds of low-end travellers who dawdle in obesity. On approach of the escalator they come to a complete standstill of non-committal lemmingness. They can't figure how the electric staircase will carry them, their flab, and dodgy, snide luggage of Blurberry, Vuittend and Slamsonite. I hate unprofessional travellers.

Iggy and I get lost in each other's eyes, the world could pass. But the stupid lame-ass, inexperienced pond scum slugs with luggage are still there...

Iggy takes his arm around my shoulders, sticks out his chest, takes my luggage, and strides through. People feel they should recognise him and stop, awestruck, which enables us to move efficiently through their hick ineptitude. His aura shelters us, bound within his black leather.

'Be good when we've got someone to help us through airports, eh?'

'Most bands can't stand up without their crew. That's what my Dad says...'

'He's been nursemaid to a few, alright. I knew you were his daughter, y'know?'

'Seriously?'

He looks at me like he has a million questions. My dad was the connection to the truths so insane they can only be passed aurally to those trusted as troupers of the rock n roll family. That's why Iggy wanted to be with me. He saw something that I wasn't even in possession of.

'That tour with The Wyld Stallions... did he ever tell you about that?'

I shake my head. Iggy kisses me on the cheek. 'Legends.'

And I think he means it about him and me.

Our names are called on the speaker, we scram slowly, get past security, down the tunnel towards the big doors to the sky. Walking on clouds before we've taken off. Iggy stops before we board, and kisses me, for what seems like forever. He's so happy to see his career aligning.

Seated, belted, we lift off, micro-bottles of champagne poured. I am apprehensive of the journey ahead. As the sky softly cradles beneath, we descend into plane detox. He asks the girls on the plane for blankets, but it's a European flight so they have none. We are allowed to cover him with my sarongs which he then throws to the floor. It feels a bit Buddy Holly,[17] constricted, entwining with the nylon seat-belts, I hadn't realised how much dope he'd been doing. Nor had he. The plane vibrates. He goes for his emergency stash in his secret pocket - and locks himself in the toilets as we hit thunder, lightning zaps with deliverance, the staff knocking on the door. He reemerges, cool, the man I am in love with. Falling in and out of sleep with each other, by the time we touchdown, the sun

---

17. Joe Meek was regularly attempting to record voices from beyond the grave, particularly Buddy Holly's, and accused Phil Spector of stealing his ideas. The producer behind early Tom Jones, Screaming Lord Sutch, The Manish Boys, Gene Vincent, Billy Fury, Shirley Bassey, Diana Dors and many more, died age 37 (3 February, 1967) on the eighth anniversary of Buddy Holly's death. It was still illegal to be gay in Britain when Meek killed his landlady and then himself. Only later that year did the Sexual Offences Act come into power, making homosexual acts illegal for those under the age of 21 (excepting anyone serving in the armed forces until 2000). In 1994 the age of consent was reduced to 18. At time of writing any woman over 16 in Britain can be legally fucked by a male. In the author's humblest opinion, we are sexual beings, and our sexuality, like our consciousness, are primary properties.

Brian Epstein, manager of The Beatles is another music industry visionary whose death could partly be blamed on the illegality of homosexuality. He died of a Carbitral (sleeping pill) overdose in 1967, mixing seven pills with alcohol. On at least one previous occasion he had written a suicide note.

The first disaster of contemporary rock n roll - "the day that music died" - gained its name from American Pie, the song by Don McLean that sang tribute to Buddy Holly, Ritchie Valens (only 17, fresh from the hit, La Bamba) and J. P. 'The Big Bopper' Richardson who all crashed and burned together in a small plane. The tour trio had changed travel plans at the last minute, when their bus driver went to hospital with frostbite. They thought it would be warmer, and faster, to fly.

Both Lynyrd Skynyrd vocalists, Ronnie Van Zant (age 39) and Cassie Gaines (42) died alongside guitarist, Steve Gaines (38) and the band's assistant road manager, pilot and co-pilot when the plane ran out of fuel in Mississippi, 1977. The band are best known for singing Sweet Home Alabama and Free Bird.

aerates the plane as the door springs open, my nostrils kick back on their little deck chairs. Pretending to be Jackie Onassis (as I always do when leaving a plane), I glide from top to bottom of the airstair, looking dead ahead, never peering down beneath my shades. It's my favourite of catwalks.

Welcome to Barcelona Airport. In five languages.

Wire-haired bitch booked non-direct flights, we've only got halfway.

'Double the chance of going down like Lynyrd Skynyrd, amazing,' says Iggy.

We lug our hand luggage to the bar, sample the local cerveza for six hours until the connection flight. Iggy is a strict rationer of his gear - he's very controlled about it - would never do it all, for the hell of it - he likes a constant drip. He's the same with beer. I drink at double his speed.

The last thing I want to become is a manipulative wife of rock.

'You don't want Malachi Wright on tour with you, y'know... try n get one of his associates to tour manage...'

I order another double.

# CHAPTER EIGHT
# GONZO GAZPACHO

*We've been dancing with Mr Brownstone, he won't leave us alone* - Guns n Roses

Ibiza airport is a soup of red-faced shell-suits with croutons of Drank It, Shagged It, Lost It T-shirts. Students splatter through, clunky stains of gazpacho sunstroke, unaware of the rucksacks on their backs bashing people around them. Chunks of hippy ravers jump on love buses - or former ambulances - to the north of the island in their threads from India, holding guitars from Mexico, drums from Tangiers. DJs slice through everyone, their aluminium record boxes on wheels spooning consumption.

My heart rockets through my chest with anxiety.

Iggy pushed to stay in some place with a Wham! history:

'Where the drinks are free... and membership's a smiling face... fun and sunshine - there's enough for everyone...' he kept on singing, laughing his head off. No way are we going back to the eighties, we're gonna stay at Jack Bentaloiz's place, El Tigre Pelado. It's part of his Kalifornia Hotel Group. It's new, it's modern. I discussed it with Ruby.

He's so excited. I've not seen this less self-conscious side of him before. I like it. He's fun.

One of the good things about going out with a singer is that they sing when you're with them. His voice is pretty. His T-shirt hangs from his shoulders perfectly, his arms, muscular - he's got a Gonzo fist in black ink, tattooed to his right arm. I kiss him. He kisses back.

'Are you on holeeeeday?' asks the driver.

'Here for some business,' explains Iggy. 'Music business, y'know, the worst kind. We are coming to meet a booking agent. I've got a band.'

We fly through ley lines of hysteria which lead to the giant, glass-domed disco-bug houses of Privilege and Amnesia, taking a road where pine trees needle the sky, sandy dust spreads beneath orange groves, and orchards promise olives and almonds. Whitewash fincas glimmer, clinging to the hills like snow. Pale birds fly against the cloudless blue sky. I feel all Eddie Cochrane and Gene Vincent[18] as we speed past a donkey cart and hippies walking barefoot across the island.

'Her name is REEEEEIOOOO and she dances on the sand...'
'Rio! Baam...' sings Iggy as we pass posters for pill parties.

The driver knows Malachi.

Iggy leans forward from our back seat, offering him a cigarette. The driver takes one, pushing back long black curls, turning down his Deep Purple tape.

'Eeeee has big 'ouse. Big parties...'
'He's been here for a while?'
'Not long. But he make good friends. That is what is important in Ibiza.'

Looking out of the window at scrubland hills. We fly down into Ibiza Town, levelling with the sea. It's stylish here, old Spanish, tree-lined avenues, bohemian breeze.

---

18. *Gene Vincent's first demo was Be-Bop-a-Lula and landed him a contract with Capitol Records after a discharge from the Navy. Released in 1956 his band, The Blue Tops' music also appeared in the films The Girl Can't Help It and Hot Rod Gang. Emigrating to the UK to avoid American tax, he had eight top 40 hits in the UK by 1961 and while on tour with 21-year-old, Eddie Cochran, he re-injured his leg in the car crash that killed his friend. He had little success over the next ten years and died of a haemorrhaged ulcer on October 12, 1971. He was 36.*

# CHAPTER NINE
# VODKA LIMONS

*Shake your money maker* - Fleetwood Mac

Jack Bentaloiz is not present at El Tigre Pelado but his general manager looks upon us with love, in his striped, faded orange and white Moorish kaftan. He picks up the phone, gets hold of his boss, who is passed over for a quick, 'Hi darling, how are ya? How's yer father?' chat before proceeding to comp us rooms.

'Stay as long as you like, angel!'

Jack is almost an uncle, an essential part of the rock circuit having hotels in every land and Class-A hook-ups to match. Everyone who's ever been on the road knows to stop off at Le Panther Noire in LA, the Maxilizardo in Manchester and La Rock Folie in Paris for all their special needs. He also makes kaftans. Like the only kaftans anyone would ever wear. Jack had a string of islands out in the Pacific in the seventies. Kept different chicks on every one.

'What does Pelado mean?' Iggy asks the manager, Ziggy.

'Bald. Or punk, depending on who you ask...' Ziggy's British, posh, been living out here since 1989. He's smoking beedies. I ask him for one, which he fondly passes over.

The hotel foyer is more of a lounge. Miro rugs and Keith Haring originals hang on white walls. Neon Indian psychedelia is painted upon terracotta pots and tiles.

'Go out there, get yerselves a couple of vodka limons whilst we sort your rooms.'

We follow his pointing hand to a pool and bar beneath a Hawaiian-roofed hut, womanned twenty-four-seven, she serves cocktails and DJs, currently playing ELO and Tangerine Dream. We each grab a lounger and sip long, cool drinks, gazing over an infinity pool which blocks out the town below. My look is kinda gothic for such climes. I strip off, slip on a bikini and dive deep into the pool. A midnight swim, the perfect entrance to the island, cool and refreshing. Water cleaning the dust of the city away. The skim of the pool halos the edge of our universe - the sea roles out to the horizon. I snort five pints of pool water as Iggy joins me.

'I'm so bloody nervous about meeting Malachi,' he confides, shaking his hair from left to right as he rises from the depths, and I bluff my way out of an embarrassing nosebleed, shifting to the side of the pool, getting out, drying my nose and self with my leopard-print sarong in the moonlight. I feel like a poster-girl for fuck ups but Iggy doesn't seem to care, and comes out of the pool to kiss me beneath the crushed velvet sky. 'Yeah, he makes me feel like that too.'

I can't even consider going there tomorrow. I hug Iggy, offering him all the life-force I can, stroke his cheekbones and jaw, and tell him it'll all be fine, he's gonna be the biggest star on the planet. We make plans together, for me writing about touring with them, for doing clothes for them, for maybe writing some kind of porn-opera together. We're lying by the pool, when Ruby and Orlando roll in with Filmmaker Paul. They landed hours ago and have been hanging out with Marie Villotta, the fashion editor. 'Why didn't you come and let me know, I could write for her...'

'In Spanish? Hardly, Scarlet.'

They're wasted, and talking about a thousand parties they want to go to. Orlando starts singing a Heroshima song at me and Iggy:

> *I want you - crazy horse*
> *I want you - because...*
> *Your eyes are mirrors, disco-balls*
> *Fall across this dance floor to me...because*
> *Stars on fire.*
> *Burn the haze of our lies.*
> *Fly me a line to the future.*
> *Fly me a line to the future.*
> *I'm a rule breaker,*
> *A heart shaker.*
> *Risk taker, oh yeah...*

One day, he's going to want to record his own album.

# CHAPTER TEN
# YOU ARE ALL YOU CARRY

*I'll be your friend* - Robert Owen

Pills are waiting on our pillows. How cool is this? J'adore the anonymity of being miles away from any truth about one's identity: the four walls of a hotel room are the boundaries of our conscience. They allow a freedom of fantasy to dance from the semiotics of our possessions, the things we carry upon us, the only clue as to who we are, or wish to be. It's good to be possessed by such a uniform, it makes life easy, there are fewer decisions: Favourite shoes, sexiest underwear, the books, the music. When you travel, you are all that you carry. I am the sum total of glitter, a few cool dresses and a couple of notebooks.

*In prison, I came with nothing. I am nothing. Destroyed. Zero. You know what you channel, the patterns you assimilate from your environment, like the affectations of the archetypes played by stars in your favourite movies, or the eyeliner you wear like your favourite musician, the people you hang out with - these things become you. You are what you fuck. You are who you follow. You are what you consume. You are as old as what you're fucking. I soon became that person who is always more wasted and crazy than you. The person who never sleeps, wears the most transparent clothes. Has the most bruises. And I always feared my secrets. I couldn't look within myself, only out, so surrounded my life in a social whirligig. A lot of people's hate for my abandonment of convention was rotting me from the inside. The poison of my truth. The muddy trauma of rock n roll would kill me. That's why I got involved with fashion: Sleek. Clean. 90s. So fist-icated. Post-techno. Direct from the underground. Mysterious. Cliquey. Fabulous. Nu. I always knew rock n roll would kill me. Because never mind what we pretend to be, we are the sum total of our experiences.*

I remember the jasmine perfumes trailing through the windows, citrus candles and purple, white and pink oriental flowers plucked from paradise parading from bright ceramics upon Balinese bedside tables. The windows above the sheepskin headrest open to luxuriant, medicinal Mediterranean air which rolls forth towards our sweetly-intoxicated bodies. I remember us smiling, blissfully rescued from city cynicism. Spas are the best rehab. And we've got drugs. It's fricking beautiful. This hotel room is love, our bodies come together, power, suction, raw lust and gentleness. We boot history over the horizon. Feelings of whooshy purity hit with the heat of the night. We are in It. In Love. Love Inn. Great neon trails of dust sparkle cherub-arrows through our vision. Bodies meld, liquid gold. Clothes drop in slow motion. Heavy bass to the floor. The heat from our skin condenses as films of slidey-snap skin oil. The wind brushes an electric current over our naked flesh as we fall onto the thick, white, cotton sheets and we roll over each other, belly to belly, forehead to forehead. Lightning aerials touch. Forceful, playful, deep waves. The moorish dome of his cock pushes against me as I hold onto his neck and he spins me around, floating in a space ballet. I am in love. Blissed out, tripped out heaven. I cum like an AK47, ratatattat. He shoots me with silver, across my stomach. He tastes so sweet, and we lie together, as one, he's apologising for a quick show. I love him. That was not fucking, it was making love. Music comes from outside our open windows and our hips groove in unison to the bass.

I pray to Ruby Moon that she is right. I focus on Step 1: Iggy, me, together. I visualise it, and pray to the God who wants to save me that Mr & Mrs Papershoes comes to be. Ha ha. My eyes cheer with obsession and roll under my skull, they clean my internal scalp, I feel like my eyeballs are about to fall down my tongue, and bounce before us as my jaw unlocks, drops and swims from left to right, not fixing into a clamp. His lips move over my thighs and I pull my hands up through the thick air and wipe the magic, powdery, sweaty sense of my palms through my hair. The skin on my upper legs is buzzing, there's multi-colour energy sparking out. I try and press it back in. Breathing the air through my mouth like a tunnel, my eyes close and open again to describe the surrounds in a mantric dictum of fuzzy fractals. I am at one with the world's pulse. This is the essence of being. It's overpowering, and I tumble off the bed towards the bathroom as Iggy discovers an Octopussy wall of fish-tank and whacks his beautiful, naked body against the glass divide, doing some bizarre post-Bowie performance art. Laughing, he glides his cock along the glass. Pale. I press my chocolate-chip nipples to the other side of the glass.

'I love the way you look,' I tell him.

'I love the way you look,' he replies. 'I love this.'

'I love this,' I laugh.

'I love us, here, now, together. No-one else,' he says.

I agree, is this real? 'I love us. This is cool, Iggy. This is sooooo cool.'

'I love you,' he says.

I feel like crying at the beauty of this moment.

'I love you.' I giggle - there's no going back. We move together, clinging to one another for life. He's so straightforward. Gets his emotions. Goes with them.

'What do we do with this much love?' he asks.

'You can write a song about it.'

'No, we should do something real. Y'know what we should do, Scarlet, to make this really special?'

He gets down on one knee, naked, his balls hanging like poetry.

'Will you marry me, Scarlet Flagg?' he asks.

Ruby is going to die.

# CHAPTER ELEVEN
## EL ROCK, 'ELLO ROLL

*You gotta fight for your right to paaaaarty* - Beastie Boys

'Hilarious. Bloody hell. Let's do it. Yes. Iggy, it'll be funny as all fuck, we should do it here - love island...'

'It's fun, huh, being in hotels, with you, on ecstasy...'

Orlando is rattling at the door, 'Open up, farkwits.'

My husband-to-be and I hang onto one another and wrap a sheet around us, answering the door together.

'Meet my fiancée,' I say to Ruby. She's giving it a showbiz smile. Totally frozen.

'Get in there, my son!' congratulates Orlando.

'Riiiiiiiiiiiiiiio!' sings Iggy. He can be a bit of a knob, and I don't care.

# CHAPTER TWELVE
# THE LOST CITY OF ATLANTIS IS HERE

*It's a nice day for a white wedding* - Billy Idol

Buzzing down a cobbled hill through sandstone castle gateways in my favourite black dress (yuh-huh, forgot to list that one, it's Mark Spye) with glitter sprinkled over my eyes and Studio 54 red on my lips, the noise of the night pulls us into its inferno of balearia-infected disco freaks flowing through a cosmopolitan web of alleys, which twist down to the harbour, a pluralistic rapacious mycelium.

A group of stunning girls march towards our gang. If Andy Warhol were alive he'd be art-directing Mac cosmetic commercials with these yankee-doodling, half-op cats, toddling their hypothetical perfections of womanhood past us.

'Adopt me!' caterwauls Orlando behind them.

'You're welcome, sweetheart,' says the girl with the big, pink beehive, matching heels and yellow rubber dress.

'You alright if I take a walk on the wild side with this lot? See you guys back at the ranch later?'

'What about me?' whines Ruby.

'You're here. Have fun!' replies her brother, and he's off.

I take Ruby's dejected hand. Filmmaker Paul films us, she gets her pout back on, and we stride down to the harbour. Boats dance like fireflies around Disney castle yachts on a black ocean. Stalls of jewellery surround the harbour, synthesised sounds from every traveller Mecca on the planet join Janis Joplin[19] clothes and parades of weirdo-fab caterwauling from bar to bar. We wander past red velvet ropes and the guy on the door recognises Iggy.

'Dude, I saw you play that festival in Austria with The Luzers a month ago. You were so wicked. Come in, this is the first night of

---

19. *Janis Joplin, the singer who really wanted a Mercedes Benz, had been off heroin for a while but fell back under its spell for one last fleeting romance and died of an overdose at the Landmark Motor Hotel on Franklin Avenue in Hollywood, age 27, October 5, 1970.*

this place, we'll look after you. Welcome - welcome to Viktor's...'

Whisked past cloakrooms, into a black space of girls teasing, dancing in nothing, luring with designer bottles, the club is in an ancient castle that was used as a training ground for old Spanish sex spies, we are told, whilst asked what we'd like, on the house. The guy who waved us in suggests EEEnglebert Humperdrincks - eeeasy on the eyeees pink bellinis from the star-themed cocktail menu. He sends a tray by a waitress on roller-boots, as we sprawl as the crown jewels, atop Ottoman cushions, on a glass floor of this swish private balcony in a supper club where no-one eats. There's a dancefloor below, where people make dancing look easy.

Iggy shrugs, falling into my shoulder with a drunk smile.

I check my reflection in the crescent of the moon, applying lipstick and eyeliner in the safety of the night, before reclining back to the mellow house music. I usually hate house music.

The drinks are good.

Ruby works it like a pole dancer for what seems like hours, us watching between the brim of Sindy dolls n Flesh Gordons, bat gals n leotards n rhinestone freedom fighters, bikini warriors and stiletto-strapped, tattooed beefeaters. Everyone's skin glows. I get up to go somewhere, to wander, but Ig wants us to stick together, so I reach to sit beside him and misjudge it by three metres, falling through to another dimension. I'm in heaven, floating on clouds with the cherubs. Shooting stars of sapphire and diamond drop like bullets above.

'You alright, love?' asks my fiancé. Ha - ridiculous.

I molest his amazing ankle. He has excellent ankles, long and lean, brushed with dark hairs, snowdrop white skin. I chew a little.

Ruby soon collapses next to me,

'I am so poor, Scarlet. So ridiculously poor. The shops are doing terribly.'

I don't know what to say, Ruby's always been the grown-up. She can't be as skint as I am...

'I'm going to have to ask Mally for hush-money...'

I groan.

'Sorry, don't mean to be a downer. It's like rave never died in here...' she shouts.

'It's like being in a room full of Bobby Bandits...' announces Iggy.

He's right. Bobby was born over here. And serendipitously enough, someone blocks our view, standing directly in front of us, his voice bellows: 'Jeezus fucking Christ - you lot... what the fark are yous doing out of Shoreditch?'

Bobby is dressed as a rubber devil in a milkmaid's plaited wig. He has a woman dressed as a German army officer by his side. His wife, the one who knows everyone. A cold metal wham-blam of a rifle goes up my back—I'm so impressed by her networking society shizzelle, her parties, I've heard so much about them. 'Jeezus farking Christ, Bobby. We were just talking about you,' I scream, jumping up from where I have fallen on the floor, I kiss him on both cheeks. I do the same to his wife, introducing myself.

We'd forgotten Bobby's brother runs clubs around the world. Malaga, Miami, Montreaux. He's here to help open this joint for his partners, the Varenzas.

'I advised them to launch on a full moon.'

'How totally kismet,' I say, wondering if that's how to use the word properly.

'You know the moon is bigger out here, in Ibiza?' he says. I nod.

'Bobby - we're getting married.'

'Who? You and Ruby? Finally.' Bobby hits me on the arm, in delight.

'Congratulations,' says his wife, in the sexiest overflow of a voice, she smells of vanilla and cocoa.

'I can give you a certificate of marital union, no problemo amigos!' offers Bobby. 'I'm the shit at casting my flagrant magic upon lovers, you know it was me that put Baron Rhinehart together with Pontessa De Seine?'

'Really?' says Iggy. He's such an A-lister slag.

'Let me do it, please,' Bobby begs. 'No-one I've ever married has split up. Not yet, anyway. We should do it now, get married here, start this club going properly. Nothing worse than a spun out engagement. It'll be amazing, sooooo beautiful. Soooooooo romantic. Your kids will be beautiful. Let's do it here, on the rooftop tonight...'

Iggy is not sure.

'Where you staying?'

We tell him.

'Oh really? Fuck off doing it here then. Let's do it there, at dawn, on the poolside terrace.'

# CHAPTER THIRTEEN
# YOU CAN'T HIDE THE LOVE IN YOUR EYES
*Meet me at the top of the sky* - Spaceman 3

'We're getting married in the morning...' sings Iggy, 'Tick tock, the sun is going to shiiiiine... I should probably call Mother.'

'Not for the first time...' snarks Bobby Bandit, in a Hawaiian shirt, leopardskin posing-pouch and platform boots. A police dog collar is around his neck. He's dosing us with hierbas, a local drink with healing properties, he says. I swear to drink nothing else ever again.

The horizon meets us with the glory of an atomic bloom.

Bobby wants us to find Orlando as witness to our union.

We locate him in his hotel room between two dishevelled friends from last night. The hotel cat, Schlurpie stalks in behind us and licks the make-up trashed face of an askew pink wig wearer. We shoo its love away, for drugs, whispering to Orlando: 'You'd best have something to wake us up properly.'

'Sure your friends will oblige,' giggles Bobby. Last night's fun looks stone dead. The cat nestles up in a pile of nylon hair.

Our wedding gift chopped out, thus commences the least paranoid hour of my life. Confident as the disco-morning star above, dawn emerges, kissing us with a rose-petal breeze. Magical. I wear the pink jersey dress with the devoré flock, Iggy has never seen it before and makes me feel like the most beautiful girl in the world, kissing me, placing the flowers from the hotel room in my hair.

He has his bashed-up, black sweatshirt with the arms chopped off, some elegant black trousers, flip-flops flapping on the bottom of his feet. The urgency of London, long disbanded, like a finished glass beside his shit-kicking, motorbike boots. I am knocked down by society's conditioning me into the importance of this event. I feel momentarily guilty my family aren't here, but know this is everything I've been born for, where I become truly emancipated from them.

I sit on a lounger, as instructed by Bobby Bandit, who stands by the pool, singing: *Weeeeeeeeeeee* are *eeeeeeeee* - the old hardcore song.

'Mate... sort it out.' Iggy asks. 'I am not getting married to that...'

Bobby nods in mock seriousness, eyes to the ground before starting: 'Let's get on it, then... ha... We are gathered here today, tomorrow, forever... does anyone know what time it is?'

No one responds.

'We are unity, and all we want is your bodies to join the spirit of Ibiza with Old Street. Time is only an image of our consciousness, it is going on everywhere, for everyone, at all lateral intersections of the cosmos, so when two people's times align, we must celebrate. These two are made for each other. Like,' he pauses. 'A Reflection...'

Iggy walks over and scoops me up to stand in front of our binder of marriage, or whatever the fark this ceremony was; Bobby Bandit deadpans the Heroshima lyrics:

> *As we walk from Saturday hills to Monday's bay,*
> *Golden sands sit by the ocean and our hands touch out to pray.*
> *We knew nothing from our pasts could stay forever*
> *Our hearts are mirrors, sun comes up for another vain day*
>> *Reflection*
>> *Reflection*
>
> *I see your reflection*
> *You can't hide the love in your eyes*
>> *Reflection*
>> *Reflection*
>
> *You are my reflection*
> *I never wanted more*
> *I'll buy you everything you want*
> *You want more?*
>> *Reflection*
>> *Reflection*
>
> *I'll give you the stars in my eyes*
> *Can't give you more.*

> *By the Tuesday, we hit tow paths and out-skirt city locks,*
> *Wednesday's alleys lead to Thursday's docks,*
> *Friday comes, you stand by my side,*
> *Outsiders outside, we light the sky with our pride*
> > *Reflection*
> > *Reflection*
> *You can't hide the love in our eyes*
> *I know what you're thinking*
> *As you stand by my side*
> *Hound-dog smile and fly-away-with-me eyes*
> *My love fades into yours*
> *Lick our lips with glue*
> *Fix me good, Our smiles take over double the room*
>
> *On Sunday's grave we walk by the chapel*
> *By next Saturday we'll marry down the aisle*
> *On the Tuesday we'll walk to the cave we will share*
> *Pilgrims to love, we'll always be there*
> > *But Reflection*
> > *Reflection*
> *You are my reflection*
> *Our morrows, our mirrors*
> *Our sorrows are scarce*
> *If there are two of us, there's so much more to see*
> *I'll give you the stars in my eyes*
> *And always know my heart will mirror thee.*

A few hormones get released from my eyes.

'Do you take, ha, do you take... a lot of cocaine, ecstasy, heroin?'

'Quit fucking around, Bandito... we're trying to do the honourable thing here...'

I am still amazed as to why, unbelievable fluke of existence, this.

'Do you Scarlet Flagg, take Iggy Kevin Robert McFerguson, AKA Iggy Papershoes, to be your awful wedded husband?'

I flinch. What the fark? I don't know him well enough, his real surname is news to me. But then I look in his eyes, and he in mine, and the chakra fizz of my knickers fires from my mouth: 'I do.'

'Do you, Kevin Iggy Rock Rrrrobert McFerguson, giver of stage-love, taker of the universe, accept Scarlet Flagg, T-shirt queen, writer of fashion, erstwhile muse of the infinite, and potential gold-digger, to be your awesome wedded wife?'

'Of course, yes. She shall write me epic poems of erotic fashion, and I shall offer songs of what could be, and hymns of wonder.'

We exchange our rings made with black straws from the bar.

'That's it, you're hooked up. Fast, fun and painless – I trust that's how it will continue.'

Toasting to nature, sucker in, pout up, shades on, this is love, this is love, that I'm feeling. We groove to the bass from the bar señorita; she plays *Red House* by Heroshima, the Sue Ditch and Tech Nick remix, then mixes in the audio of Edie Sedgwick[20] on The Ciao Manhattan Tapes.

'Sign here...' Bobby passes some hotel paper, swipes off a signature. 'We're all sorted. I'll get you some photocopies...'

A lavish ceremony of a true, tropical island sunrise commences before any of the other hotel guests return to recuperate in the sun for breakfast. Every grade of rainbow ripples afore us: palettes of Levi's blue to Biba purple, Benetton red, Hare Krishna orange, Valentino cerise, Escada yellow; a massive, great, fruit cocktail of dawn.

---

20. *Edie Sedgwick died age 28 on November 16, 1971. She was the original 'It' girl, being a rich socialite, and featured in many of Warhol's early Factory films. Andy and Edie once got in trouble stealing silver from the Ritz (her father had an account there, which he thereafter withdrew). Edie was castigated by Warhol after she started seeing Bob Dylan, sought Hollywood fame, and left the Factory circle. Her intake of anti-anxiety drugs was intense and she died of barbiturate and ethanol intoxication, after four months of marriage to Michael Post who she met in a rehab. Mr Post, in true pop-style, ended up working in a post office in Miami.*

And yet, I am too neurotic to sleep. Fearful everyone may blackout for the night, leaving me with my thoughts, my trepidation for having to face Malachi again, my

# HATE.

# CHAPTER FOURTEEN
# VODKA LIMON

*Just wear that dress when you die* - The Pixies

'Been trying to track you kids down.' Malachi Wright's smoked-out voice, with a tint of Irish.

I feel like an idiot taking his call which was put through to the pool bar. I didn't check who was on the other end of the line, in another world, gazing over to my beautiful, dozed-out husband, lying on an outdoor bed, covered in bathrobes.

'I'll send Augustin, my assistant over for you, aye?'

'Just the boys, eh?'

'I want to give you ALL some per diems. And you should meet the wife. Ruby ain't with you, is she?'

He hangs up sooner than I can say Abortion.

I down a couple more vodka limons. The palm trees scissor-flick, their silhouette veiling us from the overwhelming, magnum stupidity of everything that's going on here.

I pull Iggy upright on the white outside bed; he's narcoleptic.

'Guuuuudd morning, sugarbunny, hubby lover. You wanna beer?'

'Scar, go back to sleep.'

He crumples over, turning away from me. Is this how it's gonna be, is everything gonna change?

'Vodka limon?'

I fear he's going all grumpy monkey, Ian Curtis[21] on the other side of his diagnosis, before we've even woken up on our first day

---

21. *Ian Curtis. Epilepsy and depression collided with a coil of rope around the singer of Joy Division's neck on May 18, 1980. He was 23. The band had hardly left Manchester.*

*Both Pete Ham and Tom Evans of Badfinger also hanged themselves. Mentored by The Beatles they fell victim to the dissolution of Apple Records and three days before his 28th birthday, on 24 April 1975, Ham committed suicide under financial pressure. Tom Evans reportedly never got over his friend's death and was quoted as saying in darker moments, 'I wanna be where he is.' On 19 November 1983, Tom Evans, age 33, hanged himself in his garden.*

of marriage.

'Do you feel different?' I ask.

'Like I may be coming down.'

Ruby rolls over from her doze on the sun-bed next to us, laughing at me, she's so jealous. The Plough constellation (which I always think looks more like a shopping cart) realigns as a bullseye target from a gun, disappearing in the sun.

Iggy's eyes open, the green always surprises me, and I fall in, hang over him, sensing volatility, ignoring it.

'Darling,' I explain, stroking his chest. 'Malachi wants us to meet him? Are you coming?'

Ruby sits up sharpest, 'When?'

She gets up, aware her false eyelashes are all spider skewiff, and scuttles to her room. Farrrrk.

Iggy wakes, suddenly in control of his future with me a mere accessory. I am an extra, a woman.

'Scarlet, listen, I wanted to have a word with you about all of this. I'm, uh, really grateful for the intro to Malachi, y'know... Let's go talk to Orlando about this.'

My flatmate's in a pornographic situation, and takes a while to emerge from his room, in a bathrobe, with an unsatisfied cock. Not that it hasn't been.

'I was saying, explaining, we don't need you to start acting like a manager - we just want Malachi to get us the gigs, y'know...'

Orlando interrupts. 'We both are... really grateful'

What have they been concocting?

My new husband bats his eyes, 'But um...'

I think I secretly wanted to manage them. I looked after bands when I was growing up, with Dad - got them gigs at school, youth clubs.

'Uh, yeah. I get it,' I thought we'd discussed this. I kinda need the money.

'Y'know I may have to split over to New York, they want to shoot me for Parc Benches,' announces Orlando.

'When's that?'

'Not sure. Maybe tomorrow,' avoiding going back to his room -

scooping up Schurlpie, bringing him to sofa. The cat is a pleasing, purring, bag of fur. 'Can I wear some of your gear, Stig? I came out here in what I was wearing.' He roots through Iggy's clothes, selecting my black T-shirt so his belly shows. Iggy gets dressed, first selecting, then ditching a D.A.R.E To Keep Kids Off Drugs T-shirt, instead choosing a white Jesus top and eight strands of brown beads, the necklaces hanging to his white jeans. It's a good look. Like he's just arrived in Bangkok's Khao San Road from years on an island, aside all the kids drinking buckets of cocktails, spunking their gap year-allowances on silver pendants that will survive them through university, until they join the mainstream. Iggy reads my terror for meeting Malachi in the wrong way.

'We should have asked your dad,' he mumbles.

We're both wondering what the fark we've done.

### March 1998

*Dear Mum,*

*I hope you are well. I really hope you are well.*

*You remember when we used to sing Amazing Grace together? I wish we could do that now. I sing in my cell here, quietly, it's just me, for almost every hour of the day and I feel like you must have felt, coming to England, knowing only Dad, having rockstars as your guiding lights, when you worked in the bar, in your silly titty costume, speaking limited English. I also know how it must have felt when I left you. I am beyond sorry about everything. About how I treated you, not coming home. That I never trusted you. I wish I'd listened more. I wouldn't listen. Being alone here, alone as we are, everyone a loner, I know you're my number one, perfect friend. I cannot find the words to explain how gutted I am to realise that I have done everything wrong. I have lost everything. I was in such a* rush to the finishing line, now I'm here. I am waiting for you, and if you do or don't make it, I wanted to share something I've learnt - <u>we reserve the right to be emotional about what happened to us</u>. It's not something I can see we will ever fully recover from, but to give these things the right to dominate us, no.

So I arm myself with forgiveness, it is all I can defend myself with. And I hope you can too.

Tôi yêu ban,

*Scarlet.*

# CHAPTER FIFTEEN
# LEGS LIKE JAMON

*Die young, stay pretty* - Blondie

Malachi's assistant, Augustin, is an exceptionally attractive hombre. My posture goes ninety degrees when I hang around beauty as international as his. My cleavage racks up in my bikini, an offering beneath the gauzy animal-print mini dress, mules high. Ruby arrives in the hotel foyer wearing a black and white polka-dot dress, giving it equal chutzpah. We wouldn't be here without such prostitution. I carry an ironic pink handbag and excuse myself for a final, nervous pee, having a word with myself in the pink and orange rococo mirror.

Clinging to my crew's side, Orlando, Iggy and I slide into the back of Augustin's running, vintage sports car. It's Hank Williams'[22] Cadillac, sky-blue with a cloud-white leather interior. Orlando puts his arm around my shoulders and kisses me on the cheek.

'I love you, Mrs Rockstar.'

'Not as much as I love you, beautiful...'

Bougainvillea flaunts its violent pigment over the pavement. Augustin opens the passenger door with a slick fandango swirl, slams Ruby in. Almond blossom scent assaults us before we smoothly rev to a killer speed, flying out of Ibiza Town. Augustin's elbow hangs over the side of the car as we skirt the harbour, dark eyes hidden behind gold lenses. His perfect white shirt beats hard against his sun-licked, Latin God chest - the Moons drool.

'¡Qué bueno!' they exclaim, in sibling-synchronicity, laughing, as we drive away from the populated city through parched, rolling landscape. The pine trees. The dabs of fincas. Donkeys. Eternal blue

---

22. *Hank Williams was the same colour as the blue Cadillac he was found dead in on New Year's Day, 1953. He was 29. Born in post-Depression Alabama, hard drinking and herbal medicines were de rigueur. Fame and money arrived for songs like Cheatin' Heart, Angel of Death and Lovesick Blues. He flashed out on guitars and lived a roller-coaster life surrounded by shysters raining him with pills. He was full of morphine and chloral hydrate when his heart stopped working.*

sky, and occasional hippie garb swinging in trees. My pulse races. I hold on to Iggy. He holds me, yelping *Rio*. I enjoy the forcefield of being covered by my favourite men. I open and close my eyes like they're on a slow shutter speed.

After twenty minutes, we jolt down an invisible right turn and disappear over the horizon before swerving through ancient and redundant country-pile, iron gates - their once-adjoining wall now a dilapidated pile of sun-scarred stones, rolling into the rock-covered earth. I nest in the thought of the managers and label execs who we join in this entrance, the Playboy lodge of touring. Heritage elite.

'There ees wild animalez on the ground 'ere. Occasionally we shoot, roast and 'ave party,' informs Augustin.

Ruby turns around and whispers to me: 'He 'ave legs like jamón, maybeee I like to chew.'

Rumbling up a stony road, "ave—' I ask. 'Sorry. Have you ever lived in the UK?'

'My main woman 'as many connections in London. Sheee tries to maike me live there, but on thad island I am useless, I no know the council, I no know the police, I no know the judge. I am like... no cojones... so we back here now...'

'How long have you worked for Mr Wright?'

'Eee's been here for four years only. I 'ave familee 'ere, blood, so I 'elp 'im, yes?'

An orchard of lemon trees cascade before a courtyard of pale stone garages which shelter in the shadows[23] of a palatial farmhouse. Augustin bleeps his garage door remote.

'The dust 'ere eet arrives in evereeethin. Eee's time to get out!'

Security cameras on the outside walls follow us. I'm gulping my gut as we walk through cars parked everywhere.

---

23. Jimmy McCulloch had several mentors. The first at age 11 was The Shadows' Hank Marvin. The second was The Who's Pete Townsend. Born in Scotland, June 4th, 1953, he is best known for playing lead guitar in Paul McCartney's Wings but also played in Thunderclap Newman, Stone the Crows and Glaswegian psychedelic band, One in a Million (formerly known as The Jaygars). He appeared on John Entwistle's Whistle Rhymes. McCulloch died of heart failure caused by a heroin overdose on September 27th, 1979 in his Maida Vale flat, age 26.

# CHAPTER SIXTEEN
# ENTER THE DRAGON

*Give me all your paper money, give me all your cash* - The Psychedelic Furs

I keep my revulsion behind my shades, avoiding his outstretched sausage-fingers as they extend from the arms of a psychedelic smoking-jacket, beneath which Malachi Wright is shirtless, in navy and white Hawaiian surf shorts. His dyed-strawberry blonde hair springs outwards, all Crusty the Clown. He stands by the door to his stately hacienda.

Iggy dives in to shake his hand. Orlando gives him full-fat obsequiousness.

'Welcome, to my house - my rules,' he glares at Ruby. 'Who are you, darling?'

She plays along, 'Ruby Moon, pleasure to meet you. I believe I may know your wife?'

'Well if you do, young woman, you had better keep a lid on yourself,' and louder, to us. 'Heroshima, Scarlet Flagg. Thanks for coming. Always a pleasure.'

He looks over at Ruby: 'My memory - you know it's the sacrifice of the business, having to prioritise what we remember, so many good times. We can't keep them all, can we? There's simply not enough space in my canister, for that... Although Scarlet, I do have an image of meeting you once, at a festival, years ago when you were about this big...'

He holds his stubby hands a baby apart.

Ruby is incredulous, she's trying to slag him off in my ear as we march behind him, 'What a fucking cunt, I've got every mind to tell his tart ho of a wife that he cheats on her...', tunnelling down a whitewash corridor, halfway to fuck knows what. Iggy nudges me excitedly in the ribs, impressed by the glinting boasts of framed, gilt records.

Augustin has vanished.

'You look after Speaking In Tongues, right?' asks Orlando.

'Absolutely. And The Dandy Lions.'

'I'd love to meet them.' Oblivious.

'Of course you would... Did you get any decent food here yet? Of course, you lot probably don't eat. On the rock n roll diet are we? Bloody Spanish food, I get half my stuff flown in direct from Fortnum's. Work with the best, eat the best. My acts are the best. I am the best. You do know that don't you?' He waits for us all to agree. Thinks he's Dick Dastardly but he's just a dick.

'You are the best,' says Ruby, sarcastically.

He doesn't give her the time of day, and flings open wide, oak, double-doors to his left. Jesus Christ[24] there are metres of shiny, silver Bakelite curving around the room, edges disappear into velvety-white wall-fur.

'I love it,' says Orlando. 'Clockwork Orange meets Biba and Barbarella.'

The centre table is an enormous, silver, mercury drop, mantled with traditional silverware holding a bounty of Spanish patisseries and a glistening spectrum of spritzed fruit. If I didn't hate him so much I'd want to do a shoot here. The window is an open arch,

---

24. Jesus Christ, an original, much imitated and yet-to-be reborn superstar, goes back to the days before special effect movies, when story-telling was spread from person to person as aural entertainment. Jesus was a fan of the Old Testament, much of which was written around 1450 years before his birth. It suggests a man calling himself Jesus would be starved, shamed and murdered on a wooden rod after years of Robin Hood-style moral performance. One Bible classic story says Jesus was put to rest in a tomb but four women, including top groupie, Mary Magdalene, found the tomb open after an earthquake of some sort. Jesus was later reported to be found breaking bread, sloshing out wine and being an all around top chap and party boy at a supper party, singing in Amharic or Hebrew about the Lord freeing him from the snares of death before ascending to heaven forty days later.

The New Testament, which is largely filled with accounts of Jesus' existence, vary in interpretation from ethical symbolism to literal. Life expectancy at the time of his birth was around 50, and it took such a lifecycle for accounts of his preachings to be written up - long enough for literary embellishments, extra jeopardy and drama to be constructed and passed down another story-telling generation. Sponsors of such writings are suggested to be women, later written out, or Romans, wishing to gain power over Jews, or simply autocrats for control.

Such philosophical explanations and moral guidance are found throughout all nations through time. Religions are formed around such writings, codes and beliefs; rights are exploited, money is made, communities are united and divided.

Throughout history there have been eras of psychedelic consumption, often developing into periods of mass psychosis, hysteria and united beliefs. The boundaries of reality and fantasy are a constant tool for control of the human race. From mass entertainment to news rhetoric. It is generally said Jesus was 33 when he died. He'd be 27 if he died again.

one of around thirty of equal size which line three sides of a patio courtyard which spread into smaller gardens beyond. There's a sculpture by Picasso in the centre of the terrace space. It plays with cubist motifs of musical instruments and the face of a bull, it's tired in burnt iron, but brought to life with black and white paint.

We stay inside, taking seats in white, punctured-leather chairs.

'You like these?' he asks. 'Bought them off Bono.'

'Nice,' says my husband. I think Iggy wants to have sex with Malachi.

'This is the reward for years without sleep, eh? You know your dad, Scarlet, he was out here, not so long ago, after your mum, y'know... an angel, your mother...'

'She didn't die. She got through it.'

'Well, send her my best, love. It's never good, once it's struck once, is it? We were the first people to play Russia, me and your da, y'know? 1979 with Elton. It was actually Flash Barry, your old man, who made Elton play *Back In The USSR* that time.'

'I hadn't heard that one.'

'I put him up to it. We'd been on the old wodka, y'know?'

Iggy laughs, putty in his hands. 'Bit of showbiz sherbet too, eh, Mal?'

Wright looks at him, like he's shafting his flow, then smiles a fake one, before continuing. 'They tried to pull the plug, but what, with everyone watching, we knew he'd get away with it...What can I get you to drink?'

'Whatever you're having...' purrs Iggy. Orlando too, seated elegantly, to the manor borne.

'Shampoo aw'ight?' Malachi pours champagne and cherry syrup. 'To business. I'm gonna take twenty-five percent of everything, no squabbling, including the record deal I'll get you, and publishing.' He toasts. 'And listen, there's a lot of cannon fodder in this business. You guys listen to me, and I'll help you. What are you doing about a drummer?'

'We don't have one,' explains Iggy. 'Makes us a helluva lot easier to move about, cheaper, y'know. I want to get a holographic drummer...'

'Well, that's a shit idea. Expensive, I mean. Do you want any cake, be a shame to let it go to waste?'

He passes a Third Reich plate, gobbles a pastry, kicks off his flip-flops, puts his feet on the table, heels full of ravines, cracks dehydrated deeper than the Grand Canyon, red with blood. I feel the band beginning to emulate him. He's sticky like fly paper. I want to leave the room.

'You're druggies, aren't you? Losing that drummer already... I don't care what you do as long as you're gonna show up to gigs I fix up.'

'I'm off the gear now, y'know,' decides Iggy, without consulting me.

'Gunning down gear is so Gram Parsons[25]. We're over it. Finito, big-time!' says Orlando, like he's ever refused a line of someone else's drugs. They're getting hypnotised by Malachi's wealth as if this is some Gatsby party.

I play with the shades on my face, 'Of course they'll turn up, it's what they do.'

'I don't know what it is about your generation, taking the amount of drugs that famous people overdose from before you've even had a hit record... but anyway, Wright States International Touring, it'll be exclusive, you'll have to work at the US market, that's where I make most of my dough, a'aight?'

---

25. *Gram Parsons was a singer with a country constitution. He played in The Byrds and The Flying Burrito Brothers before going solo. He overdosed in 1973 in the Joshua Tree Inn. It was a favourite hangout away from LA for communing with cacti and getting rooty with nature. His friends tried to save him with an ice cube suppository (a street treatment for ODs) but he was called dead long before he made it to the hospital. His stepfather fancied taking control of burial (which would mean he could control his estate) and ordered the body to Louisiana. At LAX, Phil Kaufman (Mick Jagger's so-called 'executive nanny' and friend of Gram's) turned up in a borrowed hearse to snatch the corpse under a promise between he and Parsons that whomever died first, 'The survivor would take the other guy's body out to Joshua Tree, have a few drinks and burn it.'*

*There was no law against stealing a body in California but burning the coffin carried a fine of seven hundred bucks and personal fines of three-hundred each for Kaufman and his accomplice, Michael Martin. To cover the bill, they held a wake/fundraiser called Kaufman's Koffin Kaper Koncert, featuring performances from a new band Kaufman was co-managing, Jonathan Richman and the Modern Lovers. They sold beer with hand-drawn pictures of Gram Parsons and the words, 'Gram Pilsner: A stiff drink for what ales you.' Parsons was 26.*

'So what are you offering?' asks Iggy.

'Well my dear, I think you should find it quite irresistible,' he says, licking his thin, crustacean lips, outlining a verse deal which they'll see a tidy profit from, a minimum guarantee regardless of box office, and if it really sells, they'll get a full chorus line. It'll be as amicable as business can be.

Thanks, Dad, you've finally proved a use. Maybe the rape was worth it. I catch a drift of my BO, smelling of everything we consumed last night, I remember the manorexics shouting flaccccieeeed on the dancefloor. I want to spend time with Iggy, come down on a good bottle of red and a Michelin starred meal - I know you, my love, you smell of muse. Your neck, hair sweated in to your nape, you are everything I love. Cock like a sepia. An umbrella. Pushing up inside me.

We all cross the courtyard, passing through the brushed-concrete naya towards the grass gardens beyond. All the rooms face into the terrace, each bearing an individual, pimp-dripping theme offering varying levels of salacious guts and mis-taste: sedans and lurid occasional chairs, green leopardskin and purple chaise-longue creep around a corner, bone-bead fly-screens, swashes and drapes of fat, black silk. Space age inflatables, silver, swathes of yellow plumes, electric orange paisley acrylics. Beds show rock spots and rolling stripes. It's off the-o-meter decadent. Flobber-guts has filled this place with his lavish self-belief.

'I'll get the paperwork drawn up, if you want to hang out for a while, there are people by the pool, why don't you go and meet them? You'd be welcome to stay here rather than a hotel, y'know boys.'

'Wow - thanks,' says Iggy. Ready to move in forever. I put my arm around him.

'I like the hotel. Jack's sorted us right out.'

'I'll get you kids some cash for this deal upfront. Least then you can party a bit - put your faces about, eh? You must have already laid down a load in expenses, getting here.'

'We have that, Malachi,' agrees Iggy. 'I pawned my guitar.'

'Jesus, what I would do NOT to be a musician...' laughs Malachi.

Ruby is next to sidle up for the hand-outs: 'Malachi, I'm here for money too.'

'What for? Slut Of The Decade Award?'

None of us defend her, not even her brother. He just laughs really loud, in agreement with Malachi, rock n roll dogs, and pulls her back, grabs her wrist, 'What are you doing?'

'He fucking owes me.'

'What are you, a groupie?' Orlando knows she hates being called that.

'I'm a businesswoman, Orly, you know that...'

'Act like one then.'

I'm glad he pulls her into line, rather than me having to. But Ruby can't bin it, and springs back to Mal: 'At least pay for my plane tickets here... and the fucking abortion.'

'Are you going to come in and meet my wife, and behave yourself? Or am I gonna have to remind you what I said I'd do to you...'

Ruby tries to put her arms around Malachi. He pushes her away.

'Behave yourself, love.'

Passing around the far corner, we enter Mal's office through a metal-welded back door, he thumbs security codes into a calculator screen, and we are admitted into a glass-encased, seventies futurist pleasure palace. It's cinema black, but there's a sliver of laser light shining from the silver desk lamp which exposes a mezzanine floor above. The floor is covered in cream leather, the walls are slate grey. There are pale leather sofas. One side of the room is a glass wall, covered by miles of slatted metal, all shut.

My eyes become accustomed quickly.

'Have you met the wife?'

A dark shadow of a creature wearing a leather apron lifts her arm, as she reclines on a sofa. She's smoking a weed and cocaine joint. Raising a remote control, she points it towards the windows where it triggers a phenomenal Disney vista to be projected upon the glass: white bunnies eat dandelions and pretty, colourful birds tweet.

'Top class,' applauds Orlando.

Metal shutters unlock, sounding like a shooting squad, and the chrome slats that kept the sun outside, slit open to reveal a pool in the shape of a guitar, hanging over the sea. The sun rages, people beyond are all drinking and laughing on the patio. The light reveals Suki Varenza, she smiles smugly and gets up. She is foxy and sultry with huge zeppelin tits, tiny waist, everything a woman should be. Her taste accounts for at least half of this place.

'Suki!' shouts Ruby, 'It's been forever!' They squeal and hug and dance. It's like a lesbo-porn vid. Exactly the kind I don't wanna make.

We shake hands, and she kisses me on both cheeks, smelling of heavy myrrh perfumes, eyebrows painted with a Liz Taylor brush.

Ruby is Suki's cadet. Like I am to Ruby. They've had good times together, working the free drinks scene in their teens, invited to promo parties where they needed good-looking It people. Both desiring as much popularity as the Queen on a rolled up twenty.

'Tell them about the course we went on last week, Suki, as a couple.'

'Oh, you are better at stories than me...' Her accent is Spanish, or Italian.

'How To Love Without Money - cost the equivalent of four thousand quid. I shat in their eco toilet and forgot to use the spray to make my shit disappear, they told me off, I told them to biodegrade back to what they started as and burnt their feckin, wicky-wocky, tipi-camp down. Hippy feckz. Shoot the mutha feckin crusties, that's what I say. They need to stay in the north of the island or...'

'It was funny,' she purrs.

'It was a laugh, wasn't it petal... Listen, Scarlet, love, Missy Manager, go out to the pool, I'll sort everything,' he orders, putting on a top hat, his nose the shape of a pile of bat poo.

I skedaddle out, fast as I can.

Outside is as trashy and showy as inside. We speak to an assortment of surgery-rich, style-poor women - they wear the jewel-encrusted bikinis I never thought went further than the catwalk. Orlando fawns around in amused-hilarity. I would have thought Iggy would hate it but he works it like a pro. Young and old relax and frolic in the hot tub, pool and loungers. There's a guy who looks like Rod Stewart, I can't work out whether it's him or not.

Suki introduces me to international jet trash. The ladies wear shades so big, covering the cash they've spunked on skin-pumps and eye lifts, their mouths pout like Bart Simpson. I tell them I got married last night.

'You go, girl,' applauds Suki. 'Me and Ruby got married once, didn't we love? Yuh huh! Tell you later,' she winks, all cat eyes, flicking her long, perfect hair.

A squat, spunky guy in his early twenties bomb dives the pool, he's buff in a bronzed footballer-stylee, bleach highlights. Suki tells me he's one of Malachi's kids. He swims over and shouts up at me from the pool, 'Get in here, pussycat! It's lovely!'

I get an approval look from Iggy and strip my dress off, bikini underneath. Tightening the strings, I take a long sweep underwater. I love swimming. The release into another world. Football Boy pulls my feet and tries to keep me submerged.

'DICK!' I gasp, finally reaching the warmth of the Med air to my lungs, coughing up pool water. He finds it funny. I want to leave.

'I was only messing around. Geez. Sorry, I just get a little overexcited when young blood arrives here, those who haven't yet begun injecting themselves with the semen of Hitler Youth,' he pauses, then points down the hill. 'There's a private little sauna house down the path, none of these people know about it. It's for real friends and family. It's where we keep the decent drugs and drink, go down there, and maybe I'll come down in a while... make sure none of these vampires find out where you've gone.'

'I'd rather hang myself, mate,' I say.

I get out of the pool, grab one of the gratis towels and Iggy's arm. Freshly bleached hair, easily quiffable with its hardcore straw feel, it dries fast, and I pull on net stockings, peel the gaffer tape from my tits, and check the gold Screenface eyes and lips haven't shifted. We talk with the scraped-back, plastic faces. They drop names like footprints in sand. The drinks hit, one after another, cocaine rushes. I congratulate myself on surviving this confrontation with my past, but maybe I'll just have a heart attack - and leave in a body bag. Ruby and I snort a few bumps of smack that she's got from Suki. Slows me down.

A rippling champagne bellini light reflects upon the lilac silk marquee of billowing sky. Cosmic, green-touched hills hit the canopy above. Cardamom Cavalli paths lead to turquoise Chanel pools flashing around vanilla and gold Versace villas. It's all so false.

Suki picks a kaftan from a hook, and takes me and Ruby into Ibiza Town. We do coke in the convertible silver Mercedes; I'm shown where Nico[26] fell off her bike.

In a square in Ibiza Town, Suki is surrounded by shopping bags, full of trinkets and tartery. I buy a black vest. We drink vodka limons. I gave Ruby some of the cash Iggy gave me, he's gone to some legendary studio. I miss him.

Suki wants to go to the beach. We drive past fields of salt, the sun hints that soon it will be replaced by a moon, and silver mirrors of sea. Dumping the car beneath corrugated iron shade, we totter down a sandy strip to a beautiful cove, decorated with sexy couples, gorgeous girls, blissed-out beautiful people. The vibe is far cooler and more so fist than anything I imagined for Ibiza. Suki leads us to

---

26. Nico - German chanteuse and model, best known for her work with The Velvet Underground was originally produced by Brian Jones for Andrew Loog Oldham's Immediate label, despite her earlier attempts to work with Berlin-based Manuel Göttsching. She fell in with Andy Warhol and Paul Morrissey, being in New York with Bob Dylan. She could only hear in one ear which accentuated her detachment and nickname of Ice Queen. After the one album with The Velvet Underground she went solo, releasing six albums between 1967 and 1985. She lived at 29 Effra Road with the good Doctor John Cooper Clarke in the early 80s. He doesn't remember much of it. In 1988, she was clean, pursuing a more healthy existence and on holiday with her son, Ari Delon, in Ibiza. On July 18th she was knocked off a bicycle, had a minor heart attack and later died. She was 49.

a driftwood bar at the end of the beach.

'Best DJs,' she states, and flits to kiss players and those who have forgotten everything beyond the horizon. 'I am getting my brothers to pay them a fortune for gigs at Viktor's.'

Candles sit in jam jars behind the bar. Shanty, mellow, trance-y house music plays.

'You want Ecstasy?' Suki asks. This island kisses my skin, there are no pimples on foreheads, no drooling madness, no parched lips or dry skin; the sun cures everything, the happy rays of light make all smile. No unkempt fish-tank mouths in Ibiza. No broken hearts left to sizzle on sticks as warning signs. We are festooned with healing, sonic happiness. This is love. I want to tell Suki about what her husband did to me, but I can't. I want to tell Ruby what Malachi did to me, but I can't. I decide to focus on the happiness of love I feel with Ig, smiling as I get introduced to ex-pats and ex-everythings - people here assume new names and past glories, eye-bleaching sun blitzes a blindingly superficial, fantastically optimistic, island-life beauty. Their biggest concern is watching the sun go down. I'm grinding my teeth. I drift down to the sea to feel the bubbles lick my soles, rich minerals of the Mediterranean curing everything. At the water's edge, boys cruise in the breaking water.

*Have I just been to the toilet?* I wonder, and look behind.

I gulp, and swallow a paintbox of colour. Guided by white, lunaris illumination, emerging at the rocks at the end of the beach. There's a massive Om sign carved onto the fascias like in Northern Goa, it's so Aleister Crowley[27]-on-a-good-day. Pictures of seraphims, sea monsters, pyramids, evil eyes, third eyes, Krishnas, Shivas, Ganesh,

---

27. *Aleister Crowley (1875-1947) is an all time pin-up for the esoteric and occult. Cited as a key influence on Kenneth Anger, Jimmy Page and Iron Maiden, he developed a religion influenced by his travels for the British government, his theory became the Hermetic Order of the Golden Dawn. A keen actor at Cambridge who swung any way, he felt his life was full of personal tragedy but he kept up wacky-appearances establishing a sex magick commune in Italy called the Abbey of Thelema in 1920, for which he wrote a songbook. Expelled by Mussolini in 1923, he published The Book of Thoth in 1944, 'strictly limited to 200 numbered and signed copies bound in Morocco leather and printed on pre-wartime paper.' He died in a Hastings boarding house, skint, taking heroin in an attempt to ease a respiratory infection.*

Hannuman, music notes and hippy hieroglyphics, all chiselled into pediment stones. It's very ethereal, fairy ethereal, I whisper.

'Hello!' replies a voice. My echo? The words are repeated, moored to a handsome Viking fiend, hanging from a rock. Awe-striking blond dreads, an eastern, round-necked, white top with faded, black, vagabond shorts. Supermodel-esque, a warrior. By his side, a simulacrum with burnt acorn skin, black goatee and a brightly-coloured, cartoon-print T-shirt-body of a sculptor's muse.

'We saw you in the water, we wanted to check you're okay.'

'Yeah,' I reply, swallowing my first rush from the pill. 'Yeah, she brought me down here.'

We all turn to Suki's silhouette down by the music shacks, wrapped around someone younger, fitter and less financially viable than Malachi.

'Mmm, yeah, she's been around here even longer than us. Different toy-boy each season.'

'So what are you lot up to tonight then?' asks Blondie.

'I need to find my band, Heroshima, we're at the Bald Leopard.'

'I saw him, the singer, down here earlier, there were a few of them, loads of girls.'

'No, I don't think you did.'

'I swear it was him. Not that long ago.'

That's it then.

Goodbye sobriety.

We nosebag coke in their champagne-hue beach buggy and they promise some brown. The powder is strong, smooth and pure.

'It's cut with ant powder back in Blighty, believe us,' they say.

You never ask someone in Ibiza what they do for a living, that was what Augustin said.

# CHAPTER EIGHTEEN
## NEW LEAF

*I lost my heart, under the bridge* - PJ Harvey

I wake up alone in the car park. Lying where the beach buggy was. My legs are splayed open. A girl could wake up with nothing sometimes. So fist.

# CHAPTER NINETEEN
# BIG DADDY BASS

*Modern man does the best he can, nowhere to go, cigarette in hand* - The Bolshoi

Back with the girls - we guess we'll find the band at Space, the club Orlando was going on about. First stopping at the hotel for a line and a change of clothes, then the croissant shop, a parallel universe to the beigel shop on Brick Lane where club workers, cab drivers and groovers hang. They have elegant patisseries, I rave on with the best of them, ordering a straighten-me-out boccadildo. I recline aside it on the pavement, its energy does not transmute, I cannot eat, I am communing with the sandwich, it's too beautiful to kill, it smiles at me.

The sun flickers through the acacia trees; none of us can remember where Suki left the car. Riding a cab to Playa d'en Bossa, a concrete car park emerges, with nothing for miles but fields of scrubland, there's a cymbal jazz of heat-scorched grasses and the rolling licks of the shallow beach beyond; it's a no-man's land broken only by the the rumble of a Boogie Down Productions[28] big daddy bass-line from the club, and the deep charge of the planes flying overhead: one plane a minute, one hundred and fifty beats per minute, one hundred and fifty passengers leaving, one hundred and fifty passengers arriving.

We get let inside the club by saying we're on the guest list and still have to pay. There's an inside and an outside. The outside

---

28. *Scott La Rock, the DJ and producer from the South Bronx was the sound behind Boogie Down Productions and early KRS-One. He was shot down, age 25, whilst defending D-Nice, who had been in the Highbridge area, fooling around with someone else's girl. D was the youngest member of Boogie Down at 16. KRS-One and Scott La Rock had just signed a deal and were breaking bread at a McDonald's in Manhattan. They got a call and went out to investigate at 165 and 166 Streets when .22 calibre bullets shot down their jeep. It was August 26, 1987. Warner Brothers withdrew their offer, and Scott, a former social worker, who represented a different sound to Marley Marl's Queensbridge-based Juice Crew (who included Big Daddy Kane, Roxanne Shante and many of the Red Alert artists like Monie Love) never got to see the rise of friends like Chris Lighty's Violator Management, or Russell Simmon's Def Jam.*

terrace is a casualty department of international goon squads wearing wigs and devil capes, vampire teeth, blood: the full garb. Angels flutter. Gargoyles spurt hellfire. White feathers float. Silver antlers buckle. Shiny, superhero cloaks flow. Ten inch heels spike. Half-dressed man-fauns parade. Alpha baboons boom. A Brazilian athlete sucks his own cock, surrounded by a wall of flapper girls. People from every country wear national dress. Moulin Rouge girls swirl and swing. Full-grown Ewoks twitter around trees. *Sound of Music* extras bob along with out-curled puppet plaits. E-munchers chew their rubber faces. A Can-Can line of girls are gurgling and gargling red liquid, gobbing it as far as their dreams. Australian surf dudes in lifesaving shorts and matching hats bling their white teeth as they crawl across the floor, leashes in their mouths, attached to a Herculean being wearing a long, princess wig which they take turns to sit on.

Inside is all eighties' discothèque with silver scaffolding podiums. It smells of stale sweat and smoke machines. The walls: black. People are curled up in corners or having euphoric moments of rare confidence, pounding through the BPMs.

I wander alone, leaving Suki and Ruby with some guys they know. It's difficult to see faces. My sight is a lil blurry. Plotting up back on the terrace, I get nailed a Bentley for a drink. A Nordo-Samoan guy with psychedelic tattoos appears next to me and offers his condolences about the prices. His cornflower eyes speckle with saffron, his hair swishes around, windmilling like spaniel ears. Looking down at his sportswear clad body, his white shorts reveal long, deep SAS-scars chewing the curve of his calf muscles. His mouth is hypnotically chewing.

'Where you from... What you on?'

He's hoping to make contacts in the music industry. I keep schtum.

'The band Heroshima?' I ask; met with blank stares.

There is a reason rave died, and that is because not everyone should have to speak with anyone. Gurning like Muppets did not save the world.

'They're going... to be... massive,' is all I can say.

It's painful feeling my synapses fail. Spannered. Hammered. DIY-fail. Escorting my drink, I weave to an outdoor seat and watch my brain bounce from the safety of my skull to a bad comedown. Everything is connected. It's true. On cue with the cartoon cerebrum bouncing towards the dance floor to get pecked to death by kids thinking it's a giant E, in struts Malachi Wright. Flunkies aside. I run inside to find Suki. She's on the poles with the troupes of Congolese strippers, slipping her dress down from her shoulders, tits out. Grinning with ecstasy eyes, she's performing a yoga/pole-dance hybrid, legs spread lotus akimbo, she flips to a handstand. Backlit, eyes so wide her thoughts require separate rooms - her smoothness, and finesse, long gone.

I walk next to Ruby who's clapping like a seal. Our paranoid peroxide stands on end when I tell her Malachi's here. Neither of us want to get caught in his errant wife's nest of vipers, but Ruby owes it to her friend, who's holding herself upside down on a pole with splayed scissor legs. Snap snap, pull yourself together, girl.

'Thank fuck she's put her boy-child to bed,' Rubix whispers.

# CHAPTER TWENTY
# DRUGS MAKE THE APOLOGY

*I promise you anything, get me out of this hell* - John Lennon

I slide through the self-important gesticulations of people shouting about themselves and crawl to the floor, skirting the dark sides, shuffling behind the Technics. The DJ, Kris Needs, a cat weebling on his ninth life, looks bemused as I gurn up at him, hoping the drugs make the apology I can't.

I manoeuvre towards an exit which turns straight into Malachi's legs. My bravado melts. Stealer of my youth, and life.

'Awwwwight, darling. Told you I know where everyone is on this island.' Except his wife when she's banging someone better than him. 'This is Suki's party trick - stripping. She loves to be adored.'

Islands are too bloody small. There's no place to hide. Particularly for us girls.

Suki slides off the stage - coming to the wing of Ruby. They're gossiping together.

'You still up then?' he asks me.

There's no hiding my manga puppy dawg pupils.

'I went back, to the hotel, but you know how distracting the ol' disco lights can be. Do you want a drink?'

'Oh, bless you, my sweet little disco-pixie, I virtually own this place, doll. Where are the band?'

'I thought they were with you.' He undoes an extravagant number of gold buttons on his black shirt, a scraggy Bagpuss-scattering of pubic chest-hair perforates skin that fails to protect itself from his cream cake bulges and deep, cherry Med glaze.

This place is as bad as Macclesfield. Or the carousel of Old Street. Everywhere becomes claustrophobic when you all go to the same places. Fifty people, and the rest is done with mirrors. Our world is an ever-shrinking circle. Like my brain. My cortex has over-flexed, rollicked to its grave.

A flunky appears to Mal's side with a tray of champagne flutes and a magnum of champagne. Refreshment, thank fuck. Dancers flock around him like the sherbet butterflies that flutter in my knickers in anticipation of being back with Iggy. The girls greet their paymeister as a hero. He shoos away their champagne-whoring and they canter off to lick the wallets of other egos. His feet splay out in star-bound confidence. He's wearing horrible white loafers. They're so pseudo-Chelsea. The shit side of Chelsea.

Malachi recounts my dad's old band, The Moody Tuesdays, their greatness, turning his back to pour, before handing out glasses of pink champagne.

'Get that down you, pet! Never know how long the bubbles are gonna keep on popping for...' I've worked out what it is about him: he looks like a pirate gnome. Lubricated with a vagabond's wild heart. 'And your suggestions - you've got me thinking, Baz Jnr - it'll be the most insane tour I've ever done, but I think we should start in Australia, end in Zanzibar. No-one's ever done that. A complete A to Z of Rock - the whole gamut. Do the tour in alphabetical order.'

'It's like a statement that you do things properly,' I add, laughing at the paradox. Shame I feel sick. He attempts to put his arm around me but I excuse myself for the toilet.

I remember stumbling into the hospital-style facilities, swaying from side to side, arms flailing, grabbing the left and right of the cubicle, lowering myself down towards the loo seat. There's dried piss all over the floors. I rest the rear of my thigh on one side of the seat, rather than letting my pussy anywhere near the old disease-ridden infestations. Outside the door, I hear Ruby and Suki. They're plotting. Suki's scared Malachi is going to smash her face in, again - he suspected, but couldn't prove, she'd been cheating. She'd had a rib broken in the past, her nose had a weird dent in it (I'd thought it was a collapsed septum, or bad nose job; it was probably an amalgamation of all three). She always made excuses for him, saying they'd been out of it, or that she'd started it. Ultimately, she took drugs to increase self-esteem knocked out of her by brothers from an early age. And boredom. And sex with someone you don't love is improved if you're out of it. Her looks were her only tool of dominance and never enough to prevent her from deep guilt that she deserved a good kicking.

I stand by the sinks, holding myself up as they plot some girl-on-girl action to placate him. I am so wasted. It makes me forget to look in the mirror on the way out, I try to hold it together as I return to Malachi. Being seen stoned and drunk is part of my life, my identity, but incapably out of it is another bag. I pull myself together, smiling as I return, hoping friendliness will win me favour. Malachi leers back like he's about to eat the teddy bears' picnic, his army of guys with sleeves rolled above their biceps.

I have the same feeling I did when I fucked up meeting Cass Vet and The Four Flaws, years before.

# CHAPTER TWENTY-ONE
# TWO TIMES A LADY

*And then I woke up... right in the middle of a horrible dream* - Adam and the Ants

Superstar azure bubbles froth, I blow them, starboard to port, fore to aft. My tide comes in and I go under, holding my breath, letting my hair swish all silken mermaid. Gold leaf floats to the surface, dissolving seamlessly into my skin.

I don't remember leaving Space, only have a vague memory of stumbling down a shaded, warm slate path to this alpine lodge. I must never forget, in my guilt, that Suki and Ruby, planned to perform a fe-love-in, pimping me out as a decoy slave...

Marble stairs swish up to a sauna and steam room above. It's seventies' Chic-sheik; gold everywhere, dripping from the mirrors, the goblets, the wine buckets, a chopping out table suspended by chains over the middle of the Jacuzzi. Disco pimp paradise.

Beneath trefoil window arches looking out to sea, gilt tiles display scenes of Egypt: pyramids, a pair of solid 24-carat Sphinxes and a Tutankhamen share the view of the bay[29] from inside this private pleasure-dome.

I'm counting - 1, 2, 3 - but only reach twenty-seven as a Godzilla leg appears beneath the waves. I go back to air, and screech hysterically.

'Get out of here.'

'But you're in my bath[30], pet.'

I start screaming, 'Just make him stop it. Get him out!' Louder

---

29. *Otis Redding never got to hear the success of Sittin' On The Dock Of The Bay - he and four members of his Bar-Kays band flew out of the sky to their death on an icy lake in Wisconsin on December 10th, 1967. Otis was 26-years-old.*

30. *Diane Arbus was a photographer of the superficial. She was drawn to creating snapshots about intimate oddness and freaks. Experienced in mood swings, she was found dead in a bathtub with a body full of barbiturates and wrists mangled by razor-blades. She was forty-eight, the date was July 26th, 1971.*

and louder and louder.

'Will you cut that out, kid? We'll have everyone on the bloody island in here if you don't stop that bloody noise. The Guardia, the cops, the whole fucking nine yards. Put this in your gob.'

Malachi's penis comes towards me. 'Join in with my balls and chain here, won't you? Actually, will one of you two sort her out - I'm not risking my cock near her teeth...'

He yanks Suki's ponytail back, so her chin juts up.

'Calm the fuck down, Scarlet!' hisses Ruby. She comes towards me and rams her tit in my gob. You are joking.

'It's so hot, I'm so wet,' announces Suki, her white bikini slithering off, tits glistening. She starts splashing water on us.

'Shut it, Junior, alright?' Ruby twists my nipple, really hard.

'You don't understand. I can't do this again, with him.'

'No, YOU don't understand, this is what we do. We look after one another... Pretend he's not here,' instructs Ruby. 'It's not like you've never fucked people you wish you hadn't before, is it?'

And here he is. Malachi, hopping around in another of his stupid bathrobes. This one is gold, he's touching himself, grunting towards post-cosmic renumeration.

I tried running away, slipping on the marble floor, running towards the house in a state of confusion. Escaping through the wild roads that camouflage into parched land. Ruby caught me before I reached the door, dragged me back.

She forces me back in the hot tub, pulling my tits.

'You used to like that, you little bitch, didn't you?'

I am woefully spellbound by our past, the idea that she's protected me through bad times - which may never have been bad if I wasn't around her... I can't leave her. She takes hold of my melted state. Guides me through the water.

'I have to do this, Scarlet - or he'll tell her...' she whispers.

The Police wail out their greatest hits.

Enveloped in the bosom of Ruby, we kiss. She has soft and full lips. The squish is enjoyable. I've not kissed another chick since the pretty girls Joe used to drag back, and there was one night, that suddenly comes back to my memory, where I attempted a debauched career-jump with F. Loozey Meringues, fashion editor with an Action Man haircut, breasts that falollop down her chest like unravelled football socks...

'It's gonna be okay,' she confides in a whisper.

I look her straight in the eyes, perplexed, locked in a chamber, Iggy wouldn't like this. I sense there are other guys arriving. Gathered on Moroccan cushions, smoking Wonderland hookah pipes. Malachi is master of the ceremonies. There are drinks given to us - we smoke weird joints. This is seriously trippy sheeeeat. I imagine Iggy Papershoes in my space, breathing the smoke from my lungs, we share a smoke ring and our lips touch.

It's not him though, it's Suki. I can taste the salt and sun and spirit of Ruby's face. Suki takes my other hand, starts touching me beneath the water. Our bodies touch each other breast to breast, our hips move like a giant mermaid.

I push the gold button in the Jacuzzi. Ruby's tits have aged since I last saw them. The silicone bubbles have dropped, she has stretch marks hanging down in arrows towards them.

Suddenly I whip my head back and realise what is going on. I hit the tiles behind. My back squeaks on the plastic tub. Suki hasn't got a cock. My head is full of drugs and drink, and this one thought repeatedly flashes in my eyes like the answer,

'You haven't got a cock.'

'Scarlet, calm down. Let's make it as easy as we can.'

ROXANNE, belts out Sting, *You don't have to put on the RED LIGHT*.

A collection of necklaces hang down the valley of my breasts to my stomach. Beautiful tits. I love my tits, I love their tits.

'Where's Orly, Ruby? And Iggy - I just want to be with Iggy.'

We touch each other and do what lesbians do - we talk to each other, we stand and flaunt, and fuck and get wet. Lick our love points and pump each other like drills. WE ARE BATTING FOR THE AWAY TEAM NOW. My body brinks in and out of orgasm. I'm feeling totally sexed up, but can't come. Malachi's presence makes me frigid, and terrified.

I'm unsure what happened next. I think I was sacrificed. Put on a slab and fucked by Malachi and his army.

# CHAPTER TWENTY-TWO
## DISDAIN OBSERVES MY WANKERED SPRAWL

*You stupid girl. All you had you wasted* - Garbage

Wow - this is no ordinary hangover.

I chuck up. I never chuck up.
We drank a lot of rohypnol-pink champagne.
Something inside feels out of sync. There's been a break in, I touch the entrance to my womb. It's thick, bruised, swollen. My index finger shows a slug of blood from the inside.
Tattered.
Iron cocks. I am raw, sopping like a halal neck. My period looks like it's started, trailing over rocks and stones. My skin is dirty, scraped. I scream out, there's no noise. The air's full of nature. Birds swoop, cliff edge, knowing not to stop near my mess. Any sound I make will never be heard. My head is knocked out. There's the smell of dust and pine trees, and sun-scorched earth. I retaliate, fighting back with lead-weight muscles to pull myself up, chest raising. Oh man, I can hardly stand. My money, the pink bag - where is it? Where is everyone? My eyes flicker into gear, there's no life, no habitation, it's all ocean beyond, a rolling thrust of fuck. Pounding bastard sailor waves of suicide-grey battle to my shore.
Relentless. The sun. The brutal sea. I am Ms. Robinson Crusoe. I am washed up. I must shelter, find a smuggler's barrel to float on to a cove. I must hold tight to this rock. I feel boneless, like I'll slip and be swallowed into the tears of a million fish. Borne, too free. A hole. To be filled in.

They fucked me with guns.

Fallen down. Shot.

Hurt.

Oh, Christ.

Malachi is the last person I remember, wielding a Beretta, waving it around - memories come in hectic flashes.

Then nothing. Floored by an anger in my stomach. My heart shakes every atom of my being. I flick through the stills of trouble.

Cutting out, raped each time I open my memory. Without knowing details, my mind invents. Anyone could have fucked me. There is a blank from leaving the toilets at Space to waking up on this remote beach, with vague recollections between, these became clearer only later. Carried. Dragged. Restrained. Forced. Fought. Broken. Movement. Struggle. Nothing. Dead. Pain. Violent anger. A small space. No air. Maybe a bed, maybe outside. Sand under my nails, seaweed in my hair, rubbly stones scrape my skin. The sunshine more deafening than the wind.

Garish voices approach. A hiding spot below, scouring my legs on limpet-covered granite, my ankles and wrists are bruised. The fuckers tied me up. Grated skin stings. I cry as Ibicenco dog-walkers pass by, maybe seeing me, maybe not.

Crouched.

Womb-huddled in a world without an umbilical cord.

Ruby - long gone. Fleeing to survive.

Iggy. He's gone.

Stitched up, put out of the picture.

Orlando's in New York.

The police will be getting paid off.

I can tell no-one, it will do nothing.

Survival mechanisms kick in and I wash myself in stinging seawater. The smile of the ocean turns from turquoise to black, the coral broken, the water is never sad and tired, it just gets angry. No-one can help me. I calm myself with songs at the water's edge, rocking back and forth. The bass of Pacha vibrates all the way around the island's water. The people are still going, and going. On and on, we don't stop. Spin cycle forever. Getting up, my knees lock and a lightning-fast, blank flash takes my breath away. A white van nearly knocks me down in a head-rush. I'm now in a car-park by the sea. Wiping a brush of blood along my skin, I scuttle towards a washing line. It's for a restaurant. I take table-cloths from pegs, tying corners together, my back against a tree, a carpet of pine needles poking my skin, I make a starchy dress of sorts.

Scrambling forth, a big, grey tube of a road opens. The dog walkers have vanished. I start a long walk of blisters. Bile rises and I puke at the side of the road. I've been multi-fucked.

The sun kicks out a brain frying heat. There could have been hundreds of them. The whole island could have done me. Careless Scarlet. Stupid, thick, floozy, daft cunt Scarlet.

# CHAPTER TWENTY-THREE
# A TIE-DYE MESS

*I stuck around St. Petersburg when I saw it was a time for change* - The Rolling Stones

A Dodge van draws up close.

'Stay away!' I stick up two fingers.

It's a girl inside, long dark plait, random pink extensions. Another lesbian to save me.

'Hola. Okay, mama?' she persists. Alone. She's safe.

'The airport?' I ask. I just want to leave.

Sufi music shambolises from a ghetto blaster which she moved from the passenger seat to the roll-up bed-space in the back of her van.

'I am going into town...' She's English, deep tan, a tattoo of Ganesh up her arm: the kind of girl who will never fall in love with a person because she is besotted with another culture. For her it's India, she's trussed up in paisley-stamped silver, silks, patchouli. A bindi brands her forehead with the ownership of a birthmark.

'You've had a wild night out, mama...'

'Yeah... I've lost someone.' I sit on my folded-leg because my fanny and arse feel all barbed-wire mangle. My make-do sanitary mattress slips.

'That happens here - all the time. Everyone comes to Ibiza to get lost, then they wake up not knowing where they are. Full of lost people finding themselves and found-people losing each other, this island. It's a loop. Hard to leave. You're a bit of an Ibiza virgin?'

'I don't think I'd call myself that anymore.'

She rambles on: about wintering in India, sharing summers between here and Notting Hill, sells jewellery as she moves around. She does the festivals, mainly selling standard folk-art trinkets, a few of her own designs.

'The jewellery used to be all about me, then I took my ego out of it, and wow - it's amazing how simple that makes everything...'

India Chica won't shut up. She talks about dance music being such a boys' game. She blames this reinforced male-tilt on the island's seizure of house music: 'There's a patriarchal cohesion between four-on-the-floor, thumping male bass, and Ibiza. It's the pure Latin-ness of the isle, machismo pumping and pounding its sexuality unsuppressed as the pretty girls pass by. Machinated, male-engineered music, only brought to life by the wails of women.'

I consider telling her what I think happened, Suki and Ruby getting it on with me to placate Malachi. Juicing me up, offering me up, their lil lamb, 'I'm just kinda fried at the moment...'

'Oh man. I've so been there,' she says supportively, passing a joint over, and her hand to stroke my hair, 'I went on a silent retreat with the Dalai Lama when I first came out to my Dad. I lost it, man, flew way too close to the sun... FUCKING HELL!' She swerves as a police car zooms down towards the direction we've just come from... 'There are so many levels to the police here.'

She takes the joint and has a huge inhale: 'I was giving up pot. I'd been smoking about an ounce a week everyday for ten years. I was so stoned I'd come back straight again, I was like, levitating, man. My head, it like took on the energy of everyone around me. I was telepathic and aware of the electricity that occurs in everyday objects. Some people say it was a breakdown, but it's when I got into Jainism and Animism, so it was like a breakthrough, not breakdown, uh, like lose the negativity, Labellers! Breakdown is such a negative word, yogis see it as a higher awareness. I'd never have changed without it. Y'know, it was an enlightening experience really. I can read auras now. The other MAJOR change I made was giving up Buddhism for Sai Baba. I mean, Sai Baba vs. the Dalai Lama, battle of the gurus, who's going to win?'

I'm unsure, Ali Baba vs the Dali Army? AC/DC? What?

She swerves over a branch. The truck staggers at her behaviour, choking.

"The monks said I was lucky to be in such a place, but after that breakthrough I checked in at Baba's ashram, said goodbye to the protocol... is a police car tailing us? Jesus, it's flashing its lights...'

I look behind. 'Why would it do that?'

Reassured, she continues. 'It just all made sense, you know when something speaks to you, and you've truly found the real answers?'

I act like I never built a Wicker Man. Which I did once - in our old garden, after we'd left the house and it sat there empty. An effigy post-Reading.

'You're spiritual, right?' she continues. 'All this London stuff, like fame, and money, and drugs and death, it's big sheeat, mama. There's got to be some kind of karmic fallout, and you have to just make sure it's not you. Some stuff has to be exchanged for glory, that's the devil at the crossroads[31] story, no?'

I nod, looking around, thinking I should really go back to the hotel rather than direct to the airport. See if the boys have turned up. The police car starts honking at us. I wonder whether it's Malachi, has he sent them, to fuck me up in some way?

Unless it's the tablecloths...?

There's an irate looking restaurant owner hanging out of the cop car window, shouting obscenities in Spanish.

'Holy fuck. I am so sorry... this dress... I stole these from the line, of the restaurant down there...'

'No shit, Sherlock... fucking hell, I've got enough drugs in the back here for half the island.'

She puts her foot on the pedal, and we start to fly through the air. Faster, faster, more, more, more.

The blue lights are upon us.

'Get in the back and take one of my dresses. Do it, quickly...' she instructs, lighting a pre-rolled joint accelerating to 120 miles an hour. There's only one Pankhurst at a party of suffragettes, and as ever, this is my riot. I jump onto the mattress and pull a silk tie-dye

---

31. Robert Johnson, 1911-1938. The bluesman who sold his soul to the devil at the crossroads, in exchange for learning how to play the guitar. His death is equally crowned with a hero's myth - Sonny Boy Williamson is said to have advised him never to drink from a bottle of whiskey opened by a stranger, to which he replied, 'Don't ever knock a bottle out of my hand'. Soon after, it is said Johnson took a bottle from the husband of a woman he'd been fooling around with, laced with strychnine, he died three days later, at 27.

mess from a hanger. My womb tears.

'Epic town names, 'round here,' I shout out from behind, trying to pretend nothing matters.

'You what?'

'Eivissa, the way it's written on the road sign, looks like Elvis, Elvissa, and just down the road, the place is called Jesus.'

India Chica tutts: 'The J is pronounced *hay*, and you mark yourself as a cunt by saying Eye-Beetz-ah. The I is pronounced like an E, the V like a B, the Ss or Z like the TH in thousand. Eh-b-eeth-a. Be cool, yeah?'

You what? Me? Cool? If cool was on the stock market, I'd own this island.

She swerves, we come closer out of the country. At a roundabout the police are close, she tells me to give her the tablecloths, and she'll throw them on the police car's window.

And that is how we lost the police, just outside San Antonio. I'd forgotten that.

# CHAPTER TWENTY-FOUR
# LOS ULYSSESOS

*I wish I was born a thousand years ago* - Velvet Underground[32]

Lesi-desi dropped me at the bottom of a hill with a war-zone of Las Vegas lighting and trashy sex. It was early evening. The streets reeked with San Miguel, margaritas and sangria. Gutters of puke roll towards me from a side street and two obese lads adding to the stream, their mates laughing around them. Further up, multiple cases of sun-induced, third degree burns in stained pairs of white mini-skirts. I ducked in and out of bars, looking for Orlando and Iggy. Or even Ruby. Or Suki. Anyone.

I nick a dress from outside a tourist shop. Its iron-on patch with a red heart reads: I Love Ibiza. I don't. I roll into some of the backest of backstreets and fall into Los Ulyssesos, the smokiest, most Spanish joint: one of those dead tortilla bars where old and young, Spanish and English, men of all backgrounds look for their lives at the bottom of their glasses. The bar's walls parade an Irish connection with Gaelic posters hanging above the sound of these schlurping, belching, refuelling alcoholics. Sixties' white and yellow tiles, not cleaned since they were grouted in. There's an overtone of motor oil, stale smoke and slops of beer. Old fat congeals with dusty marble. A mirrored ceiling, the traditional tapas displays of What The Fark Was That moulder under fag-stained glass - fly-ridden, dried-out, stained from better years.

At the back of the bar, a terrace garden, done by a woman, no longer maintained. She's long gone. The tables were salmon pink, chairs once a mossy, lime green and dirty chrome yellow - now chipped and flaking. The whole place is a bit Twin Peaks, a bit secret IRA clubhouse. Low light comes on automatically in the

---

32. *Angus MacClise - original drummer with Velvet Underground, drawn to Buddhist drones, starved himself to death in Nepal, 1979, age 41. This was after a short reunification with the band, that didn't continue.*

tiny bathroom; the pink sink is filthy. I take off the silk tie-dye dress and replace it with the long I LOVE IBIZA vest. Cold water and liquid soap plaster back tired tresses in a ponytail, I swish water in my mouth, too scared to even begin to clean below. I drip with puce. I drink water from the tap and splash it on my face. It's stuffy and the liquid evaporates from my skin before I've looked for a dryer or towels. A petrified mop rests below the sink. I need to get off this island. I rinse the napkin-made tampon which sucks to my thigh. My sinuses crack. My body throbs. I smooth the salt from my eyes over my crinkle-cut face. I clown traces of mascara that lie beneath my eyes to look like smudged eyeliner. Cover up the girl beneath.

Where the fuck is my husband?

Ordering a small glass of beer from the tap, the barman with a gut that staggers to his input, beneath a dirty white vest and once-white apron, declares they have no beer.

'Noa beer 'ere today.'

I'm on my knees on the barstool. 'Uh, cerveza, noa?'

'No, mmeeeis, no beee-ar, heeere...'

'Uh, maybe a Guinness?' I ask, desperate, hands praying together.

Turning to his drunken mate on the other side of the bar, he laughs.

'He thinks he's got all the humour of Ireland,' his ally shouted over. They chuckle hideously.

'Just a beer.' Perhaps he's bothered by the state of my appearance. 'Maybe you have a bottle?'

The barman straightens his face, pulls his moustache from one side to another, smirks at his joke, and slips the San Miguel glass under the tap.

He passes it over. Just what the world needs, comedy barmen without beer.

I stare up at the television transfixing the lonely punters.

Without the flanking of band members, sub-ordinates and associates, I'm hollow, a complete anyone. Where is my status?

Ordering a refill, 'Have you a phone I could use?' I ask them.

'Eeet's hout hof horder.'

I'm unsure if they're fucking with me, and don't have the energy to persist. The television plays football. Men the world over, keep their eyes fixed on the action. At least I'm alive; I toast to Dad, who told me Ibiza would be stupid.

Wafts of pretty nihilism strike on each rotation of the ceiling fan above. If you're born to die and recognise when you've seen your best, then maybe it's beneficial to know the time to retire. Maybe I've had my glory days; perhaps it's time Peachy, or one of the Next-In-Line Starlets, took over. The presenter of the football looks down upon me, points and laughs. I fail to catch his drift, my Spanish isn't up to much. Feeling the rips of my skin dry up a little, I explain to the barman that I had no money. He can call the police, or I can leave the bar and never come back. His joker mate offers to pay.

'We've got to look after our own,' he says, adding. 'You need a packet of fags?'

'I'd rather the cash, right now.'

He throws some change at my feet and tells me to fuck off. I thank him. I'll repay him one day, I say in deepest sincerity.

Three blocks down, at a three star hotel, the forty-fags-a-day receptionist attempts to rip me off for using the phone.

'Eeet will cast you ten thouzand pezatas.' Her oily skin as slippery as her behaviour, her black hair straighter than a line of hearses.

I get angry when I do get through. The boys haven't been back to the hotel since this morning when they picked up their bags and left.

'Did they leave my luggage? Is it there?' I ask, describing the patchwork bag.

'Yes. It's on reception.'

'I was in your reception yesterday morning...'

'I didn't see you.'

'Ruby Moon? Has she gone?'

'No one has seen her.'

My frustration is obnoxious, and justified, my husband's left town without me.

'Can you send it over to me here, L'Estrella de San Antonio, in a cab, please? Don't make it do a fucking Bolan,[33] just get it here, to me, now. Then I'll go onto the airport. I'm a friend of Jack's. Al-fucking-right?'

'We don't do that. You need to come here to release your luggage.'

I don't pay for the call and nor do I pay for a cab to Ibiza Town. Instead I do a runner from both. Guiltily scramming onto the streets where glitter spreads and love reigns supreme. Up past the main patchwork cobble, I head towards Jack's, past a stunning restaurant with outside tables on a terrace, looking down the whole hill, the vista spreads from the top of the castle to the harbour gates and beyond to the gentle ocean below. The restaurant will have great toilets.

Cruising past perfectly ironed tables, each with several wine glasses per placing and one for water, I need to straighten myself out before facing the witch on reception - and maybe Iggy will walk in.

I accidentally whack my hip to calamity; one of the tall glasses falls through to the floor, smashing with soprano conviction to my anime eyeballs. I continue in making my entrance as un-rock n roll as possible, but one of the penguin-suited army of waiters refuses to allow me to use the toilet. I offer to pay, they blank my demands.

'Cocksuckers,' I shout, for their snobbery.

'Franco sympathising fascists!' for their bullying.

'Servile farking fackheads!' for my embarrassment.

As the prissy couples stare up from their deep European chic,

---

[33]. Marc Bolan died on 16 September, 1977, making the singer of T. Rex (with hits such as Get It On, 20th Century Boy and Dandy In The Underworld) 29 when he smashed to his death in a car driven by his girlfriend, Gloria Jones, who originally recorded the Soft Cell cover, Tainted Love. She survived. They were driving through Barnes on their way to Morton's in Berkeley Square. Fellow T. Rex member, Steve Currie died in a car crash fewer than four years later.

*vive la punk rock*, I think. Watch me now - channelling Johnny Thunders,[34] the real deal, part of rock history. But the waiters lift me arm by arm and remove me from their premises. They drag me down the hill, dumping my wasted being by a running gutter.

At Jack's, the band aren't there. It's a different person on reception: dark, curly hair, officious, even ruder than the girl at the Estrella: on the phone to her mate, gabbling away in super-fast Spanish. I'm interrupting. She looks at me like dirt. She has no idea who I am. Or was. Or may have been destined to be, once, when the stars were fair.

I bolt through as she looks at her nails, running to the poolside terrace where Bobby performed his ritual. The bar señorita is now a boy, and the past has vanished. Only bad hotels feel like thousands

---

34. *Johnny Thunders played guitar with The New York Dolls. David Johansen was on vocals, Arthur 'Killer' Kane was on bass, Billy Murcia (who had an earlier band with Thunders called The Pox in 1967, and also ran a clothing label called Truth & Soul) was on drums, Sylvain Sylvain also played guitar. However, Jerry Nolan replaced Billy Murcia on drums when Murcia died in a tragedy of rock n roll street lore leading two acquaintances to try n bring back his crashed-out self, in a bath, with an ice pack on the back of his neck, and coffee poured. He'd shared champagne with friends, and taken the popular downer, Mandrax. It is said he may have slept it off, or certainly had a better chance of living if taken by an ambulance. A verdict of accidental death was recorded, caused by drowning in a domestic bath, under the influence of alcohol and methaqualone, with friends denying his head fell back in the Cromwell Road bath. It was 6 November 1972, he was 21. Johnny Thunders left to form The Heartbreakers with Nolan from 1975-1979. Other bandmates included Richard Hell. Aside star turns with all the legends, and a recording and touring career of length, Thunders commenced a solo career, before passing on, age 38, in 1991 in room 37 of St. Peter House hotel in New Orleans. In Nina Antonia's In Cold Blood biography, she says there are more inconsistencies around his death than of Marilyn Monroe (who after an affair with President John F. Kennedy was found dead in an apparent barbiturate overdose, age 36). As with Oscar Wilde, and many a rebel poet, the myth overshadows the artist, and as much as that can be fabulous, Thunders' junky reputation frequently preceded the beauty of his songwriting. Having checked in the night previously, the room was found ransacked with his saddle bags being returned to family in New York, empty. Foul play included a syringe being found in the bathroom and the police binning it, and rumours of the late Willy DeVille singing like the devil on the street corner opposite, as the maid found Johnny beneath the desk. He'd recently returned from London, where he'd picked up a significant amount of methadone, found empty. And the coroner's report also noted there being no tests done for Hep C or HIV, but did mention advanced malignant lymphoma, a form of leukaemia. No alcohol was reported in his bloodstream, but a barman says they shared a drink, and there are reports from his neighbour of 'jolts, and fights without voices', whom he'd gone for a drink and smoked a couple of joints with.*

*In 1989, Arthur Kane fell from a window and smashed both his knees. He survived, only later to be mugged and beaten up badly during the LA riots, spending several months in hospital.*

*Jerry Nolan succumbed to a fatal stroke on 14 January 1992 while undergoing treatment in a New York hospital for bacterial meningitis and pneumonia. He was 45, and rests close to Johnny.*

of people have been there before you.

Moving back into the foyer, I go through Hell to get MY luggage. I'm incapable of standing up for myself, or standing up in general.

This is exactly why I never wanted to get involved with music. Because it gets messy. Get me back to London. Get me back in FASH ON.

*I did a yoga class here the other day. The do-gooder hippy brought in neti pots for nasal irrigation. Watering cans to pour saline water through one nostril to another. I was a natural. Slipped through like the amount of money that's been through there. Like a Cayman Islands account, my nose.*

---

N.B.: Bonnie & Clyde - sexy, young and unmarried, the pair became the pin-up rebels of the Prohibition and Depression in the USA. They robbed from rural stores, gas stations and banks between 1931 and 1934.

As 'public enemies' (alongside Al Capone, John Dillinger and Ma Barker, a list which evolved to become the FBI's Most Wanted) they killed at least nine police officers and two civilians. They were finally gunned down in Louisiana on May 23, 1934.

# CHAPTER TWENTY-FIVE
# SOMETIMES THE MIND INVENTS

*One of the hardest things to do in the nineties is to have a nice time and enjoy yourself*
*- Jarvis Cocker*


At the airport I am nervous. My passport is missing.

'Passeporte and ticket, please señorita,' says the check-in chick with too much make-up on.

Lucky Ganesh bounces on the floor as I root through the bag. The boys have thrown everything in carelessly, or Malachi's been in to nick my papers, because I can't farking find them.

'I'm sorry, señorita,' she shakes her head disapprovingly at my chipped nails and melted mascara. 'I am going to have to ask you to move away from the desk whilst we check other people in.'

No-one is behind me.

'I don't suppose any tickets have been left here for me?'

'Do you have any driving licence?'

Do you think I could be in charge of a vehicle?

I go back outside the airport, scattering over the concourse. Crouched, going through everything, unrolling, re-rolling. Nothing.

A Spanish Schwarzenegger bowls over to inform the floor is for walking on, not setting up a lost property service upon. I leave a red butterfly print where I sat.

Back at the check-in desk: 'I'm sorry, señorita, but without identification, we can't tell whether you're flying with us today.'

'I'm married to Iggy Papershoes... from the band, Heroshima...'

'And I am Mrs Julio Inglesias... I do want to help you but your name is not enough, never mind who you think you are. Have you got your ticket, madam? Maybe we could start with that?'

'No, I told you, my ticket's gone. It was an open flight, you must have a record of it?'

Walking under the departure board, it's like a crossword, a riddle of numbers and places. A code. If I can add all the flights leaving, to all the flights arriving, there'll be a remaining number which may equal a destination. Maybe if I can crack it, make the numbers add up, go via the destination they want me to select, I'll be able to leave.

The problem with madness is the holder cannot see it. Sometimes the mind invents.

I go and buy a green pack of cigarettes and some weird international chocolate for my veins. Pulling the loose change from the bottom of my shoddily hand-made bag, there, an oasis had slipped through the lining, for lo and behold, hark the farking angels sing, the scent of freedom, my shiny burgundy passport. Stuck to the gaffa tape roll. I wave it like Johnny Ace's[35] gun. Dangerous, I am an impassioned patriot. I wink to God, *nice one, matey*. Maybe you do exist. I can leave this Alcatraz.

---

35. *Johnny Ace was a soul-filled, crooning rhythm and blues guy who took a break between sets in Houston on Christmas Day, 1954. Backstage, he was playing with a .22 calibre revolver (as he often did, frequently shooting roadsigns from their car) fooling around, said, 'It's okay, gun's not loaded... see?', pointed it at himself with a smile on his face... and died. He was 25.*

*In 1978, Chicago guitarist Terry Kath recounted the same line, with a gun in his hand, and did the same thing, age 31.*

# CHAPTER TWENTY-SIX
## BEYOND THE GRAVE

*Those are people who died, died* - Jim Carroll Band

The Belgian triplets buzz me in. Immaculate always, totally Helmut Newton, black dresses, black eyeliner, black smiles.

'Oh, the raver returns...' announces Orlando, wearing silver everything. 'I've been to New York and back since I last saw you. Farkin' hell, you look rough, Mrs... look what the cat's just dragged in, Iggy - it's your wifey...'

Ig and I look over at each other - a gaze of mutual disappointment.

'PLAYBACK' is shouted out:
>*You kill stars like a martyr,*
>*Breaking their hearts is your motto.*
>*Is it a burning or burial?*
>*How does it compare with the one, last week?*
>*What you gonna wear? Make it look like you care?*
>*You've been crying since dawn for the guy you met once at a club,*
>>*too late to devote, a love never known.*
>*He must be next, break him first, after you.*
>*It's another high society funeral*

'ACTION':

Orlando strolls in front of the camera, top off, stroking the blonde crab-ladder above his denim, swinging his bass back and forth like it's someone on top of him.

'IMPROV':

Iggy lies on the day bed, wearing his wax Barbour, bare chest, jeans. Mouthing the words to the song. I'm sure he's finger-fucking one of the triplets, who straddle him, moving into a pyramid of skin, the harem licking each other's torpedo tits, under each other like car mechanics. Filmmaker Paul is whipping a Super-8 camera around on a rope hung from the ceiling, a birds-eye view. They snake together. It's a dark-disco dance, a nude scrawl. Straight out of the coffin of so fist. Iggy mouths further words:

> *The love was pure, like the dress you once wore,*
> *As you slept on my grave,*
> *Dead in the eyes, in the soul, he should go,*
> *but first shall we snort, or inhale, scatter or spike him*
> *to our veins?*
> *Should we snort, or inhale, scatter or spike him to*
> *our veins?*

He does another chorus. The song is inspired by Dan the Drummer. Our space has been decorated with billboards of Orlando's face, hung across mirror-foiled walls. They've started writing songs about me recently. Ig's been singing them in the shower. He says he's going to record them. The red velvet stage curtain that splits the space in two is lit dramatically, our bathroom and bedrooms beyond it...

Cleopatra haircuts swing, the Belgian girls undress each other, touch and fence around their pounds of flesh, Iggy crawls back towards them, putting his hand in their pants. One of the girls twings off her black gauze bra. This is hardcore, I feel trust seep away. Cut like a cancer from my heart. There's a hole.

> *Was there a sponsor at the wake? Sorry, who was there?*
> *I was, you were, killer queen, psycho sheen, breaker witch,*
> *vampire child.*
> *Jack me up, hold me tight, death 'til you part,*
> *Alone as we are, everyone a loner, give me your songs,*
> *number one, perfect friend.*
> *Funeral fan. Been dead for so long.*

They CUT, and freeze.

'In one take. Masterful. You are beyond the grave!' congratulates Filmmaker Paul. He asks again if I would like to do a lil' kiss for the camera.

'It's early, man, I need make-up, decent cinematography.' I wanted to move in to directing. I take a swig on whiskey.

'I don't think you need anything.' Iggy whispers. Yet he's fucking other girls, and my idea. 'Yeah, you don't remember me from when I first saw you, do you? I used to DJ at Men Age Trois, where GoldBug did their first gig.' Iggy takes my hand, gazing softly, 'You always looked so cute, I thought. Were you alright out there?'

'In Ibiza? Fine, yeah.'

I act like his club DJing gigs are news. But they're the reason why I used to bunk the train from Macclesfield every week and why I started staying 'round at Pip The Trip's. I didn't know his name, but I fancied him. It was when he was still at art school - with Filmmaker Paul, Laurent and Photographer Paul, who was older. They all ran a club-night down in Hanover Street called Men Age Trois. Each week they'd arrive separately with increasingly extravagant haircuts, miraculously, they'd each be sporting the same style; four white wedges, four black mohicans or four sets of carrot orange curls. I never asked if it was part of their promo ploy, but it worked. Everyone went, if only to see their hair.

Last time I saw Laurent it lasted three days and the drugs have yet to be paid for. He has no home, just a studio, he's so skint he can't afford underwear, says he goes commando because he likes to feel free, but it's because his Calvin Klein fund is up his nose. He does hair now. Always wears Communist vests (says he'd never go as far as Commie shoes though - that's the problem with equality - shit shoes, he says). Our talk is always the same: how's whoever, who's doing who, where's where and when it's happening.

I wouldn't have shot their promo like this. I'm so stroppy. I leave Iggy, and go over to Ruby who is incinerating smack on the white Chesterfield. Our furniture has got better since we started the Shoreditch shuffle. We've got Eames and Starck, Ron Arad and Verner Panton. Dentist chairs, and white leather. Chrome and steel. It's all sixties neo-modernist.

'When did you get back?' I ask her.

'I don't know, no-one seemed to notice me come in...'

She looks like a carved angel in a graveyard: worn-out tattoos, smashed-up teeth, in and out of the ivy of junkie-sleep. Her skinny T-shirt rises up her body, I look at her tattoo that runs around her lowest, left rib: Glory In Excess. You are what you are tattooed with, and I was still scared of feeling lopsided if I got a tattoo.

Filmmaker Paul is so in the moment, adjusting his belt to do up at the side, working out what to shoot, he misses a loop on the back of his jeans. Sparking up a fag, he puts the lighter in his pocket, it comes out at the bottom of his trouser leg. He doesn't notice, I don't tell him.

I just want to go to bed.

What they're shooting looks good: the band set-up, the girls, jarring in minimalist electro. Filmmaker Paul casts direction behind us.

'Now, you two, if you could just mirror each other... uh, huh, perfect, and you three, sorry, I can't pronounce your names...'

The dust and grease of Ruby's existence amalgamate upon her stationary body. She's like a forlorn lamb, touched by another being, smelling of elsewhere - dumped to die by its mother. Her eyes flit open. She smiles distantly. Her spine has no calcium, puppet's lost her strings.

'Sorry,' she mouths. Her lips dehydrated. I pause. I fucking hate her.

'Where were you?' I ask. 'Why did you do that to me?'

'I came back here to read a book, drugs are so shit,' she laughs.

My self-loathing doesn't overshadow not liking where she's at. Beyond sharing her junkie crown. Her addiction was once part-time and unobtrusive, now it's a lone sport. Like countless junkies before her, Ruby maintains an impenetrable illusion of romance about junkieism. It's a solo career. The daily control.

'It's a full-time job to be properly on drugs,' my father always warned. 'In every city in every county in every land, there'll be ex-pats and ex-everythings fawning to the gods of medicinal emancipation.'

By which, he meant: William Burroughs[36] is godfather to thousands of imitators for whom dependence is a beautiful and honourable thing. Oh, to the patron saint of booze, Charles Bukowski. Where art thou, whiskey and beer-lord brother, Kerouac[37] and gay toker nerd, Ginsberg? Hunter,[38] thanks for the acid initiation. Rimbaud,[39] you are my Rambo. Jean Genet,[40] you are my genie. Blake, you will be at my wake. Huncke, you so funky. Harry Crews, we got nothing to loose. This was my reading list. Dad gave me a book that wasn't on the school curriculum every Christmas, and I read it twice by New Year. Stephen Crane,[41] John Fante, whatever...

Mum had a go at him once, 'You want her dead by twenty-seven? Like the rest of bloody them?'

'I'm so out of here...' says Ruby.

'You're so out of IT. Fucking hell, Ruby. What you did, do you know what happened?'

'Sorry,' she says again. 'It's too much, the money, the shops, Suki, Malachi...'

Slipping out to the bathroom, the orgy dances along like candida.

I sit down, on my thigh, as I did on the plane on the way over - I can't sit properly, and put the fur blanket around me, observing the madness. Iggy comes to kiss me. I am surprised. Feel like I've

---

36. *William S. Burroughs, writer, Harvard graduate and heroin lover, shacked up with the fellow Beat, Joan Vollmer in 1944. She became increasingly self-destructive after having his child, and in an unsuccessful game of William Tell in Mexico, 1951, where she stood with a glass tumbler on her head, Burroughs accidentally shot and killed her. She was 28. Burroughs lived on a family trust fund for many years and his first published book, Queer, recounting sodomy, was banned.*

37. *Jack Kerouac, writer and bourbon lover, largely credited with being the Beat master of train-of-thought writing, died of cirrhosis in 1969. He was 47.*

38. *Hunter S. Thompson, gun lover and radical journalist, pioneer of the Gonzo movement, blew himself up with a shotgun after disillusionment with American politics and increasing ill health. He was 67. At his funeral, he was blown out of a cannon to the tune of Mr Tambourine Man.*

39. *Arthur Rimbaud, writer and lover of Paul Verlaine, died of cancer in 1891, age 37.*

40. *Jean Genet, 1910-1986, born to a young prostitute, his most famous book, Our Lady of the Flowers has influenced many a rockstar. He also made the groundbreaking gay film, Un Chant d'Amour in 1950.*

41. *Stephen Crane, writer and lover of working girls, didn't quite make it into the twentieth century, dying of TB at the age of 28.*

interrupted him fucking the triplets, and he'd rather be with them.

'We recorded some tracks out there, before we got arrested, I can't wait to play them to you... you're all over them. You inspire so much in me, baby. I'm so sorry we just split, we were literally dragged to the airport...'

'And this film, I, urrr, thought I was gonna do it...'

'Filmmaker Paul just made it so easy to do it now - we couldn't wait, Scaz, the heat is on, we've got this tour. Sorry - you're a good writer, just do that. I wanted to tell you, Malachi set us up with an amazing drummer, Woolf Talese.'

I act like I know who he is.

'Your dad played with him... I think he's gonna tour with us. What happened to you?'

'I think I need a bath. I got in trouble. With some guys.'

'What did they try to do? Take your drink away?'

'Iggy... it... wasn't... like that...' I start to cry.

'Was it Malachi?'

'No, no, no, definitely not,' I fall into his shoulder.

'You sure? I'll rip the contract up right now, and I'll go back over there and kill him.'

'Of course it wasn't him.'

'What can I do? Listen, we've pretty much wrapped this, let's get out of here, away from all these chancers, liars, crucifiers and half bit wannabes...'

'You should use that in a song.'

'I have.'

I hear Orlando shouting at Ruby in the bathroom. He's so aggressive with her.

'Have you started your period?'

I don't know if I have any tampons, my periods virtually disappeared when I started seeing Joe Delaney.

'What's happened?' I shout out. 'Are you alright?'

I run through - the tutu Orlando had been wearing in the video, that used to belong to Kyrie, is massacred, strewn on the floor. It's covered in blood. Orlando fixates ahead, on the bath, freaking right out, stumbling from one foot to the other. The lights are off and I reach for the switch. Stark blood is all over the white rugs around the bath and sink. Wiping blood-infused steam from my face, Ruby lies in a hot running tub wearing Agent Provocateur underwear. Her hands look like she's put them in a food processor. Her eyes wheel. Stringy, skin-sliced veins, mangled, flapping, rising out of the water, before smashing down to the terror which waterfalls with premier cru into the carpet.

'RUUUUUUBY!'

Piss and shit leave her body. A sonar pulse oscillates towards the next world. Her brother is holding his back to the wall. I puke up into my hands, wiping it to the white wall as Iggy runs in, reaching for our dying friend's face. He's met with recognition.

'—IS SHE FUCKING BREATHING?'

I feel myself hyperventilating, yelping.

'Ruby! Ruby! Come on... don't do this... Are you there? RUBY! Ruby get back here! IS SHE BREATHING?'

I warp into a high-speed panic. Jeezus Christ. The hot tap is still running and the pool of red water is tipping over the edges.

'It's too late,' declares Iggy. The stereo in the other room blasts out his song so they can't hear, carrying on shooting.

'It's never too late,' I snap. 'Keep a fucking eye on her.'

I turn the tap off and bolt back towards the living space, I need to find a phone.

'What's all the racket?' asks Filmmaker Paul, 'Is someone finally more punk than their Sex Pistols' T-shirt?'

The petals of death rise to the water surface.

Iggy shouts at Paul. 'Get the fuck out of here, now! You're not welcome! Pack up and fuck off.'

Paul's lacey-face breaks like a hymen.

Orlando shouts at him too, 'Stay away from me.'

Everyone's covered in blood, a tide bashing in and out of the bath as Iggy tries to talk sense to her.

In the main loft space, on the other side of the velvet curtain, girls are still twisting naked with a shawl. Black on black on black. Oblivious.

Caught up in their fifteen minutes. The camera on the rope still twisting slowly, over the bare, fresh flesh of the young girls' squirming-puppy skin, torn leopard, taut leather, tight breath - they will soon be hysteria incarnate, clasping each other, skin flanked by ropes of shawls held like Venetian blinds. Alchemy camera. Gold dust.

I call emergencies.

'Ambulance. There's been an accident - on the other side of the roundabout, near the Barbican. Whitecross Market. There is no number. I'll come down and show you where.'

Filmmaker Paul is putting camera tapes in a bag outside in the stone-cold summer morning on Whitecross Market, pulling on his coat and heading back down towards Old Street, like a wild bird before a storm.

'Later, potata,' he says,. 'You realise you can leave now, it's not a prison.'

'I live here...'

'Yeah, but still... you've got about two minutes...'

'They're my friends: Orlando, and Iggy, and Ruby...'

I don't think he gets emotion.

Breathing for the first time in a minute, I take a cigarette from him and am violently sick, again. His eyes wrinkle.

'I'm outta there - gonna go edit this video - the band are gonna be massive with her dead.'

He's way ahead of me on the personal gains calculations. Self-preserving, sociopathic career-cunt.

Iggy shouts down through the windows upstairs: 'Scarlet, doll, I'm not sure this is such a hot idea...'

'What?'

'Having the authorities over. It's a bit... napalm.'

'They can still help her.'

'Scaz - it's too late. There's a note...'

'It's not too late. What do you mean, a note?'

'Rubix has signed out, man. There's nothing anyone can do now.'

'She can't farkin' die on us...'

'You don't want to get us all arrested, do you?'

I'm getting weird looks from stall holders. This is such a bad look, man. I'm crying, half-dressed, half-broken, half-covered in blood... I don't care. Nothing matters.

The siren smashes down Great Eastern Street. Maybe they're right, the ambulance people will call the police, they'll find the drugs, the scrag-end starlets, the prawn now. Las Gambas Ahoras, the fall out of Ibiza. Ruby got busted for drugs after Glastonbury last year, and her old shop was closed after the rave started in the car park on Brewer Street when Heroshima did their first single launch. We'll get in bad trouble, not hype-trouble. I throw the cigarette out onto the pavement, there's a girl wearing bad make-up sitting on the park bench - I ask her to inform the ambulance-men that she made a mistake in calling them, I give her the bottle of whiskey in my hand and shut the door behind me. Climbing the stairs up to blame and confusion. Only celluloid can romanticise this vision.

The note is scrawled in red biro:

*Bye guys, I love you.*

*I couldn't take it anymore. Orly, sorry to leave you but how I behaved with Mal showed me how wrong I've become. I don't want to be like steel. I am not. I'm broken, voices in my head. I couldn't make it to the finishing line with you guys but I'm early for once, so I'll see you, but don't rush to catch up. Please all look after each other. Scarlet, I am so sorry to have got you involved in my mess. Please survive it. I'm happier dead, I deserve to be. I always wanted to be.*

*I guess you'll want my wardrobe. Please share it equally. It's all I have. The shop is in debt, someone else will do it better. Sure Crackhead Chris will step in. Doesn't always work, being first, does it? I've been tired for a long time. It's good to take a rest. Don't worry about me.*

*Love forever, Ruby Jane Moon.*

*P.S. Sorry for the mess. If I had money, I'd leave some for the cleaners...*

# CHAPTER TWENTY-SEVEN
# THE GAK, SMACK AND CRACK TRIATHLON

*Hey, Mr Superstar, I'll do anything for you* - Marilyn Manson

'Babe, I'd go for Iggy. Do whatever makes him happy. Do it, sweetie, marry the fucker. Get pregnant, immortalise yourself, honey. I know I did him first, but he hates me. I was too over-bearing. You know how I get... but you, Junior, get yourself written into the rock scriptures. You have to capitalise your position, you're a fashion babe, they are rockstars. Very nearly. You know all rockstars get divorced. You get half. It's the game. They know they're playing. Scarlet, there's no need for sufferance, enjoy the ride, honey.'

I flashback to Ruby's teachings. My teacher has left me. And I see her in a different light, along with everything she's ever said. The worst thing is she'll never be remembered as being a happy person. Her fast exit will suggest she was down, and she wasn't, she was always a trouper, who got fed up with trooping.

Orlando is blaming me.

I am blaming myself.

I pushed her in her last breaths.

I cringe: I was wearing a policeman's hat before I ended up here, in prison. The bonnet was wrapped in muslin bandage scrawled with graffiti:

pigZ RuLe NU SKOOL.

What the fuck was I doing?

# CHAPTER TWENTY-EIGHT
# KISS AND CRY

*Atomic* - Blondie

Malachi sent a stretch limo and cleaners, separately.

Orlando's staring out of the tinted window. We could be driving past giraffes and his pupils wouldn't dilate. Nothing engages his vision. His playfulness died with his sister. No talk. Death says it all. We're supposed to be en route to Dungeoness Nuclear Power Station, to do a photo shoot, picking up their new drummer. Iggy can't remember the drummer's name, and cares less. This'll either be the end of the band or a new beginning.

The driver is French, he likes jazz. Iggy wins him over with stories of Thelonious Monk and Sun Ra. We pause the travel plans to hit our favourite drug roads in London: All Saints Road, Rupert Street, Whitechapel High Street, the back end of Clerkenwell, Kings Cross' corners, the back of the flats near the Ministry of Sound nightclub. This takes a good twenty-four hours.

Partaking in the ceremony of brown sugar in the back of the stretch, it unites me and Iggy, falling on and off the leather seats, we kiss and cry, the windows go up and down as money is passed out and goods come in.

Pausing to sit on floors that light up, smoke on baroque benches, spin, slope and stride across the shine and inner-sanctum sleaze of London, back in the cocoon of the limo, Iggy has a one-way conversation with Orlando about his plans for the cash they may receive from a record deal or publishing, aware their exposure is on the rise in light of the press reporting Ruby Moon's death.

'We should invest in a Heroshima HQ, put all the advance into that, get a place with a studio. Rent out some of the space, sell up later, we can then split the profit, if you're up for that?'

'I'm not going back to Whitecross Street,' is all Orlando says, and he never does, not even to collect any stuff. He never goes east down Old Street again. His life moves, to solely focus around himself and no-one else. It's a narcissism lockdown, a thing of trust being best awarded only to yourself.

Iggy continues: 'I think you should move in with us, Scaz, rather than us cutting you in with hard cash; this way, the drugs will get absorbed into the band's fees'.

Ruby would be vetting all of this with laser eyes. God, I want to see her - sit together, have a line. I cry as I take more drugs. I feel so bad that I told her what I thought of her.

Orlando preaches at me: 'Free drugs, home provided, plus basic income, it's why Britain's great, darling, not that you know the difference between a socialist and a guest list.'

'Free land for all!' I shout through the roof top.

'Free Orlando?'

'Free Land for all...'

'I like being called Land' he says, and it sticks. He wants a new identity and refuses to respond to anything else.

I sip champagne from one of my patent stilettos before chundering into the other as the car drives through Knightsbridge, buckling, pure weak ankle. The limo pulls to a sudden halt and the puke whiplashes back in my face. Wiping long globs of saliva from my mouth like a vampire slurping its first kill, I smile. I feel great. It doesn't matter, nothing does. Ruby's in a better place. I look behind me, Land's face lights up beneath a white Bic lighter, our reflections blend under an aluminium mirror. We ride into our moments of obliteration: our crack, smack and gak triathlon ensues.

Toppling from one foot to the other, we dance under the weight of the stars. The driver remains our missionary, we offer to leave cash for a valet.

'We are the best band in the world, and you are the driving force of the future. Without you we couldn't progress, could we?' says Land.

Iggy whispers to me: 'All we've got is the band... there's no choice but to fight. This is war to stay in the ring, to make our lives mean something, for Ruby's sake...'

We put our heads out of the sunroof window, only to fall over.

It amuses us, finally some laughter. We bounce around the limo like squash balls - Iggy continues to fantasise about the future, and his dreams are coming into focus. It's going to be insane. We high five their success and toast to Ruby. She's sacrificed herself for the band. She was never happy anyway. Finally at peace.

We buy real fruit and vegetables from a stall in Whitechapel to make divine alco-soups in the back of the limo.

'To our bad health, eh? And to Ruby, the sexiest woman. A legend forever...' Land finally grins. He squeezes tomatoes over champagne hailing them Blurry Marys. Berries bounce into shot glasses for Berry Drunk; oranges, mangoes, ecstasy and Rohypnol topple over tumblers. I can't remember what we call them.

'We're never going to stop,' shouts Land, head out of the roof, flying into a gegenschein as we pull up to the Blind Beggar in Whitechapel to pick up Filmmaker Paul who's shown a few people the rough cut of the video. He's pretty chuffed because he persuaded them he's talented.

I give up on hating him. We imbibe our collective consciousness in a cocktail of addictions, the night turns to day, to dark to day to night to day. We fly through rainbows together. We pick up the new drummer at a shit hotel by City Airport, he's all slick, and awkward and a bit squeaky, head to toe in leather.

He's been waiting for "fifty-seven" hours.

Iggy suggests he invoices Malachi.

The boys pose. This place is DESOLATE. I could get swept off the side of this beach and no-one would ever know I'd gone. I kick stones into the sea. I think of all the people I love. And of Ruby. I throw a rock for her. It sinks. We leave the limo outside a pub a few miles down the coast which is full of England fans, there's a curry house adjoined. Everyone is white. We drink pints. We play pool.

The locals beat us. They call me a Paki.

I run onto the beach. Reminds me of my life in Smacklesfield. I hate the thought of losing Mum - she gets what it's like to be an outsider.

We drop Filmmaker Paul and the drummer, Woolf Talese at the derelict wastelands of City airport. Woolf's one of those slow-burning guys. He knows he's entering a hostile situation, so he's very careful to keep a blade strapped to his ankle. Creaking in black, the way an American rocker wears black - he's kinda so fist. We think he'll be okay in the band, just different, as we fly back under the huge money tower blocks, finance centres flanked by fish markets, crumble-down flats next to reclaimed docks for millionaires. Basic pubs, clubs and boxing places housed in Portakabin shantytowns. Everything ply-board, then marble. Limos overtaking rag and bone men. Adverts for strip joints next to prophecies from The Koran.

Iggy wants me to tour with them. Says they need female energy or it gets a bit stinky.

'Land's hardly the classic stinker...'

I don't want to be just a groupie, following them around, I need to be doing something... I also don't know what I'd do if Malachi arrived, owning us. Maybe I'd want to kill him.

Land offers the driver a thousand quid tip to stay, but it's not enough. All that remains is our desire to stay locked as a pack of wolves, loaded in spirits, our mission is nothing more than a need to be more rock n roll than anyone ever before, staying up forever, we clock in a working week of caning it. By day seven we all get matching tattoos saying *Wasted Youth* from a guy in Newington Green. Mine will later turn septic. At an underground club in Farringdon we hold it down like hostages in the basement with the walls thumping around us. In Soho we meet future dead crack barons in pool halls. We sink pints in the Phoenix bar. The pubs on Regents Park Road are home to a revival of Jaegermeister. Houses of the rich and famous follow with bowling alleys and Goldschläger.

We all snog one another. There's an orgy at the Café de Paris, in the back-room to the charity award ceremony with blueberry drinks. I watch on. I can't do another group thing, I can't even look inside my knickers, it's such a mess but I've numbed the pain.

Iggy stays beside me. I hold onto him. I feel so betrayed that he's slept with the girls, but I can't let him know that. We, the pirates of tomorrow. Crashing in and out, licking Bloody Marys from my metallic dress, free-wheeling through the wilds of London's scrubland. Less stoned than we used to feel.

In a place where chopping cocaine on skinheads is as normal as crushing ecstasy behind the menus of the Yucatan bar in Dalston, Land pees in the corner of the bar, saving time on finding the bathroom.

El Dorado's near Trellick Tower sees the guns[42] come out for shooting practice of apples upon each other's heads. It's too close to Ruby and Kurt Cobain to last long.[43]

Coke gets replaced by downers, which get replaced by uppers and things that make the paranoia slip, to be taken over by

---

42. *Wonderful World* singer, Sam Cooke (1931–1964) had his death ruled as justifiable homicide, when allegedly shot, pants down by Bertha Franklin, manager of the Hacienda Motel at 9137 South Figueroa Street in Los Angeles, California. He was 33 and a civil rights supporter. Details of the murder are contested by family and Etta James who saw the body, saying it had suffered extreme violence prior to death. Cooke had been on a second date with Lisa Boyer, who accused him of rape. Lisa Boyer was arrested for prostitution one month after Cooke's death. In 1979 she was found guilty of second degree murder in the shooting to death of her boyfriend.

Bertha Franklin had a .32 registered in her name, yet Cooke's bullets came from a .22. She moved to Michigan and died eighteen months later. Conspiracy plots of murder are also suggested as Cooke's catalogue was later bought from Sam's widow, Barbara by a businessman for a low $103,000.

Other LAPD dubious deaths include:

Bobby Fuller (I Fought The Law) who was found beaten up with gasoline poured down his throat in his car, outside his Hollywood apartment in 1966, age 23. LAPD ruled a suicide. Erik Green, a relative of Sam Cooke has cited similarities in the deaths of Cooke and Fuller, whereas bandmate Jim Reese suspected Charles Manson played a role.

Larry Williams - had tunes recorded by The Beatles (Bad Boy, Slow Down, Dizzy, Miss Lizzy) and the Stones (She Said Yeah). He was a full-time pimp and dealer, sometime musical partner of Johnny Guitar Watson. Found with hands cuffed behind his back and a bullet in his head in Laurel Canyon home, LAPD ruled it a suicide. He was 44, it was 1980.

43. Kurt Cobain died on the 8th April, 1994, aged 27 - revolver to his head in a garage, two days out of rehab...

downers, then uppers and sideways and downers, which lead the way to reserved areas and private rooms where we can wear shades in peace. Diagonally. Rhombus-ly. All masked with the company of booze. It's a binge of grace and fluidity, unusually free of cling-ons and fans/wasters/police/whatevers, the conversation is imperative, but instantly unmemorable. We set the world to rights, we went places, we succeeded where mere mortals have lost their lives. And we toast every drink to the woman we lost along the way.

# CHAPTER TWENTY-NINE
# SOONER WE BUST THEM, THE LESS THEY HAVE TO LOSE

*What I want is a girl that I care about*
*Or I want nothing at all... alright* - Jonathan Richman & the Modern Lovers

We missed Ruby's funeral.

We'd wondered where everybody was.

Walking into The Windblowers like we've been fighting overseas - eight days and nights of no sleep, we smile for a hero's welcome.

An applause comes only from the secret policemen, sitting all undercover in the corner, WPC Pizza Face, and her male counterpart. A really slow, sarcastic series of claps. We look over. She's wearing nylon trousers, a wifey-ironed blue shirt. He's got the face of someone far lower than a critic, dressed as an off-duty soldier. She gets up, leaving her male colleague in the corner.

Sidling up to Land at the bar: 'Fast lane, aren't you?' she whispers.

Land doesn't even offer a fake smile.

'I said, 'Fast lane, aren't you?''

'Excuse me, do I know you?' asks Land.

'As a little warning, nothing official, of course, keep an eye on the dignity levels, yours, by all accounts, appear to be slipping fast...'

I believed our chewing gum and Wet Wipe lifestyle is somehow more glamorous than the reality of coppers watching us in pubs.

'You're talking about his sister...' I say.

'It's fine, Scarlet. Funerals are depressing. Being around depression makes me depressed. Life's too short...' His camp defence, all that remains.

Joe Delaney, who's standing with Crackhead Chris, turns around and joins in.

'You lot are unbelievable. Life is short, yes, but not so fucking short you miss your sister's funeral. You stupid selfish cunt.'

Land, Orly's new name, which came from our session, doesn't fight back. He goes to the bathroom with Bobby Bandit. Crackhead Chris calms Joe down. Chris has a shop called Biographers which stocks Ruby's clothing. He's opening a store in New York and has one in Tokyo. He's stepped in to manage Tuesdays (he later took over both of Ruby's shops, making all the money her death invited). I go up and don't know how to greet Joe, so go for something I never do, a bear hug. I'm not feeling him hug back.

'You're so together, Scarlet. I really like what you're wearing. The nappy accentuation beneath the jeans, the grunge stains, the rivers of eyeliner. The bruises. It's all so REAL. Will you be my fashion editor, for the September shows? Please?'

Chris laughs, but I agree. I need the money.

'Sure, yeah. Thanks. You know, she was a sister to me.'

The pub is in full after-wake mode. It's angry and messy. The Delsey Diners are in from New York, jet-lag is paying them respects, and they pile together in a hush in the corner. The Chelsea lot are arrogantly out of their depth on this side of town, swanning around, too scared to touch anything, or relax. All the Portobello people can do is gossip of the profundity regarding a lack of professionalism by everyone in East London, loudly. The Camden crew have a punk edge, dated. The Soho set don't care, lost and wild. Phil Dirtfox, Skinny Lynne, Mark Spye, Kalvin Stein, the singer from Yeti and the Ravers, many guys Ruby slept with. Violet the model, The Belgian triplets, Jack from Jax's Tab, Jim and Joe Mercier (the artists we had a fight with recently)... everyone was there.

### I don't know what day it is, August? 1996?

Dear Diary,

I am a little wired, paranoid and guilty. Ruby was burnt in a Palladian death factory. The service formal, perforated with the smell of damp stone mixing with burning flesh. We missed it. Land jokes that we never got a chance to snort her ashes like we did with Craig Drake's last year in Peckham. There must be incest rules against that, says Ig. But I know he couldn't bear to be in proximity to the carcass - and how the smoke blends with someone else's so fast, there's barely enough time to breathe in their last wish after the curtain swishes them away...

The wake was in The Willow pub, apparently, down a spaghetti strap of a country lane; Ruby worked there when she was doing fashion at art school in Winchester. The first time she really got away from her step-father. An upright piano stood handsomely to the service of The Malfunctions, chucking songs against the low-slung beams. Heroshima really should have been there.

I imagine the place was the kind of joint with bugs in the tapestry benches, full of fleas falloloping around, drunk on flaccid veins. The waxed tables so shiny the beers flew off, onto a dark, red-patterned carpet, the sun shedding diamonds through the old Tudor-style windows, a galleon to share the seas to death. The marching melody of chinking glass ashtrays pattering above the hum generating from the shaking refrigerators behind the big, dark, never-long-enough-to-drown-our-sorrows bar. We missed it. I haven't said goodbye.

# CHAPTER THIRTY
# EMPTY WRAPS

*Been caught stealing* - Jane's Addiction

Turning my bag upside down on the bed, as is tradition upon arrival in a hotel room, I pull the curtains closed on the outside world of Spitalfields', where shark suits bustle through like it's a sample sale for Jean Van Chi. There's all sorts of crap from the past bender: broken cigarettes. Flyers. Empty wraps. Bar mats with random numbers on them. A candle. There's a wad of cash. Notes to myself on napkins. Abstract poetry or is it journalism? They read like plots to save the world and myself. Drawings of bizarre runway clothes. Graffiti markers.

I call up all the PRs and get room service to fax them requests to attend upcoming shows, signing myself off as editor of TBC. I am so glad Joe finally asked.

I select the music station on the TV and angle the bathroom mirrors so, should the hooded claw break in, I'll catch visual proof of my enemy before he fucks me (twice, by the same guy - I can only expect it go Oscar Wilde[44] meets Kenny Rogers, three times a trashed lady).

Whacking on the taps for a bath, using all the bubbles in the little black and white bottles, within seconds the flood of heat awaits. I love a hotel bath. Iggy left me to sort myself out whilst he scored supplies from Bobby Bandit and Fish Shop Frankie. Land's with him, he's getting a room here too. The door goes, too early for them. I edge along the wall, ready to put my full weight behind the door and crush whoever is on the other side, but it's room service:

---

44. Oscar Wilde (1854-1900), writer of *The Importance of Being Earnest* and other plays, books, poems and journalism, was 46 when he died destitute in Paris. He'd been imprisoned for two years of hard labour, leaving Reading Gaol three years earlier, after being proven gay in a libel case he had initiated. His life was an inspiration, and a tragedy of being star-fucked. 'To lose one parent, Mr. Worthing, may be regarded as a misfortune; to lose both looks like carelessness...'

Lucozade, Ribena, Orangina, Evian, Dr Pepper and French fries. I forgot I'd ordered.

Peeling off my jeans and knickers which stick to my blood-scabbed, outgrowing pubes and broken arsehole, I clamber precariously atop the built-in bathroom sink. It's a long combination vanity desk made with marble. My balance holds above the expensive taps and hump of the basin. Stretching open my legs in front of the bay mirror, I witness the damage: battered, too grim to repeat, looks like I've shat a ten tonne diamond truck. Scabs too scared to form, I'm torn to my psyché; a graffiti of bruising blossoms from thigh to thigh.

Fetching the salt cellar from the room service chariot, I dissolve the contents before dousing myself slowly, cleaning, cleaning, cleaning until the water runs a light rosé. I feel faint. Unable to sit in the bath, I collapse, belly down on the bed, legs wide. I eat cold fries before flipping to my back, transfixed by red lights flicking on and off on the ceiling, someone somewhere is recording me. Mal probably has shares in this hotel, he's keeping an eye on us, making sure I don't tell people what he did. Raising whisky, I soak cotton wool with the booze and disinfect my wounds. The lightbulb above flickers; I remember the story of Claude François, a French singer/songwriter, influenced by cross-Atlantic styles, penned tracks adopted by Elvis and others. He co-wrote *Comme D'Habitude*, the original version of *My Way*, made famous by Frank Sinatra. Sometime in 1978 he noticed a wonky lightbulb above a filled bath in his Paris apartment and attempted to fix it, with wet hands, and electrocuted himself to death. He was 39. Always reminds me to lie in a bath, that one.

The scabs need air so I stagger into the lift, in my bathrobe. The doors open to a rooftop bar which demonstrates the riches of the city. The staff look at me weirdly and the mirror of the lift exposes blood seeping through the white, fluffy dressing gown, urging me to press the buttons home where the room key fails to work. It's one of the credit card style things with three LEDs on the doors signalling a) you're locked out, b) still locked out or c) enjoy your stay. I try to slip it in nicely, like sex with someone you fit with; welcome home is not happening, the usual tricks of lifting the door, using quick or slow manoeuvres all fail. I'm locked out. I scuttle down to reception. Can I just confirm which room you were trying, Ms McFerguson? Oh, I am sorry, you were on the wrong floor. My room's on third.

Later, I lie frigid, scared my 2am thoughts will rape me. Feel I could slip out, all John Coltrane.[45] Creaking floorboards outside the room, moving walls from crews of burglars, ghosts, rapists, madmen, lynchmen. Armies of fuck forces. I open the curtains at 3am, the birds explode like grenades. I order a first aid kit from room service. Getting to the door, feeling heavy as a wet Ritz bathrobe, assuring them everything is fine, thank you. I ram antiseptic cream inside. Cover the scabs in talcum powder.

At 5am, Iggy knocks and we fall into each other. I experience an upsurge. I'm gonna rock Joe's new magazine. Fashion editor. Me. Finally. It's our choice on how we disguise our naked bodies, everyone is in drag, dear. We all wear costumes of invention. Just some of us are less concerned for boundaries. I have no centre. Or gave it away.

We stay a week. Watching TV, eating room service, taking drugs.

He demands to know who's created the mess I'm in. Strangers, I tell him, repeatedly. He'd kill them.

---

45. *John Coltrane died at 40 in 1967, of liver cancer. It was a surprise to those around him. Coltrane was a saxophonist, recording by the age of 19. He had bands with Dizzy Gillespie, Miles Davis, Thelonious Monk and Duke Ellington before becoming more experimental and avant-garde in the sixties with collaborators such as Pharaoh Saunders.*

# CHAPTER THIRTY-ONE
# PUSHING THE AVANT-GARDE ENVELOPE

*This is the end* - The Doors

Slip over-the-knee, black socks into curlicue mulettes. Stark coco legs, bruised; blood closer to the surface than anyone I know. Belt into coal-colour leather shorts. Swallow tube of arnica. Paste gallons of cover up across Ibizan episode. Pin shades to face (old school Ray-Bans). Make gaffer tape bra. Tear sleeves off Victorian chiffon spinster shirt. Rip gel strips from Neo-Modernist lampshade by hotel bed. Gaffer the strip of gel around thigh, another around arm. Tape a long rectangular piece of this coloured-plastic over one sunglass lens, down left-hand side of face, forehead to chin.

'Let me guess - Florence Nightingale deconstructed?'

He doesn't get how scared I am of going outside. I have to strut back into reality feeling tough in my crap Leigh Bowery[46] impression.

'More is more in my world, less is most definitely less,' I try to explain. We lurch out together towards the pub. Our Shoreditch family are present. JD Frank is at the bar, he's got a gig as a radio presenter through one of his old clients. Heroshima's unelected videographer, Filmmaker Paul, always documenting their lives, studying success, appears from the bathroom: 'So the video's been A-listed on MTV. Fashionheads love it. Life is so much more fashionable than art right now. We've got a cover feature about it for Jax Tab. I've got a new agent, I'm going to see her in Hollywood.'

---

46. *Leigh Bowery was a nude model for Lucien Freud, born on March 26th, 1961 in Melbourne, Australia, and died on December 31st, 1994. He is best known for trump, outlandish outfits at London clubs such as Kinky Gerlinky, Taboo (which he co-ran from 1985-1987), and Philip Salon's nights at Bagley's Warehouse. His colourful space-drag, inflatable rubber costume, and extreme blocked-colour make-up was a look that defined him as a performance artist, freaky fashion designer and outsider muse. He was 'trampled to death by pigs in Bolivia after a spell of research in Papua New Guinea' (he didn't want anyone to know he was another AIDS statistic). Highlights of his creative achievements included collaborations with ballet choreographer, Michael Clark, and a fashion show at the ICA.*

'Who's writing the cover story?' I ask.

'Rose Neath.'

'The model?' How can she write too? Is this how it's all gonna continue?

'Don't worry, love,' calms Land, 'who READS magazines anyway?'

# CHAPTER THIRTY-TWO
# A WOODEN VENETIAN BLIND WILL MAKE AN INSPIRED DRESS

*We weren't rent boys, we just wanted to get picked up* - Lee Black Childers

Alone, I do what a girl does best, put on my shades and go shopping. A luxury cosmetics apothecary and I become mutual beneficiaries. What I can't do for myself, I trust their miracle products can. This new face shields me through the boutiques of Spitalfields, buying whatever clothes aren't nailed down. In one of the Brick Lane archways, I find leather sofa seat covers that I will transform into batwing tops; I buy huge paper Chinese lanterns and a wooden Venetian blind. For dresses.

Passing back through Hoxton Square, a flock of what I'd always thought were mythological fly ahead: five rare Old Street Eagles - kamikaze birds in the habit of raiding pharmacies in our parts. With necklaces of pills and hypodermic beaks of titanium, I remember this bullshit becoming fact when Land quoted the story back to me, unaware that it had been my invention. He re-quoting this evil omen: 'Anyone who's done time at East London beer-pumps can tell you about the Old Street Eagles, Scaz - it's a completely evil omen seeing them.'

Land later recalled five flying over like the Red Arrows before Ruby died. He insists. It's not up for debate, nothing to do with shonky, burnt-retina, tour vision throwing neon-shards of morning into the reflection of his shades.

But now I see them, I cannot dispute his truth. They're like a vision becoming fact. If you dream of something long enough, you become it, if you trade that much in the shredding embers of light, prepared to take out anyone, stealing souls of the nearly-dead, their feathers strong as Iggy's long beautiful hair, like his arms, racing horse lean. *Running my fingers through, after we've held onto each other like we're all the parts on a Swiss watch, twisting around the room...*

I knew with a heart-opened acceptance that the Old Street Eagles were telling me my days are lessening. Dan the Drummer knew he was done, after he'd been swooped, and scraped, and carried halfway down Old Street, and what led him to OD, on purpose. That's what I always said: life's cruelties, taking the kindest earliest.

I stop and plant the candle from the drugs triathlon that I've been carrying around with me, waiting for the right place - and write a note beneath it, chanting the lyrics as I go:

*'Profiteer of dirge, drunk on laurels sniffing up the stench of idols was that what we craved*
*The devil invites me to a purgatory beyond - in one hand he holds my tightrope*
*The other a needle to tattoo crawling black roses to his grave*
*And I want to play cards with this friend, my enemy, hold him up with eagles of the night*
*Trade my chained mind for a castle where we rule with a litany of liberty*
*Where he will maketh me a heroine to rule our asylum land and leave us with equality, no insecurities, and peace.*
*Your beauty will always remain through good times and all that follow*
*Your love will keep me sane*

*I love you forever, Ruby.*

*Your friend Scazza Fever*

Steve, a crusty with a dog on a string, approaches. I ask him if he saw the Eagles. Never been out of Old Street, he said. Lucky to get enough cash for a hostel, let alone Hotel California. I have to explain the Ruby mausoleum. I leave him with money for a crappuccino and a bag of smack. He promises to keep Ruby safe. That is a real boundary I've just crossed. Speaking to someone who looks like that.

# CHAPTER THIRTY-THREE
# WHY DON'T MORE PEOPLE SKIP?

*I hit the city and I lost my band* - Neil Young

**DIARY ENTRY 1996ish** (I guess I thought dates were really mainstream)

The band are leasing a new kingdom with their advance. Huge, sheet-metal gates on Goswell Road open up to a courtyard. You enter through a pedestrian door, encased within a lorry grille. It's the kind of place that makes your neck click back like Pez to check the ginormity. It is pure stadium rawk. *[Where are my DRAWINGS OF THE PLACE?]* There's a covered, person-sized bridge which links two buildings on either side: we own both sides. Levering through king-size metal doors, they echo with the electric buzz of the factory lights flickering on. Pigeons flap when we first arrive. The space is the size of Wembley Arena. Acres of space, above, below, around. The floor is concrete, walls are whitewashed-brick, the ceiling is metal with transparent skylights. There are mini-warehouses within the factory shell. Enough to have one each. There are old workers' lockers which we use for wardrobes.

Kyrie's taken over the lease in Whitecross Street, I'm glad to leave it all behind.

I went skulking around the back of Petticoat Lane with Pip The Trip, my ex; he drives and was helping the move, so I wangled him into extending his services. He was always wet, and malleable. We track down nine hundred and eighty-nine black sheepskins for my satanic cell at the Amphitheatre - he pays. I wanted a thousand, maybe there are. Can't count again. We staple-gun, glue, and tack the rugs to the walls, ceiling and floor of my boudoir at the Amphitheatre of Death. I was working at Ruby's shop in Portobello when we met - he was trying to be in a band, Hemingway. They were never very good but I went to every gig and clapped half-heartedly. His hair's still long and parted in the middle, although he never brushes it, and I had to cut out knots. His skin is embryonic, freshly licked in morning dew. He's so white, brought up under a parasol made of stately-home granite, chiselled in the last yelps of colonialism. He's still in the same place I lived with him, a bit beyond where Hendrix died. A crumbling, Tsarist-style palace. Chandeliers are wrecked, dusty, few of the bulbs work. Wiring explodes from damp plaster. Long, tall windows don't shut, wood warps with lack of upkeep. There's rarely hot water and the kitchen equipment is pre-war. Everything is nicotine yellow. Even all his electronic gear. His brain is caramelled, head in a bong. Shelves have fallen out. All the books, on the floor, reshuffled backwards. Been in a blizzard to never return from. He can vaguely get away with it, being dope royalty. But Pip's taken none of his parents' risks - aristocracy funding the miracles of hydroponics, and paying for more than his education. Pip is a rainbow weasel, always has holes in his clothes and is concerned about the ecology of the planet, yet he drives a massive gas-guzzling truck, with an insane, petrol-fed sound-system. It was inevitable I'd get bored. I didn't even want to hurt him. I did think about marrying him, taking Ruby's advice, getting the house in Notting Hill, but he was convenient to start off with, he made me laugh; yet I could only take all his annoying, rich, hippy-bullshit for a year. We did 1993 together. When we split up, he told me I've been wrecked by others and my heart is caged. Pip helps me blockade the bridge to Iggy's space with old lockers. Then I tell him to leave.

After a few days of settling in, Iggy's at the door.
'Scarlet, please come out. I just want to know you're okay.'
I have more candles burning than the Vatican. Electric light is electrocuting. My husband's eyeball is staring through the keyhole.
'What is it with you and candles?' he pleads.
'Leave me alone, I'm fine. Please?' I blow smoke through the hole, stuffing it with a remnant of sheepskin, Un Chant D'Amour, yeah? I hate him, the way he goes on, telling me how to run my life.

And he's trying to ration my gear. What the fuck is that about? I've been alone, working on my special project for a while.

'I have to sort my head out. I need a little longer. Please...'

I haven't been sharing a bed with him, and have taken so much constipation medicine to prevent the butthole scabs peeling off - I'm more FULL OF SHIT than ever. I smell like a hospital with the amount of bleach I've doused on myself. Vaseline smears and Vitamin E oil have been massaged onto my fangita. Squeezes of mouth ulcer cream and various drugs have been rammed into my shithole to try and numb the pain. Stab it out with cocaine. Call the dentist, get me some Novocaine. I'm losing my mind. Hollow, hollow, hollow out the hurt. Hock it with my brain to a prankster, or gangster. Is the arsehole a mouth? I think I've absorbed bleach from sitting in a bowl of it, trying to clean, clean, clean myself. I am poisoned. I find comfort in the black sheepskin bikini I've patched for myself, fur facing in, it warms my sex-torn tools. The straps are made with metal chains, they soon leave indents against my dried-out skin. Cosy fanny tutti.

'What are you doing in there, Scarlet?' Iggy asks again, tapping the door. He's stopped shaving his head and face, cultivating a latter-day Charlie Manson[47] look.

---

47. *Singer/songwriter Charles Manson was born the bastard son of a drugstore cowboy and an alcoholic. The figurehead of The Family, branded as a murderous commune, held responsible for nine gruesome deaths in 1969.*

*Sceptics suggest this was a secret operation to destroy the appeal of counterculture to the masses, citing the CIA's Operation Chaos and Project Resistance as programmes to vilify alternative lifestyles.*

*Manson established himself as a guru in 1967 after periods in jail where he is reported to have studied Scientology. Meeting Dennis Wilson of the Beach Boys, who was attracted by his loyal posse of women, they acquired a commune in a ranch belonging to an 80-year-old man who was sexually serviced in lieu of rent by Lynette 'Squeaky' Fromme (she earned her nickname from the noise she made when the old man touched her). In 1975 she attempted to assassinate US president, Gerald Ford. But their best known victim is Sharon Tate, who died age 26. The actress was eight months-pregnant with the child of husband and director, Roman Polanski.*

*Manson, frequently described as a masterful manipulator, was not present at either of the group murders but confesses to pulling the trigger on the first victim (Bernard Crowe) when a drug deal went wrong. Some suggest this is all any of it was. 'Healter Skelter', 'WAR' and 'Death to Pigs' were some of the sentiments written in blood at the murder scenes. A philosophy of vendetta was said to have been cultivated within the commune, combining a fearful consciousness over popular current affairs such as the Black Panther struggle with a fascination of stardom in acts like The Beatles.*

'I'm working...'

'Yeah, I kinda want to get on with working too - but need to know you're okay. I'm worried. What are you working on?'

No way am I showing him. It's bigger than any of us. It's bigger than Blair inviting us to hang out at Number 10. It's bigger than any rave I ever went to, or Thatcher's privatisations. It's bigger than Marx. It's not as big as this warehouse. But I'm excited.

'We should be getting the dates through for the tour about now. I can't go away leaving you like this.'

Knew he wasn't at my door because he cares...

'Scarlet, please open the door...who's in there with you? Should we get hold of a rock n roll doctor? Would that help?'

'I'm just busy. I'm fine. I told you... got a lot coming up...'

I am making dresses. And looking for the answers, ON MY KNEES - GOD, TELL ME WHAT IS GOING ON. Christ on a bike. Inshaa 'Allah. Give it up for the tea wallah. Dali Llama. God, whoever you are mate, I'll sort myself out. Mañana banana, au revoir frambois. Later, potata...

'Jeezus... listen, I want you to know how guilty I am,' he whispers. 'I was so mashed up in Ibiza. Feck that scene. We should never have gone.'

'It's not your fault. Everything happens for a reason...'

'You gonna let me in? Show me what you're doing?'

No way. Top secret.

'I'll come down in a sec,' I tell him.

'It's safe down where we're working, really, it'll be fine if you unlock yourself out of this room, seriously, Scaz...'

'Be down in a sec... really, I will.'

---

*At Manson's trial, in 1970-January 1971, where he was incarcerated for life (after initial death sentences were temporarily suspended by the California supreme court), all members of The Family copied the X he carved on his forehead. In prison, suffering poor mental health, believing he was part of a spectacle similar to the persecution of Jews, he replaced it with the tattoo of a swastika.*

*Also note: Dennis Wilson, the only real surfing Beach Boy, was a heavy drinker and drug-taker who felt guilt for introducing Charles Manson to the music industry. On December 28th, 1983, at the age of 39, Wilson drowned at Marina Del Rey, Los Angeles, after drinking all day and diving into the marina in the afternoon to recover items he had thrown overboard from his yacht three years previously.*

The kick-kick-kick continues. Kluless fux kicking clan. My period's vanished with my marriage abilities. A poison heat takes over my body - it is not mine. This possession of evil. I am half devil. I am twisting, fighting, unable to wear butt-shaping clothes since leaving the white isle, I'm interpreting it as a kind of feminism but the sheepskin knicker-liners are depressing. I feel worthless, Iggy Papershoes cannot be interested in me as a sex object. What power am I left with? Covering my fur and gold chain bikini with my goatskin cape and ten inch heels, I hoddle outside to where they work on music. He stops. I don't deserve his love. I apologise that I have to go out by myself, get some air. Maybe I'll be better when I get back, do a striptease for him, I so want to show him my love. Give him what he should be getting...

Struggling to Islington alone, I leave my mind beneath a bar mat in a ropey pub before purchasing a Preggers Plays Pop test in the chemist on Upper Street. The nearest toilet is in a fast food joint, marching past all the Rudy Lewis[48] kids, stilettos save as I use my sleeves to lock the door. It's filthy. Fluorescent tubes buzz like fly zappers in a Mumbai butcher's shop. I tower over a sea of piss and shit in this airless hole, arm around my mouth and nose preventing consumption of the stench, I can't believe I'm still here, amid such ugliness. I wee on a pregnancy stick feeling like half of Islington's shat on my gallows.

Scramming out, gagging from the stench, I put the stick in my pocket and go back to the pub on St. John's Street, constantly checking for the colours to change, fanning myself with the error of my obliteration. My bones topple inside the coffin of my body. The test confirms nothing because I feel the devil's spawn mutating in my belly. Could be HIV cells multiplying, or Hepatitis C disseminating, but if I go to hospital, they'll want me to talk to someone, and I don't want to. I talk to myself instead. The voice of reason. Headcase. Nutcase. Put me in a suitcase and send me packing.

---

48. Rudy Lewis, dead at 27 on May 20th 1964. The beautiful singer of The Drifters was a known binge-eater and many of his friends suggested the cause of his death was more likely to be choking on food than the suspected drug overdose. His smooth voice appears, most famously, on On Broadway.

Iggy suggested, kindly, that I go to a victim support group: battered women saying they never deserved it. I was asking for it, I don't belong with their crew. If you don't stand for anything, you stand to get fucked. I can't ever stand up by the end of a night. Je suis a man-pleasing freak, keen to impress like a floral swamped hearse. I bore myself, like being out at night, the music repetitive, wrong mixes of classic records, each tune bridging the lines of cocaine swilled back with free drinks - my lack of product makes me angry.

I buy beers for the boys, and find myself skipping down Old Street, my cape flapping behind me. Why don't more people skip? It gets you there so fast. Super-happy. Super-hoppy. Tinnies bruising my legs, bouncing in their red and white plastic bag. Doesn't matter, I always heal.

I over-skip, bounce into the graveyard that links the back of Old Street with Moorgate. Consecrated ground. Blake's in here. Heya, mate. I doff my hood, tilt my head, bow and curtsy. I can't be the only one to have danced around him, joining water, air, spirit, earth and fire. Am I missing one? I'm certainly missing something. Running around the circle in the middle of the cemetery with all the poppies to the dead soldiers, I spin into the silver birch. About a metre up its spine is the engraving, Iggy loves Scarlet, darkened by time, peeling like cancer. That was a beautiful morning.

I sit under the tree and start talking to Mum. As if I am next to her. I guess I was preparing for her to die. Hallah Kebabski? Genie of my gaga lantern. Lord of my serfs. Buddha of Babylon. Ganesh of Greek Street. Maiya of Mecca. Hear my call! Yes you, with your Father Christmas face and fat, cloud fingers; I am reborn.

I am willing.
I will fight.
I am yours.
I AM SAVIOUR OF HUMAN DISGRACE.
I am a mortal coil of rock.

Actually, you bastard, leave me alone, fuck off will you, judgemental dictator, where were you when I needed you? Why show up now? Why are you always male?

All I know, is I need to be saved. Hark, will the flashing disco lights ever herald me again? I am alone, an atom with jeans split. There is a weird echo. That voice. Where have I been? Who am I? Phil Ochs?[49] Why am I? Christ. If I am the only person in the room, with a direct line to God, am I Christ? Am I reborn? What is going on? Am I JESUS THE WOMAN?

I head for the open space of Moorgate, the square that Iggy thinks hides secret rocket launchers for Soviet invasions. You see me pee in the corner? I am dedicating that effluent to you, God. See, I know you exist, I can feel your disappointment, heavy as my fall from disgrace. But it proves you're there, with your beedy lil all seeing bullshit. You've been watching me make a complete tit out of my life and career, knowing I'm too wasted to care, left to scrape the underworld in a barrel? Who's laughing now? You are. Before you go, tell me: are we both dead? Am I inhabiting your brain? I am confused, wheeling around in James Dean's[50] car, grabbing at beads of logic that float past my eyes like dead retina cells. You watch me quiver, shake and feeble out, aware I'll do ANYTHING not to die. Action that. Don't leave me here. Are you there? Give me a sign and let's make a deal. Mate? Is that you with the loud voice? Am I singing? Who's singing?

The tinnies are weighing me down, I sit on the bench and crack one open. Ahhhh. Me, myself and tinny winny woo waa. It's a beautiful moment of independence. Grown-up, not caring what anyone thinks. There's a slice of sunshine through the Tupperware

---

49. *Phil Ochs was born in El Paso, Texas on December 19th, 1940. He studied journalism and called himself a 'singing journalist' when he started playing the same scene as Bob Dylan in New York in the early sixties. He performed at rallies and political events but by the seventies his alcohol intake increased alongside his rants against the FBI and the CIA. By mid-1975 he had assumed the identity of John Butler Train who said he had murdered Ochs. Train was convinced people were trying to kill him, so he carried a weapon at all times: a knife, a hammer or a lead pipe. He hanged himself on April 9th, 1976.*

50. *James Dean, film star (Giant, East of Eden & Rebel Without A Cause) was 24 when his Porsche Spider smashed into another car in California. Sanford Roth, his photographer friend who had been riding in the car behind, took photos of the crash that killed his friend. He later destroyed negatives.*

sky, like a hot knife's been taken to it.

I could end up in a wooden box, same as anyone, dust, ash, bones. What is it with my lot always thinking they're better than everyone? I, yes, I, I, meeeeee, me, me, I will not fall the way of every other woman. I will live up to my freedom to rock. I will give hope to the hopeless. I am the new sun of God. I am going to rock the upcoming fashion weeks. I will add righteousness and dignity to a world ruled by Malachis. I will become something Ruby would be proud of. I will style this shit right out.

'Garble, you're speaking garble,' announces a figure I hadn't seen in the bushes behind me. She does up her trousers, she's been having a poo. I guess this is a kind of old-fashioned get together, like when people used to discuss current affairs over a shared crapper.

'Have I been talking to myself?' I ask.

'You've certainly been speaking with someone.'

She comes and sits aside me on the bench and asks for a beer. She has a tracheotomy piece of plastic in her neck, looks like she's done more morphine than they needed to get through the opium wars, and she's smoking. Her hair is grey, she has a long black coat, she talks like a proper poet.

'Don't worry, I know there are no free beers in this world.' Husk, spishing open the can. 'I'm guessing you are here to save me?' she asks, 'With your direct line to the guy upstairs?'

Wow, she recognises me as Jesus the Woman. Validation. Finally. Pipe Neck Woman has been sent from above to test me.

I sit down at her feet. I kiss them. YES, I have my first decibel-loving disciple. I commune with my Almighty Man, the Big Man, muttering. 'Please grant Pipe Neck Woman freedom to rock once more. Please erect her collapsed lungs to stand up in love to you. Allow her decrepit veins to fire. I promise to worship you, as you worship me.'

'Oh, Jesus!' says Joanna The Pipe Neck, recognising my divinity, that I have been sent, chosen to save her, and the world.

I choose my words carefully, thinking how He would say it. 'And what, pray, is your purpose here?'

'I am here to drink your beer,' she replies. Pipe Neck's welcome. I counsel her. She should go on stage with a guitar to preach, write the Nu Testament, about Jesus The Woman. It's the modern way to change the world. To make it ALL ABOUT MY AIMS TO REBALANCE THE WORLD. My Too Young Manifesto. Wimmmmmmmmmin rule. Iggy will sit beside me, champion rockstar on the plinth of the future. We maketh excellent icons.

'Do you do any music?' I ask.

'I was on stage at the Marquee club once, a long, long time ago, after I'd been hanging out with The Grateful Dead.'

'You want to do it again, get on stage?'

'Never go back, always forward, that's what's got me here.'

'I'll promote you as a solo artist... I'll manage you, this is destiny, us meeting - I'll get you singing to the new masses. Yeah? It must be done in a different way this time, all women...'

'Women are competitive bitches - all end up with a cock in our mouths one way or another. That's what I learnt from the seventies,' she says.

But word of emancipation must be spread. Free us from this no-woman-land bordello of incarceration. This tower of consumerist pop where the Spice Girls are the greatest chance of liberation. I can't take over the world alone, I need an audience, and preachers, more disciples. I cannot survive this alone. The answers are outside me.

Time fills with darkness. Minutes wade like hours. My brain is working soooooo fast. We smoke fags. No beer left now. We need more. I must score. Running low.

Pipe Neck moseys on my errands with me. I invite her back to our HQ. Via a pitstop in The Blowers. I conduct my meeting with anyone who'll listen. Chairman of the flawed.

Bobby Bandit's there, same old stripy top, silver jewellery and attitude:

'I'm sure this is like a naturally good mood, but it could be slightly enhanced, I guess. Then again, does it matter? I feel so fucking great... but it is a while since we, y'know... Am I manic, or on coke?' he asks. 'I'm feeling really good!'

'He's both,' I say to Pipe Neck. I explain that he married us, before I was raped by Malachi. It's just another story from the music frontline. I hadn't known DJ JD Frank was behind us as I explained about Ibiza to Pipe Neck, joking about not having been able to shit for nearly two weeks. DJ JD Frank pranged me a hug like I'd lost a limb. Now he fucking knows, doesn't he?

'I'm more wrecked than the Titanic,' I admit to Bobby. 'More zapped than the Zapatistas.'

'You look like you'll be more zapped than Mia Zapata:[51] you're doing a good advert for staying clean,' he replies.

'Two pints of Gone Too Farkin' Far?'

'Again? Can't you see we're all out of that. You n your post-chemical generation have drunk us dry...'

The good times are gone. The rising ladette culture has killed feminine emotions and everything propagated by ecstasy.

'Get us some Whatever The Fark then, will you?' I order, looking over at Bobby, sniffing my right nostril at him, asking him with my eyes. You got any, y'know?

He says he hasn't, that I'd be better off eating properly, and getting some sleep.

'Oh, come on dude! Just a bit. Look at the state of me, I need to be on drugs.'

It was obvious he had coke. He wouldn't still be standing otherwise.

'You are so on drugs, Scarlet. Jesus, why don't you just get some rest? What about your friend here, will she want some too? Looks like it's been a while since she could afford it, love, no judgement...'

I think of Iggy, our little house after The Priory. Our babies. He's my anchor around here, why have I picked up Joanna the Pipe Neck?

Bobby blows Spanish cigarette smoke in my face. He's gonna make me puke.

---

51. Mia Zapata was lead singer of Seattle grunge band, The Gits. She was murdered walking home late at night on July 7th, 1993 by a fisherman with a history of brutality towards women. Joan Jett and Kathleen Hanna wrote a song in her memory called Go Home. She was 27.

'You sure you haven't got any?' I beg.

'Man!'

He pulls a parcel of white coke from his hidden drugs pocket in his ersatz-Clash shirt. Result. Slips it into my hand under the table and on cue I visit the ladies and chop out a smallish line on the back cistern. I rip down part of the poster on the back of the toilet door, roll it into a tube, and snort baby home. Joanna the Pipe Neck is sipping a pint of bitter by the wall. I return to Bobby, pass him back his packet and again he lobs a gust of smoke from Spain into my face, which I inhale and it fills me with a shudder. I get a visceral flashback of men raping me. The room shudders. I am having a whitey.

'Man, Bobby... I'm sorry...' A huge volcanic eruption of hot, mucousy, bubbly sick hurls up from my stomach, it holds up in the air like an oil-well splurting, before cascading in a moment of unrivalled tragi-comic hell. By the time I've assessed and denied the fountain being the result of my body chucking out the reality I am inputting, Bobby Bandit is covered head to toe in my acidic insides. The watery content has a reddish/pink hue but is largely bile yellow.

'Top VOM!' squeals a nineteen year old wannabe on the table behind us, pinching her nose. Peachy chudders. The other west London tourist kids back away in case my stomach decides to expel again - it would smudge their pale gothness, glitter-revivalists, mess up their talcum-flavoured ting.

Man, I can't even talk, my throat burns. Ultimate shame package. Bobby's reaction is bad. He's so not cool with this. There is no funny side. I am your worst friend.

'Yeah, Scarlet, seriously, N.A. or A.A., I think they'd be able to find you a chair.' He seethes off through the double door exit like another blazing John Wayne disappearing off the side of Planet Shoredicks forever. I run after him. But he tells me to fuck off, and sort my life out.

Pipe Neck is at my side.

'Is he a friend?' she asks.

'No, he was never a friend, just someone I know.'

Like most people around here.

Heading straight back to the Soretits Amphitheatre, shades on, jeans slipping down my emaciated frame, my black eyes crust over with drugs and excess, we hail a cab the final block. There's something I like about having Pipe Neck in tow. She's my death doula perhaps, here to help me transition into the inevitable closure. L'étoile est sinking, eet's kaput, flying out of the sky, crashing to burn out, tune out, die. Goodbye, good life. Fare thee well, I am leaving you with the devils of my conscience, to torture and taunt, brand my reputation with worthlessness. This comedown will never end. Sliding keys in the door, dejection licks my temples, the suffocation of humiliation. I ask Pipe Neck to wait in the courtyard while I go in. I left her there.

And she waited, all night.

Dearest Diary God Of Miracles,
Thank you for sending Joanna the Pipe Neck. No. 1. My Chanel No. 5. My solid. My girl. My disciple. She has me on the right path. Thank you. I worship you. G'luck, n G'nite, sailor of dreams.

# CHAPTER THIRTY-FOUR
# MEMORABILIA ANONYMOUS

*Will they tear out the pages of the book to light a fire* - Johnny Cash

Bobby's wrong, I don't need to join Narcotics Anonymous or Alcoholics Anonymous; I need to join Memorabilia Anonymous. I went to see Iggy who was sleeping after writing and rehearsing all night and instead find Pipe Neck resting foetal in the corner of downstairs, amid half my possessions that I haven't carried upstairs. Pipe Neck seems comfortable in this cold, ratty-smelling air as I scuttle in a secret back up to my lamb womb room. I want to be zen. I want to travel light. I want to believe that everything I own is in my soul. But the clothes I wore in Ibiza. Magazine pages from various events in my life and other peoples' - none of which I attended. Ripped jackets, shirts with special stash pockets, holy-grail jeans smelling with the cock-sweat of yesterday's success. I am being suffocated. Hawkwind ticket stubs with Malachi Wright's name on them, boxes of photos, flyers. Flash Barry posters. Sydney Viscose's old snot rags. Has-beens' former tools of glory. Proof of claims-to-fame that no-one would understand: bits of ribbon from Boy George's cultured head days, Bob Marley's[52] last roach, Psychic TV's lost aerial. I consider calling Christie's or Sotheby's, but there'll be paperwork, they will want verification documents. It's all so old, every artefact of my past sits as an emotional cairn to Mum, or Dad, or whoever I used to be, in the main warehouse space. And I don't want a past. Taking armful by armful of junk, I deposit it in the high-walled courtyard and flick the tinder of my Zippo (that used to belong

---

52. *Bob Marley, whom every musician in Jamaica has a story about, was the singer of The Wailers. Signed to Island Records, his style was radical and groundbreaking and mainstream enough to break through. A pin-up for Rastafari culture, he died on May 11th, 1981, age 36. Four years previously a malignant melanoma was found under the nail of his big right toe. He was advised to have it amputated, but refused, and lost his fight, playing his last concert on September 23th, 1980, in Pittsburgh. Rumours circulated of Marley having a needle slammed in his toe by agents at his Crystal Palace show.*

to Jimi Hendrix[53]), I spark up kindlings of fire children to grow into teen-torches, to full adult phoenixes, they check their reflection of madness in my eyeballs. Game on. My flambé X-ray shows Lucifer's bones. Nature gleefully tunes its voice. I'm taking control. Watch, as I slash and burn my way to a new start. My vacancy is going to die in a rock n roll carnage of boom-shanking bonfire. I burn my bras,

---

53. *Jimi Hendrix died on September 18th, 1970. The death certificate reveals an open verdict due to lack of evidence, it lists possible causes as inhalation of vomit and barbiturate intoxication.*

*Two ambulance-men took Hendrix from Monika Danneman's garden flat at the Samarkand Hotel, Lansdowne Road, Notting Hill, London at around 11.30am on the morning of September 18th and claim to have been met by the swinging door of an abandoned apartment leading to Hendrix's body strewn upon a mattress in a sea of brown liquid. He was not registered as dead until later that afternoon.*

*Jimi had been acting increasingly erratically, drugs were blamed rather than his manager, Mike Jeffery who was said to be stealing money and involved with the mafia, and was pulling stunts which went as far as kidnapping Hendrix in New York, only to be given the glory of rescuing him a few hours later.*

*Hendrix had been desperately asking a wide-range of people to take over business management duties for at least a month previously. Jeffrey's accounts were said to be a mess and he owed Jimi cash for live gigs. Hendrix asked producer, Chas Chandler to help (whom Hendrix may have picked up the phone to at around 10am having left a distressed message at around 1.15am that morning). At 2.45am the night before his death, Danneman (a former ice-skater who declared herself his fiancee, much to the amusement of his many girlfriends) picked the guitar hero up after a 'party' near his hotel, The Cumberland. It is said Monika was not welcome at the party and Hendrix's friends shouted down insults from the window, but Hendrix went back with her and he sat up, talking, listening to music until early morning before taking Vesperax pills to sleep. Later, Monika claimed she woke up and went to buy cigarettes, returning to realise he'd taken 9 of her Vesperax and he was surrounded by his own sick. She called his friend, Eric Burdon of The Animals, who it is believed went to clean up the scene. The hotel staff claim to have heard shouts of Jimi being dead before his body was taken from the building.*

*Kathy Etchingham, who went out with Hendrix for three years prior to the scene getting a bit heavier (and later scored an English Heritage blue plaque for their old place in visitable place in Brook Street, Mayfair) accused Monika of not calling the ambulance in time.*

*James 'Tappy' Wright, a roadie wrote, but later denied, a crew of lynchmen forced pills into Jimi's mouth and topped him up with wine. He said the murder had been ordered by Mike Jeffrey, the manager. Conspiracy theories abound. Monika died of exhaust asphyxiation in 1996, after losing a libel case regarding Kathy Etchingham which she repeated in a book about her life with Hendrix, after an obsession painting Hendrix through her life. The pathologist says there was not enough red wine in Hendrix's blood to have failed a drink/drive test however, John Bannister, the doctor who attempted to revive Hendrix at the hospital said wine was overflowing from the body and it was highly plausible that Hendrix was a victim of an industry-suggested murder plot pointing at Jeffery whose motives vary from reports of collusion with the CIA's monitoring of radicals through Operation Chaos and Project Resistance, to underworld contacts, Russian relationships and life insurance scams. Mike Jeffery died in a plane accident in 1973, when an air traffic control strike over Nantes in France meant the army took control. Bannister was professionally discredited in the 90s in a non-related incident. Jimi Hendrix was 27.*

my heels, everything I used to give Malachi the wrong impression. Cutting my hair with a knife, I fling my femininity in the bonfire. Sizzle, burn, and good riddance. All the Agent Provocateur knickers, gone. Later, masturbators. Goodbye, pigeon pie. Running up to my room, I push knitting-needle pokers up my dirty gashes, splattering any baby scabs across the sheepskin walls, then collect the haemorrhages of phantom child ovaries to pop pop pop in the fire. Each re-stock sharpens the knives of flames with hypnotic butchery. No Malachi in me.

The heat chases out the cold shakes. Abortion smoke flares my lungs, I sing spells of expulsion. A syringe of flames spurts at the memory of the trails of semen he tried to leave inside me, pyre my past. Burn Ruby's beauty. What were we doing? I'd always known music was a game for the boys. A war. A flashing diorama of parties flame in a sun bomb. Amber window-panes pop, shattering from their Clerkenwell podiums, Christ-telnacht terror. Egos to embers. There shall be no remains, because destruction is beautiful, as finite as murder, suicide and rape. The Fire of London, volcanoes, a fresh apocalypse.

Taking my crown of bones, whooping from one lunged-leg to the next, I am burning everything I've ever done for anyone, and I voodoo holler:

'Oh, flame wrapeth me with a French Kiss and stamp evil in my eye, a cataract of blowback smoke, choke me and die. I come so close to worship thee, my missile of destruction free... Fire dance with me, lick the doubt from my mind, burn the memories. Charcoal my past.'

I sense bodies around me. Fire shoots from my mouth. Homeless people will heal in the shelter of the glow. Jesus the Woman will save.

Iggy shakes my body, his mouth illuminated, 'Scarlet! The roof is on fire!'

'Fire?'

'Scarlet!' He continues to shake me. 'What are you doing? Is there something really wrong with you? I just wanna help!'

Iggy doesn't know I've stopped thinking I'm any good for him. Servants, slaves, we live under the stage, like rats. Shoot me, I'm vermin, baby.

Firemen bust through the courtyard doors. The scene changes from cartoon into reality, JD joins Fireman Sam asking if I require any help, concerned by the apparent idiocy of starting fires close to buildings in urban areas. White charcoal rocks glow in grandeur, forming a premonition of deathly-still energy. Pipe Neck's gone. Everything crumbles black, a smoked joint, a blackened trail of blood. I have not finished my fight.

# CHAPTER THIRTY-FIVE
# GLORY IN EXCESS

*Drums will shake the castle wall, the ring-wraiths ride in black, ride on*
- Led Zeppelin[54]

In New York, a couple of months later, once Mum is on heavy chemo, people ask me how everything is, I tell them it is looking good. Gold-in-yer-cunt fabulous, stardust smile, an 'I'm getting what you're not' pout. Those of us who don't take the macina de sausisson de fashioni seriously are the ones who survive longest. There are many people who say they work in fashion, and don't. It is an industry that sells us more stuff than we need, as all industries do, producing ever more brilliant stuff. And it always looks good. Always. 1997 - the year of heaven... It's really, really attractive. Fuck the people who can't get clean water. Give me tailored 360 paranoia, in 3D, on loop. Fashion jungle, fashion vortex, fashion endless beach, fashion sky scrapers, fashion is everywhere. We make green leaves look better with models holding them; cars look better driven by us. My Mum's cancer, more of it, because that dead look is really inspiring. If lit and stretched and flaunted on catwalks and billboards. We all want something earth-shatteringly fresh. Yet flog-able, classic enough for people to be able to buy it... so we wait for the shows to start, to have music pumped at us, to have NEW pushed through our skin, to watch progress. I'm sitting at the Kalvin Stalin show on The Bowery. Joanna Pipe Neck is next to me. My assistant. I've dressed her in black, she still looks like she's spent fifty years on a crack pipe, it's a strong look. This show is in a gallery space. White white white. The chairs are the usual ordered boxes. Full of little gifts, so we're nice about some of the designer's lesser moments of clarity. I'm wearing a venetian blind - as a statement

---

54. *John 'Bonzo' Bonham, drummer of Led Zeppelin, passed out forever more after an alleged breakfast of a ham roll, sixteen pre-rehearsal vodkas and a session with excessive drinking at Bray Studios, near Windsor, Berkshire, England in 1980. He was 32.*

about privacy. I flip it between open and closed. NIPPLE.

'You're looking, uhm, unique, as ever...' says Joe Delaney.

'Thanks.' I say. 'And for letting me be here...'

His fashion brain doesn't compute, his eyes scrunch. 'How's Scarlet's world?'

'Which world?'

'Which Scarlet?'

'No, which world?'

'Fashion, I guess...'

'Looking good.'

'You still signing on?' he asks.

'On your wages, yes.' I'm fronting this trip myself, on my overdraft, I'll invoice him for our expenses later.

Show starts.

Neon stripes blaze across a Neo-Edwardian vibe. I write 'jazz club Rome meets Singapore with soft Day-Glo' in my notepad. I have no idea what it means after.

The next show, Donna Kernan's, a hotel, I'm next to Joe again.

'I don't even know what you're doing here,' he says. 'You're not even on the blacklist, you're on the what the fuck is that tie-dyed lace puffball list...'

'See, I'd wear a tie-dye lace puffball skirt, Joe.'

'As I was saying, no one looks at that list...'

The music begins booming. The show's sublime, vintage Chloé meets leather cowgirl boho. Pipe Neck and I sigh in lurve as a jacket with a Diana-length wedding train in patchworked white and cream furs is worn over a Stroke My Slinky Mink T-shirt, paired with white leather shorts. It's so fist. Clever Donna.

At each show the girls saunter, they soar as peregrine falcons before skulking sultry sulks like lonesome magpies, before swooping as gaggles of Old Street Eagles, paid to stalk as rooks, front it out like boxing gulls. To flaunt jewel-dripping tail feathers. Hard-lined skirts fight for the future in the desert of nostalgia. Roses, tulips and peonies pop through yards of black satin. Violet orchids explode victorious. Daisies and gladioli thrust softly around the faces of grungy, dolly-bird make-up.

Joe is at the next show. Some wise-arse fakir sat us next to each other. Neither of us will move back a row to the seats behind. And he's at the next. He's staying in our hotel. The Graham Mercy. Pipe Neck is on the floor. I ordered extra blankets, for her.

In London, every show deconstructs and sabotages the work of every previous collection. The death veil of heroin chic is thrown over the past pure-as-white-pills rave goals. We question our earlier beliefs that 2001AD would arrive as an ideological paradise of a sci-fi fantasy, and every collection reflects on the madness of AIDS ripping through tender hearts as ice caps melt, beneath the end-of-the-world-is-nigh prophecies of the Jehovah's Witnesses and Nostradamus. So we'll party like it's a movie, vagabond stars of our own invention, we collide at each show for the next three days, where Joe is, always. Every next big thing attempts to wake us with cannonball bass music.

We all jostle in the burn of fin-de-millennium end-of-the-past-can-be-found-in-the-night, nihilistic, futurist enthusiasm, layering our cultural knowledge, like Scarface meets Edie Sedgewick's pill collection. This ain't retro, it's retribution - as the song by Heroshima goes: We'll beat the hippies at something. I try to meet Joe, to discuss all my plans for his magazine. He refuses my calls and seems really into conversations with other people. I guess he's busy. It's chaos in London in his position. Outside, at this next show, Joe Delaney's debut, it's Kyrie on the door. She's wearing a white lace dress with black collars and cuffs. Her hair is in big bunches.

I stand there with Pipe Neck, waiting. She dressed herself today, she's wearing a bowler hat, and braces. A pair of clown shoes and the look would be complete...

'Sorry, love. You're late. It's rammed in there. No can do, I'm afraid.'

But I *have* to be in there.

There are giggles behind me from Joe's crew. Kyrie lets them pass and points them towards the front row.

I beg.

'Sorry, you're not on the list, Scarlet. I can't do anything about it.'

'He must have forgotten.' This would never have happened if Ruby was still alive.

Ashamed, embarrassed, and alone, I want to rip the back of the tent in South Kensington to get in. But my look, of cowboy chaps with nothing beneath won't work, not bending over like that.

I return to the Amphitheatre of Death, pigeons freak me out as I creak through the doors. The scale of this place greets me as stupid. Even if the band were here it would be ridiculous. Who do we think we are? Boeing 747s? Iggy's been on tour forever. I miss him so much. I feel like there is no heart in my body. It's with him, trailing on a string behind whichever stage he treads. Picking up grit, and dust, blood black.

I run up to my sheepskin space and huddle in the corner. I cry. I don't understand. I've made myself homeless of heart, I could have toured with them, somehow, but was too proud, wanted to have my own thing going on. I have a plane to catch in the morning, to Milan. My notes will make sense to no-one. Certainly not me. I was writing in another script, a code, to stop Joe looking over my shoulder and stealing my genius. Which I thought he was paying for.

I hear something downstairs - there's someone down there. I take my dressmaking scissors and creep out of the door and down the stairs. Holding close to the wall, there's whistling.

It is Pipe Neck. Land wanted her to be the caretaker of the building when they went away. Stop any fires starting...

'Scarlet, I know you're there... Iggy wants you to call him...'

# CHAPTER THIRTY-SIX
# WE SHALL TAKE PARIS

*She's in fashion* - Suede

Paris is where I belong. It is my city. C'est punque. I've been pounding the poetry-licked pavements, doing laps of the Notre Dame, trying to walk my brain into heel, pulling all the city rivers into a pentangle around me - Dublin's Liffey, Istanbul's Bosphorus, London's Thames, insane in Paris.

'Nice get-up, Scarlet! Only you could pull that off...' laughs Land, casting his well-toured eyes up and down my Parisian get up as we walk up the Bois de Boulogne to score. Iggy passes a bundle of ten thousand francs to an Amazonian dealer-whore, hanging by a dual carriageway, flicking her ringlet beehive, strutting an exemplary derriere in a swathe of gingham, ten inch, beat-up stripper shoes and black PVC. Brick dust opium.

Junkies don't sleep, they just nod out or crash out. Iggy and I lie naked. I watch his torso twisting in the moonlight stream, the Prussian-blue light from velvet curtains reflects on his skin in this sixteenth arrondissement family-run hotel that we escaped to. Undercover, aloof. We wanted to avoid the obvious hide-outs of Bentaloiz's La Rock Folie, or the posh places where fashion clingers-on and music fans will want to take photos. We gyrate with each other's stresses, unable to fuck through dope and tiredness, invisible lines being drawn down the bed, a barrier of my invention.

Midnight blue walls, painted with gold stars shining from the recessing boundaries.

Metres of serge-dyed muslin blow autumn in through Matisse-style windows which look across the river and down to the band's atomic tent, erected, a hard-on, pushing up through the gardens, tossing around by the Eiffel Tower. The ball-bag of a stage, surrounded by wayfaring caravans that they tour in, where Land has gone back to, his caravan of lurve. The tent only holds a few hundred people, but it means we sell out, which looks good, and every travelling blagger in every town wants a backstage pass. Roll up the wagons. Clowns galore. Roll up, roll up for the common-landers. Get your freak on. Support acts, DJs, TV rights, live exclusive stuff. And children, by having it in a circus it can be underage.

My stomach cramps. I consider stabbing up inside to kill the foetus. Cold, I put on my Jim Morrison's[55] lost-daughter leopard-skin blanket, nicked from a previous hotel, I made a hole through the middle on a metal jardin fence spike on the way to the park earlier: matched with kohl cat's whiskers and black snakeskin sandals, bought down one of the cobbled streets of København, a present from this beautiful poet of a singer. He holds my hand as we move around the bed.

Land crowned me with a Vietnamese triangle hat from the night market in Bali. I stole it from him when we sat, drunk, before scoring. I started writing a love letter to the band inside it, Land then gave me this Crowley headpiece which he'd been wearing since he found it, signalling the moment they knew they'd made it because it was when they discovered a guy in a Cucci T-shirt selling rip-off CDs of He And Sheman, with pictures taken from the Prawn No video. Land and Iggy trashed paradise in celebration, taking a rickshaw through copper-bath-coloured fruit, left past the banana plantation, fourth right avenue of papayas - through the

---

55. *Jim Morrison, poet, shaman, filmmaker, and singer of The Doors - asked an audience in Miami if they'd like to see his cock on March 1st, 1969. A warrant was issued for lewd and lascivious behaviour and three misdemeanour counts: indecent exposure, open profanity and drunkenness. Faced with a pending appeal for imprisonment, he moved to France in March 1971, continued to drink heavily and is reported to have died either in the bath or at a club, having snorted heroin in the toilets on July 3rd,1971. He was 27. Natural causes, such as heart failure are cited, as are booze, cancer of the penis, a stomach ulcer, Zionist plots, the CIA, and women, or that he had been seen boarding a plane, and was working as an intelligence officer, withdrawing money, turning up in gay bars. Only two people saw his body, the French doctor and his girlfriend, Pamela Courson, who some say he was scoring for in the Parisian club on the night of his death, after dabbling, dying there and being carried back to the bath. Pamela died of a heroin overdose in Paris three years later. Bill Siddons, The Doors manager, who once dated Squeaky Fromme (of Manson's Family) saw the closed coffin. Many people claim not to 'feel' him at the graveside in Pere Lachaise in Paris (the author thought the Greek inscription: KATA TON ΔAIMONA EAYTOY read that he was on a yacht).*

long, ivy ropes which vanished them behind king-kong teak doors opening to a kingdom of billowing white cotton with paper-walls and elegant staff in white and gold saris, all welcoming guests to wooden-stilted layers of a perfect hotel with water flowing. The gig was the 'blackmail' gig for journalists and influencers - people who think they're more rock n roll than bands because writers romanticise the roll and don't have to get on stage. All critics were bullied at school. Counterbalancing their revenge is only possible through stunts as elaborate as a circus cock tent, in Eden, proffering piles of lobster. The Heroshima States Tourship fans, who follow the band around, for a price, payable to Wright States International, with camping facilities in a variety of graded-options, bivouac to bell. They ate speed curry so they'd spin around in front of the Spin chick with foundation thick as a china tea cup, and roll with the Rolling Stone guy with the knotted-hanky, flirting around those with keys to front pages. Land gave everyone acid cocktail, they waded through rice paddies to the gig. The journalists relish the fact that I'm not there - because I'm working on a secret fashion project, or maybe our relationship is doomed. They write about the loss of Ruby, the death of Dan Shields, their drummer[56], represented as a white garlanded hologram on stage. RIP Dan. Who's next? They wondered. Things always come in threes. Never one to disappoint...

I'm wearing my long white Anthony Price dress, lips painted red, drinking Sancerre, stumbling around tiddly in my grown-up lady shoes. We get skinnier into the night. It's only five o'clock. We decide to walk through the grey, orange-lit streets, past the twines of nouveau, and the thick stone of plague-filled burial grounds, to a Mexican bar. We watch the trysts of lovers, halfway between

---

56. *Dan Shields, drummer of Heroshima, 1969-1996.*

the streets and the stars, it's so quiet, a magic radiates, the plane trees peel their camouflage and new subcultures emerge in their mottled light. Some up-all-night tourists listen to a busker wino caterwauling. We roam like bats. I feel the energies of the underclass, the commune. When I worked in fashion, I only spoke to people working in fashion - now I talk to anyone, learning that everyone has a story. Liberté.

We nod in and out some more, wake up as day breaks on Avenue George V, croissant crumbs and coffee, streets sluiced, procession of workers climbing into the city like convolvulus, up from the twisted green steel of the subways.

Sitting at the cafe, Iggy tells me what's been on his mind since he lost the touring panther in Australia and did the press gig in Bali.

'Land killed Ruby. He's a feckin' psychopath,' he tells me, through a sour cigarette.

My eyes roll up to the gunmetal rooftops of Paris. Totally plausible, but he's deluded.

'He's a nutter. No empathy. That's why he's so competitive. Has to be the best, the centre of attention, always, doesn't he?' The competition for centre stage. 'He suggested we knock off JD and Malachi.'

'Knock off? We?' I ask.

'Me and him.'

'Are you sure he isn't fucking with you?'

Doe-eyed, stoned, drunk.

'You need to tell me what happened, Scarlet, I've been thinking this all over... we're at the end of the tour. Is it true?'

'What? Ruby was a suicide waiting to happen, Land didn't need to touch the fast-forward button on her.'

'Why did she do it?' he asks.

'Ibiza - and the money she owed, on the shop.'

'I get the money, but Ibiza?'

'Malachi fucked her. Big time.'

'With respect to the dead and everything, but it wasn't the first time she'd been fucked... it seems like there should be more to it...'

The band's world tour colliding with Paris Fashion Week was

going to be perfect. But I couldn't get into any shows, not in Milano, not in Paris. Kyrie sent around faxes on Joe's behalf, disowning me. Fash sanction. Fash fatwa. He's so uptight - what harm did he ever think I could cause him? He offered me the job, in the pub. But as ever, there was no contract. Like much of the fashion world, Joe became ridiculously self-conscious and conservative, in it for the high stakes, no career risks with a wildcard like me. He cut me off. His contacts with the A-list are all that matter to him. It's class warfare. Establishment sans moi.

We sit there for ten minutes. I order more Pernod.

'Listen, I'm gonna go back to the room. You've got to go and do some press, back at the tent, yeah? I'll see you later, alright?'

'Sure. Scaz, you alright? I just wanted to tell you what I've been thinking - no secrets, right? You wouldn't keep anything from me, would ya?'

We kiss, I swoop up in my poncho and straighten out my triangle hat. 'I have to go to the bathroom.'

Land being a fame-crazed killer? I guess Iggy knows it was Malachi's crew who got them beaten up in Ibiza, and JD must have spilt about me, from when he overheard at the pub... the walls are closing in. The rope's tightening around my neck.

I go drink in a stripper's joint, the illicit minxes get foxier, strolling their passions from the moment they were born, eet's the way they were made, French, temptress manes cascading from their prams, first steps towards les petites aventures, tout le droit a la petit death.

J'adore Heroshima. Jaaaadddoooor. They shall take Paris, and every other city they play. Iggy's confidence demands it. There's no option but to surrender and give in to his power. The place goes wild for him, but first: Land Moon, he always walks on first with holy flowers, marigolds with red carnations, and performs some kinda impro christening ceremony, combined with yoga, faking a temple to Dan The Drummer - building a sorrowful tale right into the centre of the audience's hearts. Woolf Talese follows in shades, he embodies death. Iggy then appears as the lights raise, layering chords in chiffon millefleurs of angry, emotional wails - Land's basic bass slap. Mercantile warriors of what becomes a complex mathematical system which resonates deep in us all, right down to our micro-pixels of water, neons back through our eons. We are one. The audience becomes one. Atoms unite, spirit forcefield - let's go. MODEL CITIZEN starts, the drums kick, glitter explodes and a white-kiltered silver spectrum shines out over the crowd as sound bounces from circus roof, before Land circles his arm for each strike of the strings, with strobe keeping up. Legs wide, he stands still. His presence ripples through the crowd like a blood red sea. For every thousand wannabes, a few stars reach the higher sun, some get lost in the haze of self-congratulatory glory, others depart to a romance with dismal banality. But Heroshima give you hope that we're going to live beyond the after-burn... we shan't be wiped out. They are the only realistic alternative to the Spice Girls. This is more than cyclically re-marketed conclusions that society is being taken over by an increasing army of slush head, part-time humans who have no power to unite against the machines they program, where corporations have board members negating responsibility. Lucidity. We're ahead of the curve. After thirty-four bars repeating and building, a spotlight strikes on MY HUSBAND, MY HERO, guiding us all through darkness: he doesn't even acknowledge the audience for the first few tracks, they just start kicking through the same records they've been fine-tuning along their A-Z tour of the planet. Their cosmic energy feeds on whatever is around it, the audience become sound magick, believing they should leave school, leave work, leave the system that screws them into forgetting they're breathing. Heroshima offer saviour from a world getting fried by ozone depletion. Iggy Papershoes, please captain us to float away in a space elysium on some re-constituted plastic bottles that once contained a vitamin elixir to cure a world populated by piss artist politicians who wax lyrical from totemic, ego-licking pantheons. He looks at me as he performs. It's a song he wrote after we first got it on, *Fête of Love*. It's the most romantic thing in the world ever.

Only a smallish crowd, but sold out, and they encore with Diana's Dead:

> *Riding down the underpass, riding down the underpass, I can go so fast, I can go so fast, Pap pap! Pap pap!*

The backstage analysis is minimal.

Iggy's caravan is strewn like a carcass between production and catering. Land's truck roosts, straight out of backstage - the immediate hang-out, we edge our way through thirty people - plumes of ker-powing feathers bounce and scatter like dandelion seeds above heads, parting, slightly reverentially for the singer. Woolf Talese stands in a corner, entertaining in his deep voice and still with his shades on. Land shows off his latest Champs-Elysées wares, as my man works out what to do about him. The murder plot they seem to think one another have for each other. I look at the pair of them, Ambition's twin is Desperation.

They talk about where the tour ends.

Land thinks Zanzibar is in South America.

'Wait up, Gecko,' Land shouts at the rigger who's just about to dismantle the circus tent. 'Where the fuck is Zanzibar? Do you know?'

'Fucked if I do, mate. I don't even know what day it is. We could be in goddamn Zanzibar now, for all I know. I just put the fackin' tent up and down.'

I want to stay with them.

'Nice one, Geck!' shouts out Iggy.

I sympathise for the relentlessness of it all like a true depressive, not seeing the fun of the road: I find trouble with the non-stop-ness of touring, the Betty Blue vistas across the

States that they're heading to, the backdrops for Natural Born Killers. The adrenalin of insomnia, handcuffed to a treadmill on a vertical assault to neuro-collapse. The shingles, the herpes, the rock n roll. The groundhog of selling the band. It's no wonder I sometimes speak to Iggy and sense despondency, he's slagging off the music, the catering, the audience (yet totally amazed by their presence and reliant upon their support). I hate it mostly because I want to join them on tour but am too proud to ask. I wanted to be more than a groupie. I wanted to have my own thing going on, but I have nothing.

'Has Malachi been out?' I ask.

'Nah - keeps on saying he will, but not turned up yet...' says Iggy. 'I'm ready for him, when he does...'

Photographer Paul snaps the boys looking better than ever before. Dragging them out of the kerfuffle of fandom and worship, he pulls them to the side of Land's silver bullet caravan, Iggy has one leg folded back on the truck, he's focused on Paul's lens and the image he's projecting is nothing other than pure anti-hero cool; he cares for nothing but the music.

After the shoot, we drink through the night. I have a craving for grilled cheese and ignore it. We get a campfire going in the gardens of the Eiffel Tower. Land behaves as if he's performing to a bunch of latchkey journalists who aren't there, there's only one hack, from Austria, who appears to be up for adoption. He's been with them for a week.

'Zanzibar is the end, it is closure!' wails Land.

The four of us escape the masses, and scuffle back into Iggy's for a sneaky line (me, the hack, Iggy and Land). Iggy's on-the-road studio has top-end playback and the four hundred and thirty eight-channel mixer is soon to get shipped to the States. He has it under lock and key - covered in a stainless steel flight case when he's not in here. He's talking about collaborating with one of the New York hip-hop guys to do the beats on the next album. Fred Zeich's producing the live album, from this tour - Iggy wants to be him.

My Dad was well-impressed we'd got Zeich. The uber-producer's stories rival my father's, sounds of permanent synæsthesia, or too much acid, buzzing around his head like dragonflies whilst he composes the levels to mix the most golden-honeyed blend. He swells undercurrents up like rich, ripe-budded pollen crops, drawing ley lines of cohesion towards the fragile nature of the earth. Layers are grooved together with a sophisticated palette of subtle echoes. His touch lighter than a mother burying her baby. It's psychedelic, and modern. He's returned to his studio on the beach in Western Australia somewhere to mix it, walkabout, dance with his shadow beats alone in the dark, then he'll send them through, they'll get couriered somewhere, hopefully next month. He's taking more points than anyone else. Making the dreams sound real.

There's a rap at the door.

'Oh, enter the virgins!' I remark.

It's the old release forms that need to be signed.

'ENTER!' shouts Land with a dirty, dirty laugh. Clouds part as a blonde kid with a stripy cheesecloth shirt, limply hanging off his skinny frame, parades his wares to blinding rays.

The kid is nervous, his skin unmarked by time, emerald eyes yet to see any of the world's vain deceptions.

Land sings a vodka-charmed serenade to scoop up this vulnerable seraphim.

'Come over here,' encourages Land. 'Did you enjoy the show?'

'It was awesome, dude.'

'Oh, look you even speak like me, how cute.'

'I'm with the Tourship. Only until America. My Mum wouldn't let me do the whole thing.'

'What else is going on tonight?' I ask.

'The Tourship kids have been invited to a party in a squatted hospital.'

Would we like to go?

'In a squat? No,' I say. Sounds a bit retro.

Land looks relieved, winking over to us. 'So you understand, this is a film release form, so that we can, um, use you in any way we want? Like, do you wanna get involved in any extras, you know, behind-the-scenes shots for this video?'

'Cool.'

Land escorts him back into his caravan telling him it's all about practice making perfect. I hear them shooing away the hangers-on - kicking them out towards the dawn. We could put Land on a boat, send him out to sea. Yawning, I slope towards my own demise, reaching into the side of my boot for another hit.

Iggy and I think about drinking and doping until the sun comes up, around a fire, or he suggests I watch him mix the tracks he's working on. No thanks.

'We could go back to the hotel?'

Instead Iggy starts playing tracks for me... no choice. And they are godly. I wish I could do music.

I find Pipe Neck curled up inside one of the new flight cases with a blanket around her when I go out to see the morning.

# CHAPTER THIRTY-SEVEN
# FREE COCK-AINE

*Fell from grace, I lost my faith... wasting in the twilight zone* - Primal Scream

On the Left Bank, the red lights spy down from the Eiffel Tower where the Heroshima pirate flag still flaps. Iggy's packing down - he reckons the heavy gaze of air-controls all go back to central command, to DJ JD Frank. They monitor us. We have to play tight, he says, no slipping off-course. You gotta know the drill, you gotta read the signs. Someone always knows where you are.

I trip past Café de Flore and up Rue du Dragon, into another sleazy strip joint. Plumages waft in front of disco-mirrors, soft talcum-powdered skin, coyness mixing with confidence. Unsettled, worried about going back to London, I leave quickly and curb into the gardens of a block of residential flats, exhausted for a moment. I'm surrounded by grey walls, shutters and roses. A cappuccino-skinned, modelly-looking styler in a beanie and a hoody has followed me - he approaches over the geranium-covered courtyard on the wrong side of Rivoli.

'I saw you earlier,' I shout over to him.

'Where d'you see me?' He's from a place where the strong have survived, where teeth are big and bones are chiselled hard.

'Down by the river, on Pont Neuf.'

'What you doing, watching me down there?'

'I was sitting with my husband, watching the river under the moonlight.'

'My plane just landed, I'm over from New York.'

We come closer. 'What are you doing over here?'

'It's kinda crazy,' he puts a canvas holdall down on the ground by his side, gives a gauging gaze. 'Me and my friend had a competition to see who could get to Europe faster. We were high and decided it would be cool school to wake up in some place new. We wagered we'd get here before the other one.'

'Did you win?'

'No.'
'Where's your friend?'
'New York.'
'You winner!'

He flicks his woven yellow scarf over his shoulder: 'Game over before it began, I thought I'd hang and see what France has to offer. And I guess I'm doing pretty well so far, because I'm here with you, right?'

He points over at the stairwell to the flats. The door is slightly open, and we wander in. This is a bit weird.

'You model, right?' I ask him,

'Heh, how can you tell!? Is that why you're in Paris?'

'Model for ill repute.' I stand, suddenly aware that I look like a crap superhero, in my hotel-made poncho - my aura piss yellow and fading fast.

'It's certainly got that British flair. And your hair, it's rad. We don't get none of that European punk chic going down Manhattan way.'

'Yeah - I burnt off the dead ends. Wanted a new wave-vibe.'

'Rad, girl!'

He wears navy jersey bottoms, with safari pockets all over them and a tight, white granddad top.

We sit down on the marble steps of the quiet building, the sun is far from high as it reaches noon, reclusive after a hot summer, tired. Autumn licks our open-toed sandals towards the need for boots and scarves. I empty my possessions in front of me:

- a few weird French jazz records I bought from an old man by a bridge earlier;

- a big mirrored E that must have fallen from a shopfront, it was resting against a wall near the Trocadero, I kept it because I thought Land would find it funny, not that I now care what he thinks, if he's really trying to kill Malachi and JD, and me and Iggy too, probably;

- some Chanel No. 5;

- moisturiser (nearly finished);

- eight bracelets, sure I had more of them;

- Bach's Rescue Remedy;

- my AAA passes;
- fashion invites;
- notebooks;
- pens;
- a toothbrush (because most good days start with a clean mouth);
- and a few medicine bottles.

'Why the painted whiskers, kitty kat?'

I forgot I'd kohled myself. If I ever make eyeliner, that's what it would be called. Kohl your darling. This makes me laugh as I think it.

'It's like you got no home to go to, girl.'

'I got two homes in Paris; one caravan, and a room up over the bridge,' I point over in the direction of my hotel.

'Oooh la la, girl!'

I huddle up, cold in the shade.

'So what shall I call you, Circus Clowngirl?' he asks.

I start to get up.

'Maybe I'll call you Cowgirl.'

'I prefer that. So who do you model for?'

'I didn't do the European shows this season, but I was out with some of the Kalvin Stalin people last night, at the Graham Mercy.'

'Oh, I'll probably know who you were with.'

'Can still taste the cocaine in my body. You know it remains in a man's semen for twelve hours.' If I suck his cock, there's going to be a whole heap of powder waiting for me. Fuck it. I'm tired. 'You're not gonna go all coy on me, little rock n roll cowgirl, are you?'

'Uh, no.'

This is an event I play back, and back. I thought my naivety had long been fucked out of me. I was conscious as I stooped but my quest for experience demanded fuel. He coerced my hand around the base of his cock and like a granite column, his piece rose in service. He put my fingers to it, softening them with sweat, then wraps my mouth around, pushing my head hard, too hard. I was after free American drugs. The good stuff. Straight from the senate.

Up and down he pushes my head over his bulbous end. I hate

that. I don't know what I'm doing. I want to be with Iggy.

'What's your name?' I bumble with his cock in my cheek. I'd never ask complete strangers for dope.

'Ssshhhh. No names.'

I play this fantasy out with him, sleazy and confused. When you touch bad shit, you smell of it, no one wants to stand next to you, because it might rub off. They want to bleach it all away. Pretend it never happened. Wipe it out. Make you go away. I feel like I'm done as Denny.[57]

He fires out a round of spunk, it is not anything like a fountain of coke, it smells of prawn cocktail and has a yellow tinge. He gets up.

'That's what you wanted? Free cock-aine...'

He reaches into his pocket and throws down two ten-franc notes.

'What is this?' I ask.

'Cash, honey.'

'What for?'

'For you Ms Cowgirl, you played good at my circus.'

'Take your money!'

Who sent him?

---

57. *Sandy Denny briefly worked with The Strawbs and joined Fairport Convention from 1968-1969. She formed Fotheringay in 1970. Before her death in 1979, age 31, she had recorded four solo albums. She appeared as the only guest vocalist on Led Zeppelin IV. She was pretty wild, leaving her baby in the pub, crashing a car, and, most damaging, falling down a staircase, hitting her head on concrete which lead to a prescription of Distalgesic, known to have fatal side-effects if mixed with booze. Saying he feared his daughter's safety, her husband Trevor Lucas took the kid to Australia, and within a month his estranged-wife had fallen into a coma at her friend's home. Sandy Denny's death was ruled to be the result of a traumatic brain haemorrhage and blunt force trauma to the head.*

# CHAPTER THIRTY-EIGHT
# I'LL GET MY STRAIGHT-JACKET

*Close my eyes, feel me now* - My Bloody Valentine

Kyrie eagerly offered to promote the final show, and to keep Heroshima cool with the cool folk she promises a 'secret gig' with a guestlist of several thousand close friends. We're doing it at the Amphitheatre of Death. The place is locked and loaded with an 'if your name's not down, you're not coming in' exclusivity. Yet still, I anticipate Malachi. Kyrie has an ever-increasing posse of Pinky and Perkies to help out with event tasks - sweet, fit, young and willing to roll over for any wandering vagabond member of the laminate society.

'SCARRED-UP-SCAZZA! Whatzup, beeeatch? You've still hooked Iggy, you slut!' shouts Peachy.

I can't believe how fast she's grown up. She used to be all Cacharel flowers; now she's a blade-shouldered vixen, tapping her clipboard with the efficiency of a Pol Pot enabler.

'Not seen you for tiiiiiime!' she howls. My white latex vest clings in petrification. I sat next to a doctor on the way back from Macclesfield. I asked him to observe my sinuses and ears. Pain spread from tear ducts to throat, the middle of my cheeks splitting. I thought I'd caught Mum's cancer. The guy told me everything was going to be okay. And I believed him. I don't know why. But Mum's not going to make it this time.

Mary Marmalady is setting up the bar, stapling shelves of booze with fake flowers and tinsel. I know she won't cheat us on the bar, and has the right degree of condescension in her fiery eyebrows arching beneath a striped pink and orange quiff, pointing like it's accusing me of something. I quiver, as she asks me what I'm up to. She laughs as I tell her of the last conversation I had with Joe, about him wanting to be on the cover of his magazines. He likes no-one anymore.

'He's going to be really successful,' she predicts.

I dress in one of my own creations: a mask made from the feathers dropped by mating rooks and pigeons in the Amphitheatre of Death, and the half-breeds they create, freak birds, lonesome beasts, peck-peck-pecking outcasts, eyes blue from beyond the sea, their gaze can never cease with the fear of attack for being different, the bastards' fathers fly over them and laugh, squawking at their jokes. My mask is a tribute to the lonesome birds, trying to unify them with their mothers and fathers. I wear it with my furkini, old sneakers and goatskin cape. I made it when I came back from Paris. I made a lot of stuff when I came back from Paris. My Dad came down to recce the place, as he's doing the lighting for this show, and dragged me back to stay with them. It was nice. We get stoned and pissed. I know I won't see Mum again.

'Remember me better,' she instructed.

I couldn't see through the tears as I left the bed in intensive care, pulling my white coat off, ripping off the mask.

Iggy greets me from Zanzibar with a hug. He smells of safety. Remnants of tamarind air, sweet bananas and chilli oil.

'Fuck, I've missed you. Your taste, your flesh.'

We've been talking every day, on rotten lines. I should have gone to Zanzibar, but I just thought I should see Mum. After this gig, we're going to get out of town for a while, me and Ig, together. Wherever I wanna go, he said. When I left him in Paris I told him about Malachi - the first time - Reading. Made him promise not to react. We may snap quickly but the breaking down can take years. He was angry. I liked it.

The web of records I strung to a carnival of ropes and wires above us is ambitious and huge - my art installation, representing the patriarchal net of rock n roll, it's supposed to be a contemporary, punk-rock dreamcatcher. Everything gets intertwined in the net which hangs across the roof. I've hung vinyl from it. Took about three days without sleep. I followed the light of the sun. It's a sundial. Each string follows the exact geometry of how the light came through the windows. I want to keep the energy of the day in the building. It's my Stonehenge. Waiting for the boys to come back. I had nothing better to achieve. Life is a gallery, life was a catwalk.

'Y'know what I'd like to get Sue Ditch to open with tonight, my dear skitzy-witzy, voodoo starchild? *Tony's Theme* by The Pixies. Any idea where my records are hanging around?'

Ig knows that I know that they're the ones above us. I remember putting the silver thread through his *Surfer Rosa* album, suspending it to my sky sculpture. It's in my spider-web, a mesh of found objects netted high above. Cultural context to our building. A false sky. Like dead rock stars.

'Those are not my records up there, are they?' he checks.

'Nah, 'course not, found those in a charity shop.'

I reach for his hand, kiss his pretty face. We stare at the crucifix I've made with the supersize, pink neon perfume ad that we did for Yamucci in Japan. He knows I'm losing it. I am dying to share a bed, watch his beauty rest, to hear the birds twang through the night. To make him tea, with love, in the morning.

'Why?' I asked, when we talked about going to rehab.

'Because you're a drug addict. Take a look at yourself. You're doing your best to incinerate the parts of you that everyone loves. If you want me to stick around, we can do it together. Won't harm me. I want to see you, be with you, but not when you're so messed up about 'those guys in Ibiza'. You can't see straight. I'll do it too.'

'Alright, I'll get my straight-jacket.'

'Maybe just a health farm rather than the funny farm.'

*Eee ei ei e o, and in that band he had Land, ei i ei i o.*

'1998, the year to get straight, eh?'

'Maybe,' he replies.

Their next tour was confirmed today (the money too good to turn down), he kissed me, on my head, like a child. He wants me to go away with them for the whole tour. Maybe I'll film it, a porno without the porn, or write something else. Not a magazine. A book maybe.

And then I tell him: MALACHI, READING FESTIVAL, EVERYTHING.

'I know. I've known for the whole tour. I told him not to come, or I'd kill him,' says Iggy. It's why the money on the tour doubled. He proceeds to tell me everything I could dream of hearing, how it couldn't have been my fault, that Malachi is the biggest cunt on the planet, that he wished I could have told him earlier, that he would never have toured with Malachi if he'd have known. Exactly, I explain, and wander off, embarrassed, excusing myself to the bathroom, which Kyrie - superior woman, has decked with posh soap and towels, flowers, gold rococo mirrors, white roses & gypsum crystal. It smells intoxicatingly citrus, I like it, the layer of candy-floss flower I never achieve in any form of housekeeping (like I ever brushed a floor).

A girl in the bathroom checks her lips in a compact mirror. Her eyelashes bash like a farm of clotted-cream caterpillars, eyebrows sludgy glitter slugs. She's all pixie stardust from the fairytale she's never left. She sticks her tongue out. A bright pink pill rests on her tongue. She swallows, continuing to stare me out.

'Want one?'

If there's one good thing about being notorious, it's the free drugs. I am Kowalski in *Vanishing Point*. She jiggles in her plimsolls and pulls out a pill from her teen bra beneath her bomber jacket. She then realises they're in her knickers which read Kill Rock Stars.

'You're very sweet, thank you so much.' I neck it and smile, strange drugs, weird girls waiting for their story to begin, going to the bar to find the names they've dropped.

Land is hathawathering a warm-up, he's wearing a full feathered headdress and a new leopard-skin skirt from Zanzibar. Fine gold-tipped dreads, woven with silk-wool, hanging all the way down his back. The sides of his forehead are shaved back. He's gone Aztec alien, pure Elizabethan, his skin is slicked with a rich shine, fresher than oil haemorrhaging from the earth. The clap of pharaoh palms echo behind them, the sense of jet-plane rubber tracks in monsoon, flying over mango-lined roads and a patchwork of blacken-windowed tour-buses[58], every kind of architecture: from tinpot roofs and painted shacks selling oil in cola bottles to grand palaces of colonial resplendence. Bone-bleached sand is reflected in the tropical sealife eyes of Land. He's been drinking lion's blood with Massai warriors. 'Where the fuck are we gonna find that in East London?' asked Iggy, usual black velvet jeans and a T-shirt for some old punk fanzine. A tokenistic Massai bracelet.

'Life is a safari, man,' Land soothsays before giving me presents from the foreign lands: 'Jewellery, Scarlet. I bring you jewellery.' Torn ribbons of material, twisted ostrich feathers, pearls, bones, micro-hessian sacks of juju dust. From a plastic bag with African designs all over it, he crowns me with stitched beaded necklaces of AK47s, bullets and babies.

I run up to my room and change into a sheer black dress, simple, a symbol of my transparency, it's vintage Tuesdays, tech-noir. It complements my new jewellery. I've stopped covering my nipples in gaffer. I'm back in heels. Bouncing from one long lost drug-fiend to another as the place starts to fill up, I splat into an ex-shag, Hot Rod The Sex God Stanton who's dressed like a butcher in a pork-pie hat and apron. I tell him I like his jeans, he tells me they look better around his ankles. He came out after our third night out together. I introduced him to Diego The Yoga Teacher, who ended up rinsing him for loads of cash, locked him in a cupboard for three days. None of us were meant

---

58. *Randy Rhoads, lead guitarist for Ozzy Osbourne, was trying to land, or at least buzz Ozzy's tourbus with the Beech Bonanza F35 airplane he was aboard. All three passengers died after the wing clipped the bus and flew into a house.*

to be together.

Roving from pillock to post, air-kissing a-go-go; a queue goes around the curvature of the earth.

I look at the roosters standing in our backstage area, re-introducing themselves to each other: How could you forget who I am going to be?

The deepest of underground folk heroes, violently stylish, eyes like stars. It's the kind of have to do event that everyone makes an appearance at. Another one. Smokey Joe has completed a new group of paintings he wants me to see in Germany. Latex Lilly has jacked in her City career to do garden design. Joan Dark is making terrorist T-shirts. Fish Shop Frankie's business has been taken over by Big Buns Bill, after Fish Shop Frankie got busted when we were in Paris. The law's taken possession of his homes, cars, business down in Billingsgate, the whole shebang. Did you know how much he was hauling through? He had a massive farmhouse estate down in Essex, five cars, that office down on Brick Lane, a place in Soho, and they pulled in a whole nine-metre tuna, full of Columbia's finest. Headlines: Fishy Business, Scales of Justice, Cocaine Tuna Millions... right old stink.

Pipe Neck Joanna is cruddled up in a cosmic egg. Dad's not with her. He comes down the beanstalk of a lighting rig he's installed. I give him a beer. Happy to see him working. Functional. Alive.

I pour my own bottle straight down in a single gulp, he looks on respectfully.

'Another?' he asks. I nod, hardly breathing, heart freewheeling, thoughts trying to catch up, no brakes.

'I could drink a fish.'

'I did that once, four goldfish with...'

I interrupt his war-story, saying how happy I am that he's threaded strings of disco-rope around Marmalady's bottles, lighting where our money will be made tonight, the bar - vodka and sweet whiskey, adding, 'Y'know Kyrie's gone to work for Malachi.'

'She's the one who took on the old flat for you?'

'Uh huh.'

'Not a bad career prospect...'

He looks as though he wants the conversation to continue. He wanted me to tell him, to confess Malachi's sins, then we could legitimise a revenge.

'They're like the Stooges, girl...' pustules of spit splatter in enthusiasm. 'A feckin' two-piece. They remind me of Devo meets the Byrds, but kind of...'

Iggy has his extended family down, the Scottish side. I introduce the good, land-working types to Dad, they share the rich era of innocent pleasure, before our heads cut everything up in a punk fit, before the world was owned by a chaebol of oppression, before they sold us our liberty.

Dad is nothing like them.

I remember the days at parties and exhibitions when we thought we were the art, this party reminds me of that.

The venue fills up, our warehouse, our Amphitheatre of Death. I pick on canapés laced in cognac, carried by the Knickerbocker Wolves' groupies, the band that's formed by some of the Tourship kids. They wear bow-ties around their necks, battered Heroshima T-shirts. They're supporting later.

I'm stopped by a group of record company people, more oiled than a bodybuilding convention, loaded with gear to sweeten the taste of the critics, and the crashing egos of musicians. They're concerned Land's a little juju-jumpy about this gig. He's looking a bit performance art with Emerald, his new boyfriend who's wearing a conceptual sculpted dress in black. A vibrating crowd of too cool for school yooves and cultured amalgamate around them like bacteria, ready to hatch, and although the London crowd never dances, the arrival of DJ Milo Speedwagon playing a Laurent Garnier-sounding bootleg with Richard Ashcroft covering Subterranean Homesick Blues means the crowd soon entwine as one, heads bobbing and bubbling like a bed of black lava. Speedwagon's piled the speaker stacks all Larry

Levan.[59] Our Paradise Garage fills with the bars and pubs of Clerkenwell, Hoxton, Shoreditch, Islington and Soho. The energy bustles with the privilege of exclusivity, fanning its rarity.

I pull down my disguise, my feathered mask. People I've spent years with walk right past. Fark the people. I walk over to Land, outside of the circus cocoon of a whole band-era, he strides and paces back and forth, clocking up zillions of miles, his long, skinny fur coat catching the breeze behind him: there's a 'Mummy, Scarlet, Mummy, Scarlet, Mummy, Scarlet, are you my Mummy?' vibe.

We don't ever get deep anymore - me, a reminder of his dead sister. Closest we get is him suggesting I manage his new business venture, Heroshima Condoms: 'For when you need to stop bad explosions.'

We neck another couple of Dexedrines and share a massive weed blunt.

Iggy Papershoes comes to my side and we pose for photos, me behind my mask. He whispers, 'Scarlet, doll, you got some extra-special guests coming?'

'Why?'

'There's a helicopter landing in the courtyard...'

---

59. *The Paradise Garage was at 84 King Street, west SoHo, New York. It is the blueprint for the warehouse nightclub experience. The resident DJ was the passionate and emotionally contagious Larry Levan; he could be found polishing mirror balls before playing incomparable and epic sets which would drop everything from Pat Benatar's Love Is A Battlefield to Yoko Ono's Walking On Thin Ice. He piloted drum machines and synthesisers in his all-night sets, often referred to as Saturday Mass. Above the booze-free dance floor, the New York skyline could be seen from a rooftop with fountains, flowers and brightly coloured lights. Operating membership interviews for Saturday nights made the club exciting to dancers and DJs such as: David Morales, Danny Tenaglia, Cevin Fisher, Junior Vasquez, Danny Krivit, Kenny Carpenter, François Kevorkian and Joe Clausell. Offering 'electric punch' with LSD for the first few years of opening, The Paradise Garage embraced a more anonymous culture than Studio 54, it was a post-Stonewall scene which built on club manager Michael Brody's exceptionally black-gay previous venture at 143 Reade Street, in a meat-packing warehouse. Levan was influenced by his one-time lover David Mancuso's Loft parties, as well as the many black drag houses of the seventies. Similarly, his good friend, Frankie Knuckles ran The Warehouse club in Chicago. The Garage closed after Michael Brody was blackmailed over tax-avoidance in October 1987; he died from AIDS two months later. Larry Levan had seen many AIDS-deaths rip through his life and was left doubting his legacy. Levan was still into heroin when he died from a heart condition at age 38 in 1992.*

'Maybe the word is out, it's the assassins,' I joke. Iggy's paranoia has got no better - I get down, crouching behind the door. I'm always laughing at his imagination being worse than mine.

'I'm sure it's for you...' I tell him. Heroshima have been accruing Hollywood support of late, people are battling over song use for their projects, and Iggy is being difficult about licensing to everyone who asks, on my Dad's advice. I always knew Dad was what gave Iggy the go-ahead to fall in love with me, or lust, whichever it was. But it's like a stamp of approval, rock genes. It's how the royal family work. Rockocracy.

'I've got to sort something with the guitar tech.' He's so bored with my shit. I have to serve him.

I'm guessing the helicopter contains someone who thinks they can't get a cab, someone who likes to own the skies, to have a bird's eye view on their territory... an actor... or another disciple, perchance? Of course it's going to be Malachi.

'If it is Malachi, don't worry: I'm here, the ICF are here, we'll fuck him right up...'

I believe him.

I wait in the courtyard, the walls still mucky with the smoke from my memorabilia arsonymous episode. The air is gravy-thick with the lumpy whirl of unexpected surprise. The linen-wrapped leg of Malachi descends upon my scene. I scan the crinkly-arsed fucker. His tragic, glutinous raspberry lips ordering others to ram me, spit gobbulling upon my naked, kidnapped body, watching the frizz of his wiry balloon-shaped head. That stupid dressing gown.

He wears a Heroshima band T-shirt in the largest, greediest, major XXXCESS size. It's Ruby's limited edition by Doctor Hemp. They go for two-hundred quid a piece: pre-slouched necks, a choice of black, red, grey, white or pale blue, pale yellow, pale pink. Cotton and silk mix. The artwork is a hand-drawn graphic of an atomic explosion, the phallus tent, and the boys' faces flickering in the cinder. They're surrounded by circus iconography, animals going two by two like a Chapman sculpture. Pigs snorting drugs. Elephants on ecstasy. Malachi wears the pale pink. The back of the shirt has tour dates beneath. Today's is the last. Finally. And in the countdown to the end, the blades chop violently to a halt. He jumps out from behind the silver lamé curtains of the helicopter. He's got a black baseball hat with some kind of bad graffiti logo over his pubey, clown hair.

Should I stay or should I go?

I leg it.

# CHAPTER THIRTY-NINE
# LYNCH O'CLOCK

*I've been a wild rover for many a year and I've spent all
my money on whisky and beer - The Dubliners*

The Rioteurs play a gangster-metal-house set. They blaze off stage. Malachi is busting through the saloon doors, all cowboy, cigar hanging from his gob, spilling people's drinks, no apologies, coming towards my face like a heat seeking cruise missile.

Bolting through the crowd, tryna lose Mal, I run into Hairdresser Laurent: 'You alright?' he asks. Hairdresser Laurent's got a new product range with Mega-bionix® being sold in supermarkets.

'Yachts darling, I'm accruing yachts.'

I try bending to the ground.

'What are you doing?' asks Laurent.

'Hiding.'

Laurent puts his fingers over his eyes like long eyelashes. 'Woo hoo, I can't see you!'

I cover my head with my hands, hoping I'm invisible.

'This is serious, Laurent. Hide me!'

But Malachi is targeting closer, a dirty sponge in a cold bath. He kicks my foetus shell looking for acknowledgement.

'I only came here to wish you a Happy New Year!' My heart stops beating. I hear his voice bellowing out, '1998!'

Laurent steps in to my rescue, he flips his hand up, trying to make Malachi halt.

'Excuse me, Mr No Manners, I'm not sure the lady wants to speak...'

I scramble against the crimes, drunk and stoned. I hate it.

He ignores Laurent, grabbing my arm, hard: 'I do like a game of kiss-chase, darling!'

I'm mortified - frozen in my tracks as he flips me to his face.

'Mate, I think you should back away, you're clearly upsetting Scarlet,' Laurent attempts to step between Mal and myself, his eyes gasping with disbelief. Malachi staggers.

'Mal, you're hurting me. Let go. You're bruising my wrist.'

'Mal-ach-eeeeeee, you're hearting me, let go!'

He's dragging me through the throng of people, away from anyone we know, Laurent hurdles along behind us, legs lolloping, looking over his shoulder.

I try bolting towards my satanic cell. I kick him hard in the leg, how I wish I had the first time at Reading. Released, if only momentarily. I scram towards my room.

'Go Scarlet!' shouts Laurent.

Chased, I slip on the stairs, scraping the front of my legs as I get caught in my dress. I fly in and put my back to the door to keep it closed. I know Malachi stands at my weak stable, hinges broken after Iggy busted in during my pregnancy tests phase.

Lynch o'clock.

I struggle to keep the door shut as he pushes against it. Not again. The door explodes, I lie on the floor.

'What is this, love? A big furry cave?!'

The band's next tour stands between us as he takes his breath, examining the dried-up chunks of foetus splattered into the sheepskin walls.

'You been shooting up gear, Sca-la-la-bompiday?' he asks, welcoming himself down by sitting on my bed - legs splayed.

Deny. Deny. Deny.

Next thing I know, Laurent has an ice-pack on my head.

I'm amid my black sheepskin floor, looking up at my life passing by. My clothes are still on. Mal is looking through my piles of books - I burnt none of those.

'Where's Iggy?'

'Go find this girl's husband - will you?' Malachi instructs Laurent.

"That okay?' Laurent checks, his hair falling over his shoulders, his clothes hanging perfectly off his perfect body.

I just want Iggy here, as soon as. Mal will do whatever to me. Laurent leaves.

222

'Now the queer's gone, we can cut straight to it, eh?' Flem jumps from the pits of Malachi's lungs, littered with the rusting trash of his existence.

Why is my Mum dying, not him?

'I'm clearly here to show my support, for the gig and all, but it's Suki...'

'Suki?' I ask. *What?* 'Is she okay?'

His brow furrows doubt into his brain, considering his stupidity for marrying her. It's a momentary flicker, quickly shadowed by his super-ego.

'Turns out she was feckin' Augustin, as well as this Spanish kid. You remember Augustin right?'

'Wow! Who'd have known?'

'Don't pretend you didn't. Problem is, his family, they're old school Ibicenco, y'know what I'm saying?'

'More protected than your brother?'

'I'm not sure what you mean, Scarlet?'

My body feels like a Geiger counter, clicking in petrified anger.

Malachi falls into my ear, whispering, 'Augustin has a little film of you, me, Suki, and, God bless her soul, old Ruby, all making love, don't you remember? Scarlet Papershoes, you orgasmed about twenty three times, had shoots of cum pissing out of you, you did, had to check you hadn't wet yourself. Don't know what to tell your daddy...?' I am in Hell. 'Babe, it was amazing, really, we went all night. Then you just disappeared. I was worried, you know the amount of gear we'd been doing, enough to placate a storm of wildebeest. Anything could have happened to you after our little beach party.'

Every atom of my being shakes. I am on a battlefield with lice in my trench, ulcers on my eyelids, bayonet blunt. Fear is my only weapon of defence. He's so ugly, the vilest polarity of rock and roll. Ruby's dead because of him, and Suki's betrayal hardly seems to have dented his grandiose. He doesn't give a shit about anything other than himself.

'You told me you were nineteen. At art school.'

'Oh, c'mon...'

'You feckin' begged me to feck you, all you girls - swooning around, putting on a show for me - for my money, for my power. Don't think I don't know. And then you all pass out, kittens full of milk. Pussies full of cum... Look, this is simple: I want you to put a kibosh on the tape, then it disappears. No adultery, less alimony. More gigs for Iggy-boy.'

He pulls a fresh cigar out of his holster, and uses his old one to light it. A parody of himself. And me a stereotype of everything I've become.

'It was fun, y'know...' he grunts.

'You wish.' Trying to add consent to the occasion.

'Scarlet, you've got a wild imagination. I gave you and your little loser friends more cash than you could spend, I did it for your Da. Everyone knows you were too fecked to remember a thing. I'm hoping you've learnt your lesson.'

'I bled for weeks.'

He looks surprised, 'We got carried away, sorry, but I bet you won't get fucked by an NME award, a Grammy AND a Brit again, eh?'

Iggy enters, 'Howdy-do-da, Malachi Wright? You old shit nugget. I wasn't expecting you. How are ya, really, you old cuntybaws?'

Malachi looks at me, knots tie in his eyes, propelled by the stuttering undulation of not having enough lies left in his chamber, perspiration tracks his nectarine hairs, and survivalism sprays his mouth with the bullshit of false confidence.

'Oh, y'know, things have been better. My wife's threatening to leave me. But what about you? Heard it through the grapevine that you got into a little trouble at Viktor's? Trust that worked out alright?'

'Nothing we couldn't handle...'

I wrap my arms around the calves of my knight-in-shining-armour, pure lame love-limpet. Iggy grabs Malachi by the arm, and gives me a look to keep my cakehole well and truly shut.

We get up, pull Land from his ever increasing circle of close friends. Find my Dad. Blank the kids and the fans, and the nosy wannabes, everyone that wants a piece of Iggy-action - so he does the rockstar glaze that looks through everyone - like he's going towards the horizon faster than everyone else. I wear my mask, sling on my caped hood, and we slip out, velvet smooth.

'You're looking well, Wrighty,' says Land, putting on a fake smile.
'You too. I'm your biggest fan,' Malachi grunts.
'No, you're wrong there, sunshine, I'm my biggest fan.' I'd hate Land if I didn't love him.
'My man, it's been what...? I'd been hoping you'd drop in a lil earlier in this tour.'
'Shall we go and find a drink?' suggests Iggy. 'Get off site?'

Malachi takes a seat in the pub on the corner of St John's Street, booming confidence, his belief that I'll honour the band before duty to myself, spot on. We all want what's best for Iggy's career.

Iggy spikes a drink with liquid acid, and passes it to Malachi. The dirty fucker takes it, drinks it. I wait, drinking to metabolise my shock, hoping Malachi'll fall into a dark and paranoid world.

I stay afloat their one liners, two liners, long liners, loaded. Locked with them rather than taking the risk of being left unaccompanied. I pretend to drink, wanting to stay sober to witness the full horror of Malachi's pathetic being. Every second drags for eternity.

'What I don't get about Suki, Mal, is why would anyone want to leave you?' asks Iggy, sarcasm dripping. 'Did you not get a pre-nup?'
'No, I thought it was forever.'
'Good job I cashed the Coutt's cheque earlier...'
'Glad to be able to support you guys. Thought it was time I came to pay a visit on my extended family.'

Malachi's desperation blobs, the threat of losing his wealth leads to games of manipulation. He 'levels' with Iggy, going over his childhood, being the second youngest of five boys and three girls, never enough meat to go around. Och, what a hard time Malachi had, living in a stone shed with the livestock, his ambition coming from having to leave Ireland because he was being kiddie-fiddled by Father John at the school, Father Billy at church, and his father's friend in a fishing hut next to Wicklow Lake.

'Maybe your little wiener could cure them, dude?' asks Land.

'Happens to not be so little, but it happens to the best looking kids. Surely such a beautiful baby rogue as yourself didn't escape, no?' he asks Land.

Land ignores him.

Malachi pushes: 'When are you going to start your own band?'

Getting no answer, he pulls back his shirt to reveal tethered scars across his back and chest, 'It fecks you up, your mam n da,' he points to his back, before groaning, adding to his drama of a life: 'Flagellation.'

'That's kind of hardcore, dude. I just got into dope,' offers Land.

'Are you boys gonna be able to play tonight?' I ask. They're getting mullered.

'Same old show,' grumbles Iggy.

'Gonna be a thrilling performance,' sniggers Malachi. 'Since you ask, these marks were a present from my first wife, at sixteen.'

The boys get thick on battle scars, digressing through other bravado rich victories from band combats, promoter battles, schoolyard territory wins and girl sweeps, police-force tales and junky deliverance; they could get the night done with if they whacked their cocks out on a table against a tape measure.

'Can we make a toast to Ruby?' I ask. My Jesus fixation prevents me from slagging anyone off, I'm going through an anti-evil phase, treating no-one badly, doing to others as thy would do to oneself - I'm weak, it's a selfish move, I can't take a kicking. I can't challenge anyone, they're all better people than me.

'Now there's a gal who shouldah had her own band...' salutes Malachi.

'No, amen, let's drink to that,' chinks Iggy. 'Here's to finding what we like, and letting it kill us.'

'Heroshima's been trippy as Disney after Ruby died...' says Land, attention seeking, hoping the relevance of mentioning acid may make his spiking of Malachi kick in, for the entertainment quotient, if nothing else...

'This industry's always been a magnet for dumb bitches, idiots, puppets posing like they've got some kind of talent...' starts Malachi, the cripple-dick. I look at him, incredulous - is that what he's saying Ruby was?

'There's never any respect for the audience. People say drink and drugs are the problems in bands, but it's always the farkin' frontmen, and the girls, or management...' slurs Dad. 'Joking! It's the wannabe frontmen,' he coughs, looking at Land, now sliding tequila shots down the full length of the fifteen metre bar and tobogganing, first on the barman's longboard, then in his socks, chasing along the wooden floor to catch the drinks at the other end, hurling them down the bar, he speeds like Pete de Freitas'[60] motorbike.

'Power, that's the poison, it ain't drugs, they're just chemical warfare to control us,' claims Iggy. Not that the drugs he's spiked Malachi with seem to be having any effect.

I pull down the hoody of my white sari. I wear the drapes of silk slashed short, a mini-sari. Iggy calls it: A mi-sari... a misery - for his depressed wife.

'What are we gonna do?' asks Iggy. 'I think we should be in a band together, Scaz.'

Dad winks over at Iggy, 'Couldn't agree more, son.'

He got John Entwhistle from The Who to teach me bass when I was four-years old. Before I was managing the bands in the youth clubs.

I stare at them - maybe it is what I should have been doing all along. 'It's alright, Dad, don't have a seizure, the bar's over there.'

'Jeezus, Scarlet, give him a break,' says Iggy. 'I think you should try a stint at sobriety yourself before criticising others.'

Dad looks at him like he's gonna take him out.

Putting down another empty whiskey glass, it's time to get back and do the show. Every hack in town will be waiting.

---

60. *Pete Louis Vincent de Freitas' motorcycle hit a car on the way to the Echo & the Bunnymen's studio in Liverpool on June 14th, 1989. He was 27. The Bunnymen's drummer from 1979, he started singing in his own band called The Sex Gods in 1985 which involved a black peacock's display of destruction as he stayed up for eighteen days consuming LSD, dope, coke and booze. Pete appears on a motorcycle in Julian Cope's video for China Doll.*

*Duane Allman from The Allman Brothers, was also a session guitarist for stars such as Aretha Franklin and had the nickname of Skydog. He also died because of a motorbike. On October 29th, 1971 after spinning ninety-feet off his Harley Davidson Sportster, he was crushed beneath the bike as it bounced from the sky. He was 24.*

# CHAPTER FORTY
# SURVIVORS IN THE HOOD

*If I don't go crazy, I'll lose my mind* - Death in Vegas feat. Liam Gallagher

Laurent rushes up towards us in a big dramatic fluster, 'Scarlet, he's horrible, yuk. What the hell was that about? What a grotesque pig! Are you okay, darling?'

Arms and eyelids flap, his leather jacket off, a black T-shirt cut down the sides to show his skinny, fit bod.

'Sure, yeah, I'm fine.'

'The music industry is so vile,' he says.

'Yes, fashion crime at least has allusions to beauty.'

Band protocol with anyone we want to keep an eye on is to keep them stage right, as über-VIPs, lull them into feeling special, on the right side, kiss them with the occasional rockstar gaze. Malachi will undoubtedly stay there feeling typically himself for the whole gig.

'It's showtime,' shouts Land over to me, his tin-can cut-out silver dangles from his neck. He exudes old school charm, the kind that will float him first-class forever. These guys belong everywhere, from sub-Saharan marble flanked hotels to downtown souk bazaars to New York City palaces, their beauty always exotic on bored-filthy shores.

'Do me a favour and don't let his presence affect you, yeah?' asks Iggy. 'Don't go fainting, or passing out 'til the show's over, alright?'

They're going to rock it like never before.

'Hello, East London,' announces Iggy swaggering onto the stage, his huge eyes stare into my soul. He's about to go under, into his realm of Iggy Papershoes. Taking his stage personality to the people - winking over at me standing in the front pit. 'It's great to be home.'

The corals and turquoises of another land glimmer between us. Woolf counts in. The groove of *Devil Smile* kicks off. Metal chords, Land screeches into action. Woolf Talese is beginning to show off...

Land's so ready to front this band:
> *I don't know where I left my frown, but last night I got down*
> *and I woke up this morning with the hottest smile in town,*
> *they call me Land, yeaaaah, my name's Land,*
> *and I got the devil dancing in my teeth,*
> *I am running the Cheshire grin that makes me and Satan sing...*

He can be such a knob.

Malachi props himself up on stage right. Great big cuntybaws, tapping his toe and shaking his head in an off-kilter stagger. I receive that rare blast of supernatural healing from Dad as he smiles at me from the lighting rig.

There's something about a gig on home ground, you know mates are in the audience, getting off to the sound that's jet propelled you around the world, sharing the energy.

The jaded has-been, seen it all before we were four years-old crowd, loosen up, uncross their arms and allow their heads to nod. What an achievement, we got this London party started.

Iggy goes over to Malachi and kisses his cheek. My jaw's gone, the pill's reverb-ing, I'd forgotten about it, dope's running through my veins and I shake my head and body in the midst of the mosh pit, supported by those around me. They bridge into *Guerrilla Gun*. Malachi stands, pint glass in his hand, a stoop in his neck. He watches into the crowd of life's beauties, beatniks, blaggers, naives and thieves.

Land is busting post-ironic yogic modelling poses whilst maintaining cool. The hip audience heave for more, records get pulled down from the cotton weave ceiling, hurled towards the stage, heavens open. Heroshima hit them straight with *Rooftop Killer* and *Requiem* before leaving the stage. A wrath approaches, I can feel it. Bobby Bandit, now a photographer, snaps away at the evidence of my demising smile. He informs me he's divorced her indoors and is marrying Poppy Popsocks and asks when my rehab check-in date is.

The day I die.

He disappears to find a fresher face.

The band go back onstage for more. Iggy and Land sniff their noses in synchronicity and soak up the appreciation,

'We'd just like to thank everyone who's been involved on the tour, man,' says Iggy. 'I don't often give thanks to audiences, but y'know, tonight has been the best gig, you've all blown us away, thanks for waiting for us, London.'

He plays it glacier, his few words are master-chef in buttering up love hungry crowds. They relish in his energy like it's a deluxe spa to hang in, his treat. We all like taking drugs in Iggy's sauna, sipping piña coladas in the hydrotherapy pools, dye our hair white with peach highlights, find mazes of alternative stables selling rails and rails of vintage.

'Are we ready to rock this Sleaze House?' asks Land, 'Our Sleaze House is your Sleaze House and your Sleaze House is Mine. Let's fakkin' have it!'

*Fade to Black* plays, slaughteringly pro, energy annihilation, stopping in perfect sync, feedback fills the Amphitheatre and Iggy pulls on the chains that hang down from the sky.

'In memory of Ruby Moon, in honour of a sister, and all women like her,' announces Iggy.

A massive subsonic rumble overwhelms the breakbeat solo as the track crossfades into *Atom Split*; a shattering earthquake of vibrations explodes like a bomb for the final chorus. These pills, man. There's nothing like dirty British drugs. A City and Guilds in Chemistry courtesy of the dole office can go a long way. England so fine at industry. The lights do an atomic flash and crash, I look for the face of my father as a numbing crescendo makes a noise louder than the sound systems. Fire sparks from the crashing of metal onto the side of the stage, everything begins to tumble. There's the squeal of thousands of people... they start running to the doors.

Dad, what have you done?

I can't see him. His shoddy workmanship falling to the death of his reputation. And what remains of mine. Part of the silver-alloy ceiling rig crashes down onto the speakers, the system sounds as though it is being crushed beneath. The metal folds like a concertina and one by one the bulbs pop out to pitch black. There's a stink bomb of burnt fuses and cooked metal. I shout out for the band. I can't see anything as I jump from the crashing stage.

Kyrie grabs my arm in the pit. 'What the fark is going on, beeatch?' she demands. 'My rep is at stake because of this.'

'Do you know if everyone's okay?'

'Uh...'

All we can hear is feedback.

'You know what, Kyrie?' My fist pulls back with the power of a boa constrictor, I've waited so long for this. Frustration unleashes. My tension flies into Kyrie's face and I smash her supercilious ski-jump nose with devastating purpose. Broken. The warmth of her stinking blood splatters across my skin, she holds her thwacked up features from falling to the floor. Sheeeat. She's gonna get me back for that.

# CHAPTER FORTY-ONE
# WHACK HIM

*No future* - The Sex Pistols

Pure panic. The crowd syncopates in a shriek of hysteria. It's a feral stampede. People fight to leave, smoke, carnage, a rumble, a weird heat. My sky-web, alight with fire, it drips, lava threat as people run over each other. A boiling black glob hits my shoulder, it burns through the dress. Yow. CUNTING HELL - I scream, with the realisation that everything could be finished forever. It's a freeze-frame which stays in my eyes forever. Everyone's moving faster than me, across the factory that's bigger than several football pitches. I don't know where to go - to the stage, to check on the band? The place is full of VIP screams, more drama than RADA - all our friends: every reprobate, blagger, guest-list ligger, model, designer, publisher - running like it's there are free handbags being given out by the exit.

A strange wave of acceptance pushes me against the wave of people. I need to find the cause of the disaster, the star-gate to the mystic pyramid. The warehouse empties. There's no-one left. The fire has burnt itself out through the fire system in the ceiling. I shout out for Dad, Iggy and Land.

'Hello? Anyone?'

Pulling myself back onto the stage, face full of smoke, skin covered in grey dust, unable to see where wires or bodies could be, I pray there's no death-count.

'Scarlet feckin' Flagg? I'm feckin' dying here, man. It's over...'

Moans of death. Curiously, stage right is the only damaged area; the scaffold rig has fallen from the sky, flattening karma to a squelch. It's Malachi. He's being crushed to death under the lighting rig. I shout out for Dad. I should finish this fucker off, whack him with something.

I reach over and find his balding head, mushroom sweaty.

'I can't believe it's ending like this, stage right, hurrrrgh

hurrrrgh hurrrrrrrgh.'

Stinking vodka sweat drips like porridge from his flubby neck. Querying whether to act maliciously, to smash his head repeatedly to the ground so his brain splatters and his eyes stop working, I am unsure if I could stop hitting and bashing. The choice is soon made for me, his body ceases to grunt, fast turning into a corpse. His neck holds no life, it's curved right towards the grotty pulse of avarice. My eyes become accustomed to the light provided by the swinging doors. There's no time to register my emotions about his death.

*SO I DIDN'T KILL HIM, I think, as I get as far as this memory... I didn't do it... so why, why, why did I ever blame myself?*

Kyrie called the cops. She accused me of selling out the pictures of Ruby dead in the bath to the press. I don't remember doing that.

I look around the quell of smoke, the feedback and crackle of amps. Crowds will dine upon this night forever. Everyone has scarpered, the band and my father included. Crumbled - finally. Death by rock n roll. And for a moment I feel free, hurling in a hurricane.

# CHAPTER FORTY-TWO
# PUNK ROCK THE POLICE

*It's such a good vibration* - Marky Mark and The Funky Bunch

The Ford Sierra blazes to the cop shop, siren spinning a noir shadow down Theobald's Road to the straight-jacket of impending cells.

I can't see the copper's face properly in the mirrors; he's a uniform, black and white. I fiddle with the hat he left on the back seat.

'It would definitely be right if you put my helmet back,' he instructs.

'Okay, if you put your foot down, be good to make this seem real,' I respond.

'Do the words Hillsborough and Kings Cross mean nothing to you?' says fe-cop, his partner, self-hating rancid pizza-face, chip-fat hair, margarine grease dripping down her chin.

'The fire sprinkler system worked, I don't know what your problem is...'

'Thousands of people could have died.'

'What do you think we've got you here for, Scarlet?' asks the policeman as we pull into their yard.

'Smashing Kyrie's nose? I dunno...'

I flick my head to look back, not knowing this is the last fresh air I'll be breathing for some time: the registration plate is full of prophecy: M399 STZ. They've got me on a ninety-nine year stretch.

Traipsing down the cold polished stone corridors of the police station in Covent Garden, I land in a large room in the basement, the walls are a seventies comprehensive-school mustard-yellow, grey lockers lean against the walls.

Another dead body, another day.

Pop is eating itself.

The air's liberty fades.

My senses dim.

'You out of cells?'

'It's not always how you see it on TV,' says the policeman. His hair is a Roman road to loon town, as if a marker pen has drawn hirsuteness in a seamless circle around his face, and the short beard blends a circle to his fringe. In the middle sits a funny little nose, a mouth that refuses to smile and eyes so frozen cold they don't seem to be able to blink. No moustache - that's why he looks double-weird.

He sits upon a low, metal-framed black vinyl seat, unfeasibly tall and bulky, flubs of pallid, pre-cooked pastry are layered over his organs, his thoughts click simply without his intervention, a linear processing brain. We're in the basement, surrounded by his colleagues' lockers. Flexing his fingers as steeple towers, he surmises his thoughts.

'Death seems to follow you around like a nasty smell.'

'Oh, I get it, are we going back to Ruby again? There's a permanent site on Hoxton Square where you can join the rest of the fans in leaving messages, and flowers and whatever else to help the grieving process, y'know,' I offer. I have an inbuilt friction to people in uniforms. Especially gnomes.

'Perhaps you should have called us to that particular little scene.'

'JD Frank knows all about it.'

'Who?'

'One of your special units. He's in Special Branch, undercover.'

They look at each other blankly.

'We'll have to explore that.'

'He works for you. That collapse is nothing to do with me, love. It's our promoter, our booking agent. The dead guy. It's his fault.'

'You don't seem bothered he's gone,' she says.

'People always hate the boss, don't they?' It was Doris Lessing who said some of us like having victims. 'Call JD, he'll explain.'

I scribble down names for JD, Augustin, Suki, and Malachi's son. They do some kind of telepathic police communication and get up in sync.

'Make yourself at home, we're off to make a few enquiries. Want to speak to some of your compatriots.'

'Not guilty.' I said, as they left. My head falls back.

Why am I all alone, a loser, alone as we are, coming in on our own, leaving alone... Maybe they want me to redo the police uniforms? Give them a bit of cred. They know I am capable of managing the image of the police force, I can make coppers cool. It's my duty as a British citizen, it's something I can do unlike anybody else... JESUS THE WOMAN.

The black and silver jackets hang on the back wall. I have a root around the stock cupboards. Finding first-aid kits, metres of muslin bandage, I'm gonna punk rock the police. Taking safety pins I unpick the sleeves to make the uniforms more war-torn. Pulling out the lining from beneath the hems, I slash and deconstruct, demonstrating how hard it must be to walk around in a uniform with that reputation. I push pins through the fabric across the chest where the medals would go, I rip and feather the bandage into battered micro-tresses, signifying the merits of street battles they fight every day. I wind the white, fraying cloth around one of the trouser legs, like a memorial band. *Sergeant Pepper.* Pulling the iodine dropper from the glass bottle, I begin to paint awards onto the bandage medals, hero, icons of hearts, and skulls, and CND signs and lightning bolts. I write Street Fighting Man.

Classic.

Reaching a police helmet down from atop a locker, I prise off the medal on the front and attach it to my own belt using a thin layer of gauze. Big belt buckles are so now. I then wrap bandage around a police hat and use the iodine to write PROPERTY OF THE HEADSTATE. I wait for the cops to return with the tea they've promised, modelling my improvements.

Top of the Cops. Pretty visionary, I thought. Poetic and resourceful. Customising the uniforms into an approachable update. Making the police force look good. Did it all using nothing more than a first aid box from an unlocked desk-drawer and white board markers.

I curtsy and hail-fellow as they re-enter.

'You like it? Kinda psychedelic Seditionaries, no?'

Neo-Versace meets classic Westwood, they just couldn't see it.

'Damaging police property?' says Acne Feast.

'That's Sergeant Canto's uniform, not the most forgiving chap. When is he back on shift, WPC Bomfield?'

'In about an hour, I believe, Inspector. So Scarlet, we were just speaking with your friend, the Filmmaker, Paul Nicholson. You didn't like Malachi much, eh?'

'Yeah, I killed the boss. He deserved it, pushed down a sky rig on him... crushed his very legend. Life takes its natural course.'

'You did kill him?'

'Yes, the world's overpopulated,' I laugh, the hyena laugh, the one that makes them think I'm maaaaaaad.

'Scarlet Flagg...'

'It's Scarlet McFerguson, actually...'

'You confess to murdering Malachi Wright... we have reason to believe you would act on behalf of the music act, Heroshima, to escape contractual obligations to Wright States. There are also other factors we believe could have led you to be affected into murdering him...'

You could be right. Actually, it all makes sense...

'Scarlet Flagg, I am arresting you under suspicion of murdering Malachi Wright, and additional charges for affray, GBH towards Kyrie Eleison-Adetayo, and damage to police property. You do not have to say anything but it may harm your defence if you do not mention when questioned something you later rely on in court, anything you do say may be given in evidence...'

'I WAS JOKING! Of course I didn't kill Malachi. This is totally illegal. Get in touch with anyone. Those charges have nothing to do with me, mate. I don't know what the...'

*Even by my standards, or lack of them, admitting to murder was groundbreaking.*

# CHAPTER FORTY-THREE
# OF ALL THE THINGS I'VE LOST, I MISS MY MIND THE MOST

*You'll still be in the circus when I'm laughing, laughing in my grave* - Mick Jagger

Dream-slang ebbs in and out of consciousness. I stutter in a glitch of greys. Everything used to be black and white and simple. The nineties: minimising the minimal until there was nothing left. Simplifying the complex. We did it with a Thatcherite win in drug consumption.

I fall in and out of lucidity, tears fall as evidence, of something. I don't know if it's guilt, or pleasure. The auras of sensitivity are so loud here, where we become prisoners of new belief systems, locked in by the electricity of so many irregular frequencies from freaks, and fuck ups fucking in the shower, for contact, any previous preferences, disregarded. Our input here is so limited, psychosis becomes the common option, generally in the fact that no one here has ever done anything wrong, in their own minds. We are all innocent criminals. The hum of fluorescence in these institutionalised corridors substitutes the structuralism our minds have left behind. The muted tones of the 'relaxing' vinyl chairs, which we're allowed in for an hour a day become the most colourful occasions in our lives, staring at utility pipes fantasying of climbing Victorian walls.

I look for greater answers in tea leaves and the way shit floats in the toilet because I have no idea what is really going on. I am old now, close to twenty-four, fat on the hell of six tranqued-out months in captivity, awaiting sentence in a purgatory of drugs passed through the grille in the door, in secret handshakes, in return for you don't want to know: Valiums, Temazepams, drines, dones, Z-drugs, bed drugs, head drugs. A dolly mixture of poetry in pills, magical mystery far away places in sucrose coverings, manageable respites. If only. They are harsh drugs in this Savoy.

These are plastic mattresses: you swill in your own piss and sweat. Sliding in a landfill cocoon of your past: knocked out, foie-grassed with the cheapest sub-NHS drugs, braying guards: Up time. Get up. Time to get up. My eyelids laced together with the want of peace. I just need to rest. My skin's dry. I've got spots, forehead devil horns. Always thirsty but can't be bothered to drink water. Cold feet, and no will to warm them. Depression is so relentless, self-absorbed. There's no reinvention. A life without colour, each minute is hell with my brain. Deceived by my own rants. Too tired to move. What's the point in anything? It's only me who can lift the hazed mask and lead myself from this to the beginning of something new. I am so depressed, I can't even be fucked to commit suicide.

Shaking myself like an old plastic doll to keep my eyelids open, I get it together, for our freedom of gruel-time. I'm in a Nick Drake[61] fug. My reflexes are in slow motion, looking at the floor to walk, holding myself to the cold white wall, body and brain discombobulate, staring at a cigarette between my fingers, like it's someone else's hand that brings it to my mouth to smoke.

Everything is mushy.

A hag of security rattily[62] tells me I need clarity: I am the centre of my troubles. I am the continuing problem in all of my problems. Wanting to help me... like I need that. I think she is concerned for my health. She pushes me into the visitors' room.

White shirt, denim, black leather Nikes. He looks good, for an old person. Stupid Dad. We share the drabness of the air, interfused with static awkwardness. Wallpaper is at half-mast, carpet - a nylon burner. All the furniture is too plastic to soak up any of the difficulties that flourish here.

---

61. *Nick Drake, singer/songwriter, guitarist, pianist, clarinet-man and saxophonist, signed to Island Records and released three albums of dark folk-blues. Best-known singles include Day is Done and Pink Moon. He died on November 25th, 1974 at 26. He took an overdose of Amitriptyline, a prescription anti-depressant.*

62. *Jimmy Donley was an out of control Cajun singer songwriter (who wrote Born To Be A Loser which went on to be a hit for Fats Domino and Jerry Lee Lewis). He was 33 in 1963 when he committed suicide by carbon monoxide in his car, after several suicide attempts, including a rat poison sandwich which didn't work...*

I can smell the vodka in his skin. We hug, he holds onto me, I break away to sit opposite him, with a poxy table between us.

'How you doing?' he asks.

I can't answer. I'm in a slump. Reading my old diaries. Thinking about rock club honour. My life, a series of chapters that don't make sense.

'Thanks for seeing me, love. What are you doing with your time?'

Again. It's a stupid question. I go to meetings about addiction; maybe I was an addict. To what? Saving myself? The lawyers tell me my only get-out clause is the insanity of *addiction*. Addiction takes the blame for everything in court. Never my glamorous, perverted, selfishly indulgent life. Never the people. It's the abuse; never the circumstances. The culture has nothing to do with it. Always the effect, the result. Addiction - the catch-all phrase for men fucking me. Addiction - my only chance. In the meetings I watch Phyllis smoke to her imaginary time scale, black void butthole instead of a mouth: twitching and itching to the count of her watch, tapping the side of her chair with a tobacco finger, burning time marks into the furniture with a chain of cigarettes. Every wooden armrest in the chill out room bears her marks. Inhale, burn the furniture. Exhale, burn the furniture. The screws can't stop her. What happened to Phyllis? It's exhausting just trying to work out her methodology, let alone the cause. Obsessed with measuring time by smoking. She puts cigarettes out on her arm. Rarely other people's.

'Prison is full of weirdos, Dad. It's criminals and victims.'

'All you can do in Her Majesty's custody, Scarlet, is rest. Gawd, I know, it must seem like an even longer stretch for you...'

'Why?'

'Because you're so bloody young, you're nearly a teenager,' he stretches his arms up in the air before scratching his balls. How old does he think I am? 'I'd barely lost my virginity at your age, at a bleeding orgy, it was the sixties. Half of them went on to be in Pan's People, and the other half went off with Hawkwind.'

I wish he'd shut the fuck up. The silence was stronger. I don't know how I can be related to him. Him, going on tour, leaving my Pol Pot-battered mother working in a titty-rock bar in Shepherd's

Market under where Mama Cass[63] carked it, sending me up to Gwanny. A blue-eyed, charcoal-skinned Catholic, who liked a sherry and having EastEnders on loud enough to deafen each Ganesh in every room. There's an anger surging inside of me, but it's dead as Granddad dying to leave her to watch TV in peace.

Gwanny would go to bingo and leave me under the total cross-eyes of Dodgy Dave. Her toy boy. He worked in scrap metal. Had been in a band with Dad. Looked after her dog, Blake, a hairy chihuahua. Never seen Dodgy Dave or Blake since she died. Gwanny brought me up, largely, from age six to age ten, when my island of a mother spoke to herself in Khmer devil tongues, high on manicure fumes and medicine, waiting for Dad. Who clearly doesn't understand that women are forced into relationships because of money. He also doesn't get that virginity is the conversation of lovers and best friends. Of boasts. That's why I got so wasted. Why I avoided Truth or Dare when I was growing up, and never played Spin The Bottle. Because of Malachi. The question of virginity would always occur with these people I was at school with. Living out the oppression of their parents.

'Dad. I don't need to know that.'

'Well, I'm sorry I wasn't around to witness your previous relationships, but it's very long-term with you and Iggy now, isn't it?'

'You are joking.'

'Sorry, darling, I'm just trying to lighten the mood.'

'When you were gone, Dad, my generation grew up with AIDS. Longterm relationships would never have gone on so long without that stupid guy who rolled into school on a wheelchair, telling us sex made you die.'

HMP Holloway is not fun. It's turning me into a bitch, this borrrrring arthritic youth. Lashing out. Backpeddling, demanding, sleepless

---

63. Cass Elliot, the substantially-sized front-woman of The Mamas and The Papas, best known for Dream A Little Dream Of Me is rumoured to have choked on a sandwich on July 28th, 1974 after a report in The Times. Instead, it is said she died of a heart attack in the same flat The Who's drummer, Keith Moon died in four years later - the place was on loan from singer/songwriter Harry Nilsson. Like Keith Moon, Mama Cass was 32. The flat was later bought by The Who's Pete Townshend.

sleep. At 4am last night I was fucked by a ghost as I hovered above the metal toilet to pee. I know it was Malachi.

'Did I do it? Dad?'

'What?'

'Did I kill Malachi?'

His reaction would suggest I did. At the NA meeting, hearing the self-centred stories of others' failures, I consider that maybe I had a complete blackout. Shot him onstage?

'I dreamt he fucked me last night. Lightning ratcheting through the prison door.'

Dad takes my hands: 'I wouldn't water the vinous-faced cunt's grave by squatting on it, love.'

I feel Dad connect with the black, male cord of rock n roll I felt last night, rooting across the astral planes, I was spasming three levels inside, wild sexual energy: pussy; spunk tunnel; womb - an exploding shower of psychic glitter, until my heart stopped, and I woke. Here.

He takes his hands away. And reaches them over the table, placing them strongly on my shoulders, holding me down to earth.

'Let me tell you, kid, E. M. Forster was right, everything does connect. But it makes people disconnect from you. You've always known too much. You're like your Ma, a wise soul.' His eyes hang embarrassed, finally looking up into mine: 'Darl, the minute you admit you're a fuck up, you're done for. It's like that where you are. Here. Inside. No-one has time for the bad times, although these things create us... Showbiz is about showing your biz being good. My love, think of Burroughs telling Patti Smith to keep her name clean. It must have been a rollercoaster for him, gay, shooting his wife dead - he felt he deserved the junkie-label. That pin-up for depravity. He could afford it. But you, Scarlet. I never wanted to hurt you, or let you know that single events can fuck up someone's life forever. I've got to tell you something. I tried to write it in a letter. But your Ma did instead...'

He passes me an envelope. 'I haven't read it.'

'Is she dead yet?'

I flashback to one of my dutiful: I'm baaaaahaacks! : My daughter, a prostitute in London.

I found her pathetic. Tôi ghét depression. Tôi ghét her coughing. THIS IS LIFE. LEAVE THE HOUSE. Always thought I was going somewhere valuable with my life. But I'm just a snob. This hangover of pills is where I am at. Energy = reaction. No energy = nothing. Her purple velvet-clad memory ohm-bombs me through the ether.

'Is she dead?' I ask again.

'No. Not yet.'

The fuck ups of her past meld together with mine. I can't analyse the anxieties because they are a wall of sound. I want to see Iggy.

'Where is Iggy?'

'He blames himself for all of this, Scar. It's like you could never really love anyone, not after what was done. You couldn't accept love. And if there's one thing a singer needs, it is love. Getting on stage, Scarlet, anyone who does it is mental! Jesus on a bike. That stagepower-thing, it's a nightmare but the people who create stars, those that make them into endless, needy voids - they're psychotic at best. Fans, fanatics...far worse than the stars themselves...'

'What are you saying? Was I a fan of Iggy's?'

'We all are. He'll wait for you. Don't worry.'

I take the letter. There's a gold-framed poster of a grey fluffy cat on the wall, it's wearing a party hat. Dad speaks softly: 'I remember getting your letters in prison was what I lived for. And your visits. They stopped after Reading Festival, though, didn't they? I'm not sure this one's going to be as good. Scarlet, before you read that, I wanted you to believe anything could change, but now that seems a little too romantic to believe, doesn't it? I know romance has no place in prison. That goes as far as Jean Genet, and no further... but at the same time, my dear one, all you have to live for is romance, of life outside. I am glad you found love with Iggy. He is here for you - imagine him as he wants to be. Love is a reflection of what we desire, like the fantasy of escape, of being rescued, of all the walls falling down around you and there being a freedom that you now regret taking for granted. I understand all of that. I am too much of a fool to give you advice, but I must tell you, it wasn't your doing, the death, the murder. We did it. Me and Iggy. Your confession was not your own. Do you want me to leave? To let you take your time with that letter?'

'Dunno, depends what it says.'

'I'd rather stay.'

I should have said yes to one of his visits months ago. Dad realises we only have a few uncomfortable minutes left to fill, he passes me a Rolling Stones' tape: 'They usually get me through the dark times.'

It's the best he can do.

'I can't take a tape. I only have a CD player in the leisure room.'

'The Leisure Room. Jesus, times change. But I sentence us to thirty years in the pub, the real leisure room, when you get out of here, once I'm done with the inquest. I'll take the tariff, girl. I don't want you doing another second in here.'

'I fucked up massively, didn't I?'

'You, Scarlet, no, none of this is your fault. None of it. I'm going to sort all of this out. You just get through the next days, alright? Baby girl, I love you. Just hang in there.'

I finally feel a bit more normal. Back in my room, I savour opening the letter. I decide to read a word a minute, to spin it out. My chin drops heavy to my chest as I cheat my own rules, hiding from myself like a mushroom stalk shields from the sun. My depleted septum, eroded molars, hanging from my gums like my future.

*To Scarlet,*

*It is Channary here - mother.*

*My friend, Maryam is helping me write this letter. She is nurse. You know how bad my English writing is. I can read enough, but writing is always difficult.*

*I planned to come and see you, to tell you this with my hands around your heart, but they say the germs and journey, too much. They think I am unable. But they forget, I got here, to England!*

*I hope you will be free soon. I know this is no life. To repeat what Flash Barry went through. But there is repetition in life. Yours and mine, and Dad's.*

*Which brings us to great news. Black and white, is so hard. I have to tell you this. It is a horrible secret, but the good thing is you are rich, or can be, and you will experience pure freedom when you get out. Maybe I should have done this long time ago. You know why I was sad you went alone to Reading? I am sorry it came as anger, but I did not understand exactly. I think I knew what happened there, to you. Spirits. The same happened to me, in war, as you know, but also in England in 1975. Malachi did it to me too. Malachi raped your mother too. It is why I didn't want to give you his phone number. It was one time at a party, he took me to a basement when your Dad was on tour. We always knew that your real father is Malachi Wright, but in our eyes and hearts, never. I need to tell this before I leave you. Flash Barry loves you more than you know. He kill your father.*

*Khnhom sralanh anak xxx*

I fall to the floor, the pit of my body disappears in some kind of convulsion. I am so empty, the only alive part of me tries to remove itself. I am physically sick. The screws strip me, check my body for needle marks, assuming I've overdone the drugs rather than life.

# CHAPTER FORTY-FOUR
# CLARITY

*I went out to the insane asylum and I found my baby out there -*
Koko Taylor & Willie Dixon

Dear Iggy, my rock, my roll.

I want you to take the money. Something has to pass to you from this pain. My true father. His stinking greed, foul breath clotting my path, his hammered sceptre made from hitting more like me. My mother. One of me. There were many of us for whom I squeezed the dead grey from his eyes in my armour of a goatskin coat, when you left me at The Amphitheatre of Death. My own flesh feels so old. Tarnished with the sulphur and tar of my travels. The weapons, of sex, and drugs, they were never mine. The money, neither. These were all his, like Malachi's pelt, made from parched souls of women he had run dry.

I have to scrape my skull clean. This exhaustion of being alive in a world I am not made for. This sobriety, in here, it tramples me. It is not my design. Not how you told me I would bring these bloodless cheeks to wed. To win.

Ig, I am sorry you trod upon my faultline. I know you are on the other side, flesh not ripped and torn to the ground like mine to gutters, sewers and the mouths of rats chaining me to dampness. Iggy, this chamber I find myself in now, the temple of metal frames, of spikes to hold me in, they are opposite to the spread of Malachi's indulgence, Suki's perfume, their spilling puddles of wine - I'm safe dying here. I am happy doing this. I think of Malachi and Suki, I think of vice. Their reputation is so long lost, to pleasure and partying, their flowing tankards to silks, smashing their lust to my red lips, blooded from my bones, and all those they have walked upon to rise. Fuck them, I am going out innocent.

Sorry to leave you, but this part of me, you wanted it to die, so let me take it, and free you, so you can walk alone. It is safer this way, I will take my last thoughts above the stars of the El Leopardo Pelado. And of you. I was never happier than in your arms. But I think back, and I never allowed them to hold me fully. Find someone wiser than me. And give yourself happiness. Please let my body rest, let it dry so my spirit can fly.

Anxiety, Dread, Fraud, Fear, Fabrication, they will soon be corpses with me too, their shit-fired furnace will bleed with such false gold. Fuck them. Do not allow their savagery to shadow any more than my weak soul.

This temple here, my cell, these are clean white sheets I wrap around my neck, as I imagine this place pouring with light. As our sex was. Peridot chrysolite skin, gold veins, a sapphire and beryl disco. Agate flashes of all the friends, of Bobby Bandit, Filmmaker Paul, Doctor Hemp, Joanna Pipe Neck - tell her to look after my true Dad - tell him I need to put down my weapons now. They were always too heavy. And I never believed in hitting back. Kyrie Eleison-Adetayo, Paddy Auschwitz, Joe Division. My mother will be around me soon enough. I am in a place where faces of faces morph into the character of an era as they entwine with time and nature herself. Joe Delaney. Land, precious Land. I reach for Ruby. The arc of Emerald, is she still around? This the new phase of the moon and stars.

My inner temple, here, white, as white as my mother yearned her soul to be, with all her thousand talents, and lies of wisdom.

The pearl here is death. I lie with you as my sceptre, hoping that in another world, you will protect me from the blood that fell on my lily skin that I thought was yours. It is. Rebellion, for flesh. My prison here is my heart, its bondage will never reject the ornament my life was to this final wisdom that now is the time to cut out.

Fiction is madness is delusion. Blank paper, naked skin, born, covered in someone else's blood, our first lesson in taking the beautiful byproducts of others into our existence: blood and shit, semen, cum. Reality, fiction, you, me. I have carved these notes, trying to make sense of life. They become this book, I leave to you, and all the girls like me, as I crawl around on my knees, licking the Joe Meek-wallpaper, full of microphones. Recording.

'Hello?' It took me twenty-four years surviving to write. Writing is nothing without experience, they say. Of course, I lived for every moment, but peaked too early to make it to further... the noise is too loud. I can only obliterate the thuggish by hanging my soul to rest.

Be brilliant.

Laters. x

# CHAPTER FORTY-FIVE
# MALICE AND AFORETHOUGHT

*I'm a freeborn man* - Ewan MacColl

**POSTSCRIPT:**

*Cherry Gonorrhea writes exclusively for DROGUE, December 1999. Photos: Kyrie Eleison-Adetayo.*

Iggy Papershoes is a long shadow, walking up a peppermint lawn from the riverbanks of Kerala's Cochin. He's been down by the metaphorical river for eight months, since his former girlfriend, Scarlet Flagg tragically took her life while awaiting trial for the murder of Heroshima tour manager, Malachi Wright, who she found out was her real father following multiple rapes.

**DROGUE are here to put the record straight on all the rumours, and Papershoes speaks exclusively to us.**
Lush green palms applaud and a pair of peacock flutter as though Land Moon, the six-foot blond rockstar, now solo artist, has spirited past. But instead, the original talent, Iggy approaches Drogue. He's wearing a crumpled pale cream linen suit with a sea-green chalk stripe with one of the 'I survived the Heroshima disaster, 1998' bootleg T-shirts that appeared after Wright died beneath the lighting rig he'd erected for the illegal warehouse party, attended by over 5000 people, at the end of their sold out tour in a circus tent.

In the distance, on the other side of the backwaters, saris blow in the wind, winking like groupies, in fuschias, golds, turmerics and azures.

**DROGUE:** ARE HEROSHIMA HISTORY?

**IGGY PAPERSHOES:** *[He drapes his old leather jacket, sewn together with badges, beer mats, studs and memories on the floor,* *kicks off his motorbike boots, orders us both a quinine tonic and gin, and sits cross-legged.]* Yes. Heroshima are done. I'm working on my solo project, called Rape, and I'm going to release it as Iggy Flagg.

**DROGUE:** WOW. TWO SCOOPS THERE. WE UNDERSTAND IT'S ALL A TRIBUTE TO YOUR FORMER GIRLFRIEND... WIFE?

**IGGY PAPERSHOES:** Wife. Yes. Late wife.

**DROGUE:** SO YOU AND SCARLET WERE ACTUALLY MARRIED?

**IGGY PAPERSHOES:** Absolutely. We had it signed in a legal service in a hotel in Ibiza last year. It was magical. It was everything. We carried her body to the water in Varanasi, and offered her to the gods.

**DROGUE:** DO YOU BELIEVE IN REINCARNATION?

**IGGY PAPERSHOES:** No.

**DROGUE:** DO YOU BELIEVE IN ANYTHING?

**IGGY PAPERSHOES:** No. Music, maybe, it's what keeps me sane.

**DROGUE:** SO YOU ARE GOING TO INHERIT ALL THE RICHES OF WRIGHT STATES INTERNATIONAL TOURING?

**IGGY PAPERSHOES:** I can't discuss it right now, it's in court. But obviously, regarding WSIT, you'll be the first to know. Nothing matters. I just need, a gin and tonic, where is it?

**DROGUE:** SCARLET FLAGG WAS RAPED BY MALACHI WRIGHT. DID HE KNOW HE WAS HER FATHER?

**IGGY PAPERSHOES:** I loved her. I don't think I'll ever meet anyone like her ever again.

*Iggy departs for a short while, staggering through the colonial doorways, for the gin and quinine tonics. He returns elucidating.*

In this business, we spot girls coming like snacks on a sushi belt. In all their banana-skin T-shirts, star in the movies of our minds. But Scarlet was different.

**DROGUE:** WHEN DID YOU LAST SEE HER?

**IGGY PAPERSHOES:** In my dreams, last night.

**DROGUE:** WOW. AND YOU, SCARLET AND BARRY FLAGG WERE BOTH PRESENT AT YOUR LATE FATHER-IN-LAW'S DEATH?

**IGGY PAPERSHOES:** I prefer to think of Flash Barry as my father.

**DROGUE:** YEAH, IT MUST BE VERY CONFUSING.

**IGGY PAPERSHOES:** Not really. I'm here with the man who brought her up as HER father. I felt like I knew him before I met him. Barry's a legend. His aura and passion penetrate all the pop of culture. He's real. He is the real deal. And Scarlet carried that light. Y'know she wrote me a letter?

**DROGUE:** A SUICIDE NOTE?

**IGGY PAPERSHOES:** She said she was going to start a business when she came out of remand. Clothes that naturally biodegrade, by the time you're bored with them, they've disappeared. Fresher than Tokyo fish market. Clothes for those who know nights don't last forever. I'm going to launch a collection based on her ideas when my album comes out, in her honour.

**DROGUE:** WAS THAT IN THE NOTE?

**IGGY PAPERSHOES:** Maybe one day I can share that. But not now.

**DROGUE:** AND WHAT DO YOU THINK HAPPENED TO WRIGHT?

**IGGY PAPERSHOES:** Malachi died of a heart attack.

**DROGUE:** WAS IT THE DRUGS?

**IGGY PAPERSHOES:** No, it was a heart attack.

**DROGUE:** NOTHING TO DO WITH THE LIGHTING RIG?

**IGGY PAPERSHOES:** Again, it's in court, so I can't truly comment, but what I've said before, publicly, he put up the lighting rig that collapsed and nearly killed us, and our fans. Tragic, eh? Mal signed it off himself. He was the health and safety officer. I think that was what likely killed him. The shock of his own bad performance.

**DROGUE:** SO WHAT HAPPENED WITH YOU AND LAND, THE ARTIST FORMERLY KNOWN AS ORLANDO MOON?

**IGGY PAPERSHOES:** He's like an orangutang on ecstasy. An ADHD spider snorting on cocaine, netting everything for himself. He's just a dopehead for fame. He wears a top hat to the side of his head, lilac feathers splurt from the arms of his long morning suit jacket. Doesn't that say enough? Do I need to be on stage with something that maximus, and gaudy? My music says enough.

**DROGUE:** SO, YOU DON'T SPEAK ANYMORE?

**IGGY PAPERSHOES:** How would we do that here? I've been travelling with my guitar, and Barry, for the past eight months.

Listen, there's a punk-hubris which is Land Moon. He's a master of change. And I look forward to his next projects. But they're a spectacle. It was him that wanted the circus tent. I'm just a troubadour. There's a thing, growing up in our classless street society, of Old Street, and Soho, Portobello, London, nightclubs, where we make connections we think are real, but it doesn't always cut both ways, y'know? He had a hard time with his sister, Ruby Moon, I don't think any of it's done yet. He'd take a bow at a funeral, thinking it was for him, y'know what I mean?

**DROGUE:** DO YOU THINK THE DEATHS OF DESIGNER RUBY MOON AND DAN THE DRUMMER, AND SCARLET FLAGG WERE INTERCONNECTED?

**IGGY PAPERSHOES:** I think we've just experienced something like the HIV wipeout after Studio 54, but grunge. They were dark times. I'm hoping that energy, maybe it came from Malachi, has died with him. Scarlet was the echo to my song. I am devastated to not have her with me anymore. Can we move onto something else now?

**DROGUE:** WHAT ARE YOU DOING HERE, IN INDIA?

**IGGY PAPERSHOES:** Getting suits made. Seeing the monkeys. Getting rid of bodies.

**DROGUE:** AND YOU'VE BEEN AWAY FOR A WHILE?

**IGGY PAPERSHOES:** You probably would have been too, if you'd lost your wife, your band, your tour manager. The album's in my head now. It's about the patriarchal system of rock n roll. I wrote it, as we drove here, through French vineyards, past Turkish sufis, Iranian markets, Afghanistani deserts. I recorded with the chanting ragas of the priests by the Ganges in Varanasi, you can maybe hear Scarlet's body burning, with her mother.

**DROGUE:** WOW. DEEP. AND JOANNA PIPE NECK,

THE ONE TIME GROUPIE TO THE GRATEFUL DREAD - IS SHE HERE TOO?

**IGGY PAPERSHOES:** Yes, she was a major part of our lives, looking after us all through much heartache. She manages a lot of our stuff. She and Flash Barry, outside Jordan, they felt they were spoken to by God, or one of his messengers. It's been an incredible journey.

**DROGUE:** WILL YOU GO BACK TO LONDON?

**IGGY PAPERSHOES:** Scarlet used to call that place we did the last show The Amphitheatre of Death. I think she saw it coming. She liked Paris. Maybe there. Maybe New York.

**DROGUE:** DO YOU BELIEVE IN THE POWER OF THREES?

**IGGY PAPERSHOES:** What, with Ruby, Scarlet and Malachi? No. Because you're forgetting Dan the Drummer.

**DROGUE:** WHY DO ANY OF THIS?

**IGGY PAPERSHOES:** Anything to be remembered.

# ACKNOWLEDGEMENTS

Writing is often prophetic when it's doing it right, and after many titles and drafts, which I began talking about in the 90s, musician Gil De Ray appeared at a reading for Tony O'Neill that I was attending with my best accomplice, Kelli Ali in around 2014. Psychomachia was largely drafted by then, in my first marriage, to Alex, through fiestas dancing with the devil. I have Alex and his mother, Sybil to thank for that accommodation. Thanks to Ris and Rob (& Suki, and Schlurpie) - for believing, by your pool.

Falling in love with Gil, as he performed at the Sylvia Plath Fan Club night I'd started, he suggested I send the manuscript to Shane Rhodes at Wrecking Ball Press, after two agents hadn't managed to place this book with their contacts with larger publishers. Although I'm very grateful this wasn't published in earlier forms, I believe it's because Psychomachia is an unusually brutal and an exceptionally druggy story for a female to write, this was before Me Too, and I feel it's found its correct home.

Thank you eternally to Gil, and to Shane for sending the message that he was going to realise this into paper, which I read lying in a bed in Berlin having been out all night after a Cold Lips party in October 2017 - my life began to come into focus. All I ever lived to do was to share this story. I went for a drink with Shane after he'd trashed the London Book Fair, telling me stories of Dan Fante. I like him very much. Thanks from my deepest heart, and to his partner-in-crime, Dave Windass for his grounded steer, and Elle Grice (for wrangling me with great wit). As a Londoner, I'm forever honoured to be taken into the Northern fold, aside some of my favourite authors.

Two people have made me believe in this along the way: Johny Brown, whose enthusiasm is an insurmountable honour, and Sarah

Nuttall, who actually bothered to read it, and make suggestions. But more recently, Malik Ameer Crumpler, who I'm honoured to work with on Vagrant Lovers (thank you to Das Wasteland Records for putting out our first vinyl this summer). I was reading in Paris, hosted by he and the great Nina Živančević (one time assistant to Ginsberg) and Malik instructed me to remove my limitations, which are words to live by. All of his are.

Sophie Rochester, for subtley encouraging the Sylvia Plath Fan Club, and Tony White & Sarah Such. Sarah Norris, for establishing Women In Art, the manifesto still stands. To the old days, Lee Bullman, who introduced me to Siena Barnes who created the Babylonian sigil of the art for this cover. Fee Doran, Lucci Daddo Fuzz Orchestra, Windscale, the Peppes, Piers Thompson, and Salena Godden (whose Book Club Boutique was where I really began reading poetry, other than terrible early goes with Ambit and at open mics). Performing with bands allowed me to express ideas and frustrations, get increasingly weird, because painting with words as a performer allowed me to break up the styles I was getting trapped in by day jobs as a writer.

To the London frontline of Murray Lachlan Young, Tim Wells, Cymon Eckles, Pallas Citroen at The Bomb Factory, Doc N Roll, Dipak at LFB, Robert Pereno, Chip Martin, Babette. David Erdos. Sophie Parkin. Lev Parker at Morbid Books (for consulting on Manson aside Gil), Phil Dirtbox. Le Gun. Cate Halpin. Peter Cross at the Union. Anna Goodman. DJ Claire Conville. Fiona Cartledge. Gallery46. Ben Osborne. Sean McLusky. Soho Radio. Daisy Wake. Jeff Barrett. And beyond: James 'Hound' Marshall at Please Kill Me consulted on a couple of footnotes. Roy Gregory at the best record shop in the world: Clock Tower Music. Byline. Neu Reekie. Bella Caledonia. Razur Cuts. Ben Osbourne at Noise of Art. Lazy Gramophone. Jim Sclavunos. Steve Norris. Carl Loben. Tayba Mason. Mark Reeder. Danielle De Picciotto, a rare female role model whom I'm honoured to share a friendship with because after being introduced by Chris Bohn, I found someone else rolling across mediums.

You'll note many of these are men, we're still in female infancy, but respect to the men who also work to break the patriarch's power. The hardest part of writing this was changing from girl to woman, as the characters became their own, dancing over the pages in free will - that's the same as people that guide, there's usually some mutual gaze and wonderment - so thank you to all the people that invoke that. Many of them have died, it's taken so long: Sebastian Horsley, Gary Fairfull, Mandy Wright, Jock Scot, David Kilburn, Bill Macklin, Howard Marks, to all muses dead and alive. Cannot believe Andrew Weatherall passed, without me saying thank you for opening his Convenanza Festival. Little more than I can believe I've performed with the good Dr John Cooper Clarke, Thurston Moore, Youth.

Being a journalist, growing up in glitter and nightclubs, interviewing so many legends and stars, and being on TV at 19 is a bizarre life. But being a poet is truer. Thanks to Dave Barbarossa - one day we will tour again (I write this in Lockdown v.III). Thank you to all of these people who have trusted me, and all the amazing venues and galleries and artists and promoters internationally.

Sincere thanks to the living. My solid girl squad of Jacky Edwards, Amy Vallance, Kate Reed, Kate Clews, Melanie Sturges, Amanda Dayeh, Rebecca Bartels, Louise Kennerley and Marina Formesyn-Baker (sorry about fucking up the boiler in Cannes, Linda), Sophie D'Angelo, Letitia Thomas, Jacquebelle Purnell, Margarite Werner, MC Feral Is Kinky. To Mark Nunn, his secret writing lodge, & Suzi Browning, and Jemima. Pat Whelan. Metso. Miles Cumpstey. Felix Unger-Hamilton. Donna Kernan. Neil Smith.

To newer associates and inspirations, Rob Doyle, Lias Saoudi, Kieran Leonard, and my team at Ambit - Briony Bax is a wonder (and isn't a blood relative, to the founder Dr. Martin Bax, her father was the poet Adrian Mitchell). But to Geoff Nicholson for scooping my peacock feathers from the slush, and Travis Elborough. Ambit gave me a 'proper' lit fam publishing my first fiction back in 2007, and as the incoming editor, I intend to maintain that. To 3:AM. Dean Stalham and Carlotta Allum. Paul Waters. Peter S. Smith. Dallas Athent. To my former students, especially the stars, and those such as Heidi James-Dunbar who entrusted me as professor. Jim Frank at the BBC. All I met and learnt with through consultancy and training, you're all amazing. To Kevin Pocklington, someone I like to drink with. Actually, that may be a thread.

Irvine Welsh - one of my longest friendships in this Milky Way sarcophagus. It was good to make up with my old toxic twin, Kris Needs, from being a resident at Mike and Claire Manumission's Motel. And back to all the self-starters, The Social, where I first had a picture taken with Miles Cumpstey, which led me through the door at Loaded, opened by Michael Holden, for that special training when they were shifting half a million editions a month (and half of Columbia). Tessa Williams and Laurie Long Legs at X, Jefferson Hack for giving me the blank book to fill before I ran off to Glastonbury from Dazed. Derek O'Hanlon. The tabloid poetry school. Teachers, particularly the great printmaker Peter S. Smith and TV-iconoclast Juliet Alexander. Sue Stemp and St Roche fam. Huge thanks to Ernesto Leal (and all the Leals), and the Scream Team for allowing me to look in, and associated great friends from Andy Fraser, to Marion Sparks for all the gigs I've reviewed, performed at, and been a part of. Boy George, thank you for paying me to make clothes, and Simon and Bryanne, for employing me as teenage milliner, and Tracey Moberley for inviting me to show poetry-films in the Tate. I know this is sounding like a really bad Oscar speech, but it may be the nearest I ever get, and I found a rejection letter from the early noughties, when this journey first began, when doing the image research for the world class designer, Stephen Barrett, so it's been brewing for a while. Thank you so much to him for realising this cover with instinct, style and precision. Neal Fox for the bat syringe, and Pure Evil. And massive thanks to Graham at Human Design for beautifully typesetting.

Cold Lips, the publication I began was enabled by a great crew: to Nick Winter the printer, for showing me the ropes, Justin Taylor,

Kedge, Anne Cathrin and Jason McGlade, Doug Hart, Judy Nylon, Stuart McKenzie, Nina Antonia (who also read the Thunders footnote), Anne McCloy, Ana Sefer, Dave Barbarossa, Richard Cabut, Greta Bellamacina, Robert Montgomery, Jeremy Reed, Dr Noki, Sam Jackson, Dr Golnoosh Nour, Olly Walker, Mat Lloyd, Lisa Moorish, Gail Porter, Graham Bendel, Wildcat Will, Barnzley, Niall McDevitt, Julie Goldsmith, Danny Fields, Will Carruthers, Jeffrey Wengrofsky, Sarah Lowe, Zoë Howe, Vivi Carr, Paul Sakoilsky and fam, Scott Temple, Trinity Tristan, and Sophie Kennedy Clark, Ana Sefer, Win Harms, Heathcote Williams, and all I've published (except maybe a few) and all of those who have joined the stage and floor - sorry to miss naming out the full register, to the brilliant people I've undoubtedly forgotten here, or not named. Martyn Goodacre, a pleasure to run into you again. Anjelika Barbe, Rawly Myles, Cindy Fournier, Millie Radaković, Joshua Hart, Seb Bowden, Ollie Hardman, and the interns, and to Luke McLean for designing the cover of my first hand-stitched poetry book. To all the people, reading this, I hope you've enjoyed it.

I'm very grateful to the Society of Authors for awarding me with an emergency literary grant when Covid kicked in, ALCS, and all of my Substack subscribers.

My younger brother, Jim, and his family, Nicola, Isla and Archie. Also to Voirrey and Chris, and the fake-god parents, of Bronwen Young, Barrie Barker, Annie Heath, and to Christine Miller and Alan, Chloe and Alex. To my blud, Morgan Young.

Kirsty Allison
May 2021

Psychomachia
The war of the soul

Prudentius d. 45AD, Spain

Luxuria: 'Flowershod andswaying from the wine cup,
Every fragrance

Beauty and pleasure her attendants, her weapons,
rose-petals and violets
the army of virtue surrenders, before
defeat

Idolatry and the vices struggle against faith and virtue
spirituality
religion

Kings of barbarian bondage stand against our hero/ine

Faith squeezes the dead greyeyes from the bloody soul
her fans wear robes of flaming purple

Chastity's virgin armour. Lust's shining torches.
They fight, chastity's eye is hit with

burning pine, knotted, dipped in sulphur
and tar
She pierces Lust's neck sucking fumes, blood clots
foul breath from her throat

The hammered sword stained red

Patience, the long)suffering soul took over from chastity
when she retired

Wrath's black mouth foams. Patience's eyes don't flicker at Wrath's
spears, the frenzy, till nothing remains
~~/////////~~
Wrath dies in her own Fury, after throwing all her spears.
No virtue lives without patience.

Pride wears a lioness pelt atop a high spirited horse,
big hair, fine linen cape rises mad to Lowliness and her
motley crew of waifs and strays, penniless upstarts
against Pride's fame.
Lowliness's cheap spirit, surrounded by Justice.
Honesty and parched Sobriety, fasting their past y faces
Purity and her bloodless cheeks, Simplicity, exposed
to injury
All to be trampled
but Deceit builds a trap for Lowliness
which Pride falls into, and it is
her true companion, Hope
who rescues her.

Lowliness takes the sword of vengeance from her, bends
Pride's neck back, and cuts it.


Indulgence belches perfume and puddles of wine,
Reputation means nothing to yer, for it is long lost.
She lives for pleasure, and she weeps as everyone surrenders
to her party of banqueting from from flowing tankards spilling
on silks, dragged/////  by Wantoness and Drunkeness
"Abandon this den under the flag of Sobriety, my sweet"
and Sobriety hurls a rock.
Chance found the stone, smashing the red lips of Luxury,
so her teeth loosen in her bloody /////  mouth
broken bones consumed she vomits.

Sobriety: Drink up. Enjoy your morsels.
Your stomach can taste your body.

and Indulgence dies.

Her drinking friends throw their cymbals, and scatter.
Lust also flees Pale. Vanity, stripped naked,
leaves, her robes in a
pile with Allurement's garlands.

Strife and Pleasure depart in trails of hairpins,
ribbons, buckles and veils.

Sobriety and co trample on the sins, into the gutter.

Greed then folds her robes, and picks through the dirt

for gold.

Her pals: Care, Hunger, Fear, Anxiety, Dread, Fraud,
Fabrication, Sleeplessness and Sordidness.
Greed grows strong stripping their corpses
of their wealth.
Greed's infamous pestilence is followed by Pride of
Possession never sated, and Gluttony who robs his
own children. In the wake of Greed's wrath, all
living things turn into shit-fired furnaces, bleeding

with gold.

Seized by Greed, only Reason can save.

Greed puts her weapons down in the name of Avarice.
In the form of austerity, she becomes the virtue
of Thrift.

Bellona, goddess of War steals her look.
 But hides plundering thievery and miserly
   hoarding of stolen goods beneath the commendable
   name. Gullible men fall to the monster, shackling
   themselves to her fiend.

Good Work comes to the aid of the faultline
 in the battlefield.
She had been poor. Looking to Faith in Heaven with
 the accrued interest of her toil. Greed strikes her
   with lightning. Numb, her neck is iron but she
  retaliates, turning to Greed, no wound, - the body
is strangled in the agony of death. Nuggets of gold,
gems, decaying cash leaks to the poor. Good Work
 claims the desire for gain is gone. With ascetic
chants, she says to leave not thinking
   of tomorrow
    because daily bread will come with sunlight.

 Birds, fouls, sparrow will not perish


   Their troubles ended.


Suffering, Fear, Violence, Crime and Fraud lay their
    bugles
    down and Thunder smiles.


   Concord reigned after the chaos, a miraculous
      highway opened up for all, a storm
   troubled Peace.


Discord joined Concord, imitating a friend. She
  carries a knife, caught, she announces:

   "Belial is my teacher, and see God and mock him."


Faith takes a spear to her tongue, pinning her to
the ground of bloodshed. Disord's flesh is ripped
  and torn to the ground, to gutters, sewers, the
 mouths of dogs and animal chain to earth
     and air and fish to fire.

Faith and Concord sit on high, watching the settling skirmish of their work over Vice.

The entire camp and tents open, no niche of body closed.

With equal command, Concord speaks first:

"What will Faith offer now? Victors to the savages. Your homes must be united or we will be divided. Virtues produce peace. Peace is the end of labour. The temple is our Kingdom., guard it from the wolves in soft white lambskin."

Such as, Discord.

Concord was hurt but Faith defended.

The twelve names of our senate mark the gates of the temple with a single stone entry.
Precious stones match that number and pulse collectively.

The temple pours with their love and coloured light. Peridot chrsolite with gold veins, set between a sapphire and beryl light disco. Agate flashing with its amythyst neighbour, crimson striking the sardonyx, jasper, topaz, carnelian arcing. Scattered fresh cut grass emeralds. Chrysophase as bright as stars.

The inner temple had seven crystal columns. A white stone centre with a thousand talents. The pearl the prize purchase of Faith, paid for with a thousand talents.
Wisdom lies enshrined.
Asceptre of live wood.
A sceptre of shell holding pearl.

A sceptre of live wood. As the nadir of solstice wrote the winter, that wandering kick. The wander years.
The stem never wilts. It s prouts roses and willows.
Red as blood on lillies.

Here we worship.

Sin falls.
The throes of rebellion for flesh.
This is what surpresses the spirit. Yes, the prison of our heart, its bondage rejecting the filth of flesh. Light and Dark that is what builds our temple, the soul, an ornament to delight Wisdom -

for she reigns glorious in her throne.